SNOW BLIND

Richard Blanchard's debut novel *Snow Blind* was completed in 2013. It draws on his life experiences: being an avid skier; becoming a father late in life and losing close friends too early in theirs. His previous short story work generated critical acclaim.

Born in 1962, Richard Blanchard grew up in Liverpool. After graduating from the University of Westminster, he built a career as an executive in the retail industry. He still lives in Liverpool with his wife and two sons.

Praise for Richard Blanchard

"… a superb piece of prose, and really engrossing. His writing really has dynamism."
Chris Dukes (London School of Journalism)

"In my opinion Richard Blanchard is a staggeringly good writer with his own unique original voice."
Mark Davies Markham (Playwright – *This Life*, *Taboo* – *The Boy George musical*).

"With prose as taut as a guitar string, Richard Blanchard dissects the workings of the male mind."
Jan McVerry (TV writer – *Clocking Off*, *Forsyte Saga*, *Coronation Street*)

"All that is necessary for the triumph of evil is that good men do nothing."

Edmund Burke
Irish orator, philosopher, & politician (1729 – 1797)

SNOW
BLIND

RICHARD BLANCHARD

Matador
9 Priory Business Park
Kibworth Beauchamp
Leicestershire LE8 0RX, UK
Tel: (+44) 116 279 2299
Fax: (+44) 116 279 2277
Email: books@troubador.co.uk
Web: www.troubador.co.uk/matador

ISBN 978 1783061 747

British Library Cataloguing in Publication Data.
A catalogue record for this book is available from the British Library.

Typeset in 11pt Adobe Garamond Pro by Troubador Publishing Ltd, Leicester, UK
Printed and bound in the UK by TJ International Ltd, Padstow, Cornwall

Matador is an imprint of Troubador Publishing Ltd

For John Young
(1967-2005) RIP
Peace, love, hugs 'n stuff.

Author and John Young skiing the Valée Blanche

Prologue

"Haaar…Oomph!" I am falling and laughing, ripped from a skiing heaven to an icy earth.

It's a juicy fall; the impact of which bellows half-used air from my lungs and sloshes the water content of my body around like a drunk's glass. Maybe I wasn't in skiing heaven though. I am falling head first into abundant off-piste snow, casting suffocating ice particles into my mouth, which I vainly try to spit out. My red carving skis are in the sky above me, chopping air like un-tethered helicopter blades. The perverse laughter is because my body is actually relieved to surrender to gravity after so much toil. I try to set a defiant smile into the gorgeous late-afternoon sun for the sake of both my ego and my friends, as I flash rapidly over their elongated Lowry-like shadows. Pompous parents sneer that pride comes before a fall, but I am not sure I have much.

But you may ask myself, how did I get here? My fall may have started twenty yards back when I tipped off a narrow track, but its source was surely when my stags arranged for me to ski off-piste on Vallee Blanche under Mont Blanc. In hindsight this was unwise when I have so little experience; but I had made so much progress. Maybe the fall was inevitable when I let this stag group come together. My latest fall adds scorn to the disdain, embarrassment, hatred, panic and unerring inevitability that my stags are individually feeling. Perhaps I should blame it just on that bastard Robert, who hijacked the destination of this trip from Johnny, my best man. The worst fate I would have befallen there would have been vomiting the whisky produce of a Macallan distillery over trampled Highland heather. Perhaps setting foot on the plane last Wednesday was the real downfall. All of this is prefaced by the embarrassing moment I was told by Sophia's dad that we were getting married on Saturday the 25th of April because he had secured a slot at his country club. I accepted this fate far too easily.

My soul travels downhill uneasily; I am a pollutant, stripping away the high mountain snow, producing floodwater and misery in the valley below. I curl my neck upwards to try and pivot on my shoulders and pull my skis under me. An unseen hump does it for me, sending me airborne where I can manoeuvre my skis. I now slide faster from the combination of the flip and a more severe slope, but feel more control as I am almost in an upright sitting position. The view would be awe-inspiring, mountain peaks jostling for supremacy, some cloaked in patchy snow, some nakedly showing their body of jagged rock. I read a sign way back at the top at the Aiguille Du Midi station that said the glacier below me is moving at a centimetre an hour. Apparently it takes ninety years or so to ride this natural escalator into Chamonix, as proven by the recently discovered skeleton of a climber. The heart of a crevasse defies all expectation; how can something so white be so vibrantly blue? You keep staring at it to build up your belief that you haven't gone colour blind. This beauty is now a life-threatening beast. Blue lines drop away in every direction, encircling my journey. My flight instinct kicks in. Stop my fall. Alter my fate. I cycle my legs frantically, casting off huge splashes of snow. I turn my torso to the hill; my ski gloves claw vainly uphill at nothing fixed. My last desperate acts are slowing me but not enough. I am sucked towards the cavernous crevasses and shattered seracs. Stalactites glisten and welcome me to their wintry desolation; they may soon present their sharpened edges to my supplicant body.

Hell, I fell because of me. I surrendered to this downfall. Pompous parents sneer that pride comes before a fall, and so they should.

I lift off and silence falls, no scraping and clawing just heavenly silence.

WEDNESDAY 15TH APRIL 2009

CHAPTER 1

Dan 13:13

"Oh, yeah!" Prince rips a vocal chord and cranks up his rubber-taut funk in my iPhone earphones. His lyric invokes the spread of AIDS-induced death and hysteria from France, the destination of my journey ahead.

Sophia, my wife-to-be, drives me onward to Manchester airport; but I exist in Prince's visceral music and a splendid isolation. She drives hunched forward, compensating for the ill-positioned steering wheel and seat. Glancing into the rear-view mirror she seeks the face of our son. Her straight, brown bobbed hair curves achingly down her cheek as she lifts her chin. Her lips wriggle, as she engages him in some reassuring babble. I often see this scene, but am often outside its intimacy with or without my musical exclusion. This beautiful device was released from its box yesterday; a pop of compressed Chinese factory air landed in my Chester office as the bottom of the Apple box hit my desk. This perk from work will undoubtedly result in more for me to do.

A plane hangs low in the sky alongside our rear view mirror, a monumental cacophony of beaten metal. Banking south over polluted devalued properties; I speculate its destination to be the wonderful free-spirited San Francisco, the plane crammed with pioneers going west, exhausting both spent fuel and Virgin's Cool Britannia brand presence. The fumes trouble me personally; the brand hurts me professionally. As a copywriter working for the mosquito-sized budget airline ByeFly, I wince at the challenge of feebly attacking them. Working on their account would be a dream. I squirm anxiously in my seat and imagine pitching my latest campaign idea to Richard Branson; a poster campaign to attract new customers for them. I press the projector remote to reveal a photograph of a naked couple reclining discreetly in a business-class seat: the lady astride him with her right arm covering her breasts. The strap line underneath would boast: "Lose your virginity in style". I also imagine the sneers the plane is now attracting from the irate ruddy-faced Cheshire set nearby.

Sophia had picked me up on time outside my flat in Chester. I had waited on the street, sat on the guitar case I am interestingly using as a suitcase this weekend. It was very chilly down low so I had pulled my purple velvet lapels across my nose. The early commuters must have thought I was a sulking under-confident busker awaiting a sufficient audience before he would perform. I counted the nights I will spend under my flat's roof till I move in to Sophia's parents' house in Wilmslow south of Manchester; ten more nights minus the four I am about to spend in France. Must make the most of the days before life changes. Her mum and dad are good strong people but I fear I will be overwhelmed in a household with their grandchild in it.

Prince is still unhappy in my head; now bemoaning man's sheep-like behaviour in pursuing life threatening thrills like going to space on a rocket. If he was to sing for another forty verses he might produce an attack on the environmental impact of skiing, the reason for my travel. More specifically to an event that at forty years old I never thought I would live to see, my own stag weekend. When did the stag night, essentially a huge piss-up ending in a mixture of pain and embarrassment, stretch to become a weekend? When did a weekend become five days? This extension adds the inconvenience of having to carry on drinking for days on end and living with pissed people, most of whom you only want to converse with once a year. I have meekly succumbed to this generational change.

I turn again and Sophia is talking directly at me. Her mouth is speeding now, showing strained dimples around her chin. The sweetness of her face isn't lost, but there is exasperation there. Her head flicks between looking at the road and trying to get my attention. My last

4

moment of contemplation is lost. I pull out my embedded earphones too sharply and my right ear stings.

"Where in hell are we going Dan?" asks my tetchy wife-to-be.

Answering Manchester airport would not help, she must mean which terminal. The weak spring sun flashes across the papers on my lap and I flush knowing she needs a decision fast.

"Probably Terminal 3."

"I am in completely the wrong lane. Are you sure?"

She scowls and lurches her Daddy's obscene green luxury car into the right-hand lane with a skid. The leather seats squeak with our body weight, emitting an opulent odour of brushed clean death.

"Err!" The number three appears to me belatedly from the e-ticket and I let her drive on without interruption.

"How come I get a Hen night in Manchester and you get a five-day skiing holiday in France?" Sophia protests with childish petulance; she doesn't think I have earned enough credit to take this liberty.

"It wasn't my idea. You know it was Robert who sorted it all babe." I try to carry the conversation beyond argument by blaming someone else. I know what really irks her is how come Juliet my ex-girlfriend is going on my Stag weekend.

My son Giuseppe, or Bepe for short, fires orange polystyrene pellets from a Scooby Doo pistol. He hits the front windscreen twice.

"And how did he get that?" Sophia frowns at me as we negotiate a series of roundabouts. I had succumbed to his whining to liberate the gun from the front of his latest magazine.

"Good shot baby," I humour him in an overload voice.

Juliet scowls and I think she says, "Who is the child around here?"

The airport rises in front of us, screaming nonsense from ill-conceived signs at my word-alert sensibility.

"For Terminal 3 follow T3" the sign suggests coyly; I never would have guessed. Terminal is such a bad name to be associated with such a risky way to travel. It threatens a trip with no return, a destination with no way out. Partnered with cancer is its most succinct and compelling usage, but is that just the wordsmith in me?

"Manchester – Gateway to the World." For some maybe, it must be the prison of the North for others. Is our passage helped or hindered by this boastful nonsense?

Relieved to see the "Short Stay and Rental Vehicles" sign we enter the gloomy car park, accepting their extortionate fee unchallenged as the barrier lifts.

I stop Prince in time to hear the engine turn off.

"You got me here in great time babe." I thank Sophia. I think she was motivated to be here early to see the group assemble, but most definitely to check out the surprise stag Juliet.

I get out of the car to seek a trolley but the signs fail me and I am lost scouring acres of this desperate space. The low phosphorescent light brings to mind oozy images of stolen affairs between illegitimate lovers with collapsed home lives. Eventually the bashed metallic crate I need appears, abandoned in haste across two spaces but hidden from plain view. I feel proud to have rescued some unsuspecting traveller from denting their bodywork and losing their no-claims bonus, but my chivalry is at a personal cost. The plastic panel screwed onto the hand luggage basket advertises my own crafted words let loose in the real world.

WAVE GOODBYE TO BRITAIN; WAVE GOODBYE TO OTHER
AIRLINES; FOR FLYING SATISFACTION

GO GO BYEFLY.CO.UK

My heart sinks with the over-promise. I squirm at the sure knowledge that they offer nothing but flying squalor on their planes. I wince knowing how I avoided mentioning price in the vain hope we happen to mug enough travellers who can't work out the implications of our small-print baggage and plane tax clauses. I gag at the client's twee obsession with using a Waving Goodbye theme. What is it doing here anyway; surely spending money advertising somewhere else to someone about to buy a flight ticket would be better than someone just about to get on one. I am disconcerted.

Bepe strains prematurely to get out of his car seat; compressing the flesh at the top of his plump arms. His buckle snags my fingers.

"Daddy is getting on a plane now Bepe," I lift him out with his two-year-old hands grasping a toy plane and the already spent plastic pistol.

"Let's leave them in the car for later," I take his toys from him.

"No Diddy." His face instantly frowns, threatening to reap tears. The physicality of his protest surprises me, and I accede to the Scooby Doo gun. I sense Sophia's disapproval; I have just given her the moral high ground should this be lost or cause more tears.

I place Bepe on his feet while I unload the car.

"Don't let him down in here, you know he will just run away." Sophia reminds me of Bepe's recent behaviour. I sit him on the hand baggage shelf at the back of the trolley. I put my inappropriate guitar case onto the trolley. My packing logic went haywire, lost trying to recall what is needed to go skiing and coping with the extremes of blinding heat and bone-quaking cold that accompany a trip in April. I also packed for the inevitabilities of a man in my position, such as being dumped outside in the middle of the night by my stags (a vest and long johns), being regularly doused in water or urine for a laugh (every T-shirt I own) or suffering theft from my wardrobe (spare ski pants and fleece).

"Come on guys, time to scoot," I warble to my family, revealing my nervous state.

"Scoot! Where did that come from?" Sophia barely tolerates my search for offbeat ways to communicate.

We head out of the gloom, crossing two parallel lanes. Cars line their kerbs spitting bags and passengers towards the terminal building.

"Listen, you are going for the purple paisley waistcoat aren't you? My dad needs to go and get one today if possible. He says your wedding shoes are finished, he will get someone from the factory to deliver them to your flat when you are back." The urgency of all this is clear with our marriage ten days away, but I do not feel it.

"And the ring, did you pay for that?" I have not called the jeweller to finally approve my on-hold wedding band.

"Sorry babe, I didn't get a chance to confirm." I screw my face up pleading for help. She knows I didn't want to call because I had to negotiate the price down.

"You do want the one I chose, don't you?" I nod my approval.

"Why didn't you call them then? I will have to do it later." I leak more responsibility into her already crammed Filofax. She is in a zone of high alert. She took a call before we set off from an ungrateful vegan non-dairy-eating cousin who is suddenly available and wants to attend with her family. Somehow Sophia thrives on it and knows she will bring it all in on time, on budget and to her specification. Her wedding most definitely, mine possibly.

CHAPTER 2

Dan 13:23

**WARNING! YOU ARE FORBIDDEN TO ENTER THIS AIRPORT
WITH ANY OF THE FOLLOWING ITEMS**

A list of banned substances is attached to the entrance on the outside of
the terminal building. It is so long that it can't be read without the risk
of decapitation from the revolving door. It flows from the obvious real
or replica guns (No Scooby Doo for Bepe) to reach the impossible brief
of no liquids nor gasses. How are humans meant to pass? Will any of
my stags fall foul of the list? My throat dries a little and my sphincter
twitches at the thought of my disparate stags in one place.

The visual noise and brash modernity of Manchester Airport
Terminal 3 screams at us as we move inside. Instantly you feel the
contortion between the beckoning promise of the freedom of cheap travel
and the sinister threat of some unknown act that could blow it all apart.
The rules are unrelenting even before the security assault course of 100ml
liquid limits and clear plastic bags. Being a fair-minded capitalist system
we also get the choice to buy back anything that has been confiscated at
fake bargain prices, which can't then be taken on your next plane journey!
Can't we just have one big sign saying: "Don't carry big bad stuff or else"?

My mind is working overtime as it is also confronted by the attrition
of advertising communication. I try to decode information crammed
onto every paintable, writable, scrawlable space. I am constantly working
out the ploy, the strategy, the pun, the masked hip reference point that
makes my fellow copywriters cream themselves in quipped glory. I don't
much succumb to advertising; I can only dissect and judge it.

"Departures that way Daniel," Sophia gestures towards the up escalator as we move inside. Prince knows how our all-consuming desperation to get the hell away from reality keeps us coming back for more.

But Bepe felt differently; he pleads for release from the trolley basket by wriggling every limb. "Diddy, wet down? Get plane Diddy."

I set him down onto my only baggage; the leather guitar case jam packed with all the clothing eventualities I could imagine for the four days ahead. Sophia has already commandeered every proper suitcase for our honeymoon to Portofino.

Bepe makes three toddler steps towards the escalator, the hesitancy of each one suggesting he is likely to topple over. However, in bold defiance of his dodgy toddling he bolts back towards the revolving door. I am frozen by the contradiction of his movement, as well as being stuck on the wrong side of the trolley. Does he just want another ride around? Twenty seconds later it is clear his agenda is escape.

"Just go will you!" Sophia's command is my starting gun.

I exit through the pseudo-roulette wheel that is the door. I cannot see him immediately amongst the hubbub of arrivals. So many things move at once that I have to keep surveying and re-assessing the scene. A taxi pulls in sharply but stays closed. A South American-looking businessman pushes an overloaded trolley with his left hand; his right arm holds both a draped camel coat and his mobile. Twelve over-excited eight-year-olds spill from a school mini-bus. I keep searching. There behind the unbalanced businessman I spy his crouching figure, close to the kerb at the rear of the halted taxi.

"Bepe," I attract his attention with a gentle suggestive tone so as not to prompt him to run again.

His crouch is to retrieve the banned Scooby Doo gun he has dropped in the gutter. It could also be in loin-girding preparation for a poo. I approach slowly but as I crouch down my jacket pocket spills my iPhone, which skids onto the harsh concrete. I wince at the thought of its glass being cracked or more importantly my music collection being trapped inside its malfunctioning casing. On its retrieval a sharp edge on one corner jags my palm. I am relieved to see the Apple sign illuminate it back to life.

"Dan, what are you doing? Dan…" Sophia is five yards behind me. Bepe has gone again. He has disappeared around the taxi, into the road, out of sight.

Engines roar around me. My glands seep hot sweat rapidly into my shirt. To my right I see another taxi travelling at about 30 mph on the two-lane one-way slip road. A blue car travels neck and neck with it. He will be all right; they will see him for sure. There is no point fearing the worst. The black cab in front of me narrows the road and forces them both to squeeze closer together. The drivers are caught up in unforgiving self-imposed timetables and are accelerating to leave the terminal. The over-loaded taxi could have stopped sooner had it had brand-new brake pads; instead an unnatural metal squeal is released as the driver vainly pushes his foot to the floor. This prefaces the thudding metallic crunch of the body of the taxi. My knees hit the pavement. I close my eyes to avoid seeing Bepe's pliable young bones helplessly shattered on a radiator grill. My eyes close, my head bows, my hands and forehead find my knee tops. At the point of impact he would have been thinking of his gun, the inane grin of Scooby Doo issuing an imaginary "Scooby-Doo-be-do" his last memory. Surely nothing else would register, he would feel pain momentarily and have no explanation for it. There was no chance to fear, he would not have braced himself for impact.

"You fool. Where is he? What have you done?" She speaks breathlessly with no moisture in her mouth.

"Don't think the worst babe." She swipes me on the back of the head as hard as she can. I shut myself down, locked in a sickened peace before my life can re-start its bloody mess.

"Bepe my baby, Bepe," she calls out to the road.

"Urghh." She emits a primal scream that reverberates in my bones, which I will never forget. Both hands are cupped over her mouth but she cannot prevent the escape of this inhuman guttural moan. At first I am embarrassed that she had made such a noise in public, but I look up to see her beautiful face full to the brim with wide-eyed terror. Through her eyes I see the unfathomable well of the universal parental soul, at the bottom of which is an unparalleled vortex of demonic agony from which there is no escape. This is the unthinkable part of having a child, losing them. The blinding light of her world has been snatched away, the pride and power of parenthood is under threat. She has so often told me that once you are a parent to one child, you become a parent to all children. This never kicked in for me before. This is parenthood, why has it taken me over two years to see it? At the point of tragedy I see my true responsibility. More worryingly Bepe was our relationship, the love we rallied around. Sophia's tension disperses through her thumb and forefinger locked onto the back of my neck. Somehow I enjoy the pain, as it is fully deserved. As the most culpable adult I will be assigned the millstone weight of the blame. My left arm reaches back to offer empathy but she shakes it off and walks haltingly towards the front of the taxi.

The accident would take the souls of eight lives. With Bepe gone his stricken parents would never make their union, we would walk away from each other without a glance. She would sleep on the floor of his time-frozen bedroom for four years. I would sleep on the floor of the ad agency for four weeks. The light of life would go out for four grandparents, and each in quick succession hastened towards earlier graves. The haunted taxi driver would never recover, always the night terrors and the contradiction being a child killer took against his own family life. I could imagine living in rancid isolation, a sneered-at pub loner, the man single women cross the street to avoid. My family don't die early; I would be locked into the insufferable torment of memories of the little life I surrendered for an iPhone. I started babbling this to myself. There is no inane stag weekend now.

"Is this your son?" A male voice from my right shatters my foresight.

"Is this your son?" he repeats. In the seconds since the accident I had lost all hope of him being intact.

"Is this your son?" Bepe is alive and reaching down for me. I look up to accept the intact but limp shape of Bepe into my arms. His face is a puddle of tears and shock, his eyes swollen into slits. He went too far but has come back. His top is soaked with dirty cold water, presumably from some nearby puddle. His second coming brings more life to me than his first. Two and a half years ago Sophia's mother relegated me at his birth to being a redundant outsider but no more. His appearance then seemed like the frantic production of a coven of white witches. At first I was allowed to look not touch while they hid any hard evidence of his magical appearance.

Sophia lurches past me from the scene of the car crash.

"Sophia, he's fine, our baby is fine." She grabs her son from me and screams from her empty womb. They envelop into one, her muscular hold seems to be trying to morph him back inside her body for ultimate protection. She cries and gasps for air, jerking her whole torso.

My life is resuscitated; it comes flooding back in glorious 4D High Definition Technicolor with surround sound. An engine roars high above in praise of my recovered spirit; its burnt petrol particles are like smelling salts. Each breath tastes most wondrous. I feel the damp concrete coldness eke through my corduroys, set dead against the warmth of the spring day. It is that day, the one that bakes the earth for the first time in months, heralding an aching change to the tone of the year, real growth begins.

"I saw it all. He ran across the road, tripped and fell just onto the edge of the pedestrian island." My fellow traveller helps me to my feet. From my restored height I now see that the blue car was not an immediate danger to him, it was in the outer exit lane across the paved area Bepe landed on. However the travelling taxi must have swerved to avoid him and clipped the open door of the static one.

"Thank you. Thank you." I clasp his hand and shake away some demons.

"Don't thank me, I just picked him up. Thank God, Praise Allah and the rest of them that he is alright. Let's face it, there is nothing you can do to stop them getting into scrapes is there?" I feel unqualified to answer, having only just graduated with a scraped third-class degree in parenting. He goes back for his trolley and to offer himself as a witness to the feuding taxi drivers.

I look afresh at Bepe's beautiful wet face. Plumped, red, olive-skinned cheeks, redness competing against his brown eyes, a small bloody graze on his forehead. For the moments we were ripped apart he became faceless, I could not see him for fear he never came back. This is unconditional love, not one you can mentally re-appraise the nature and strength of right up to your wedding day. I shudder in his humbling presence.

"Why did you let him go?

"He just ran babe."

"You silly fool, you almost got him killed while you picked up that bloody phone." I leave the harsh judgement and blame at my door. Sophia leans forward to spit out the acidic pre-cursor to a full on vomit just released into her mouth.

"Diddy get my plane," Bepe gives his game away. His escape was to recover the plane from the car. I contemplate recovering it for him so he won't run again. I am damned for taking one toy and almost damned forever by leaving the other.

"Let's get you tidied up kiddo." I rejoice at the prospect of another mundane change of clothes, however incessant these demands I will never begrudge another one.

"Home Diddy? Bad Diddy." Gravitas disappears as he screws his nose and mouth into a grin. Sophia kisses away his warm salty tears.

"Mummy and Bepe are going home; let's get rid of daddy on the big plane now."

"Plane Diddy," shouts Bepe as we revolve back inside. He is my son like never before.

CHAPTER 3

Dan 13:47

My bones ache, relieved of unthinkable tension. A security guard back inside the terminal is glaring at my abandoned guitar case. I hastily pick it up and return to contemplating travelling with the inhumane chemistry experiment that is my combustible friends.

"What the bloody hell have you packed your guitar for?" My brother Chris arrives with his expected disdain for this trip and all who sail in her. I let go of it to shake his hand and find it scraping my shins through my beige mini cord trousers. The pain is not so bad, just a dull marrow deep ache in my slight shins. I grin at his rounded ruddy blonde presence. He is a ruffle of a man; he looks akin to one of the haystacks at the end of his field. I am happy he is here but I know he is extra baggage on this delicate trip. I have always loved his steadiness. Chris Greenhenge never made store by anything that could not be done manually, a world where words are hardly used. Fashioning potatoes and children from seed, soil and sunshine is his contribution to life. Our physicality is completely different; he is hewn from our father's rock-like presence, me from my mum's delicate ancestry.

"Been here long?" I ask.

"No, Sandra and the kids just dropped me off in the Land Rover." I imagine the mayhem of seven bodies crammed into the far reaches of the vehicle, some seated, some on sheep dip canisters.

"Sophia, right good to see you." He offers his grinding rough-skinned grip to her.

"Bepe nearly had an accident outside. Dan let him run out of the airport and almost let him be knocked over by a taxi."

"Are you stupid or what? Why did you do that?" He is happy to instantly blame me rather than seek further explanation. He exchanges worn glances with Sophia; both are paid-up members of a responsible parent club that I have been blackballed from. Sophia treats me like Bepe's sad older brother who has yet to leave home.

"Listen, will I know any of these characters?" Chris is worried.

"Of course. Johnny and Max from my year at school, Robert you met at college once and of course Juliet." The last name betrays information I withheld till the very last. I have avoided telling everyone except Jonny my best man and Sophia, in the hope of skipping past inevitable resistance.

"What, women on a stag do!"

"Listen, she was a good friend." She was much more but I cannot remind anyone of that.

"Sounds a bloody odd bunch." With that he withdrew his approval and sat it squarely on a fence, waiting for the appropriate time to chide my ill-judged selection. Old rogue friends and an ex-girlfriend, who I broke up horrendously with; it didn't exactly feel risk free.

Bepe reminds us he is still here by firing his gun at the stomach of the security guard who starts to move towards us. I pick him up quickly. They scowl but ignore the non-lethal weapon in my son's hand despite the briefing from outside.

"Let's go up to check-in guys," I say.

"Postman Pat," Bepe thinks the security guard has the look of a village mailman about him as we ascend the escalator which runs alongside the inside windowed shell of the building. We rise above the two taxi drivers who are now occupied with the police. The angel who returned my son has flown. A brief contemplation of what might-have-been causes me to stumble at the top.

"Face forward, can't you read?" Chris points out a sign that I would never have thought I would have needed.

I ignore SELF SERVICE CHECK-IN, a concept I mistrust completely, to find DESKS 23–26.

SEE A MEMBER OF STAFF BEFORE YOU JOIN THIS QUEUE – another sign barks at me, denying me my right to join the great British queue.

Bags shuffle forward in the dreaded line. Some owners are desperate to unburden themselves and proceed to retail therapy; others are starting their holiday right here. Chris and I pass over our luggage. We agree to check in separately so we can both get aisle seats; me because of oversized legs, Chris because of an oversized body.

"Here's Johnny!" Sophia is unaware of the grimacing axe-wielding face in my head, rolling his eyes through a wooden door. Johnny offers nothing but solace, we smile at each other knowing that there is love with no edge. No proving, no probing, just approval and openness. I first noticed his unkempt rebel fringe in class 3R and we have co-existed since. I can show him my soul and he will nourish it. We completely unite over the post-punk musical tapestry that succoured us through adolescent acne-afflicted angst. He will add a dose of calm to the heady stag brew.

"Look who I found, Dan," Johnny's appearance has a sting in its tail. Back at self check-in, I see the fit scrubbed presence of Robert. His feathered flick haircut has been unchanged for decades. At first glance he cuts a boyish non-confrontational figure, but as he marches towards me with hand outstretched he bellows confidence at my shrinking mojo. He usually pulls the strings and presses the buttons to get whatever he wants. Our college friendship was probably only due to him wanting shagging access to the less available female populace I naturally befriended.

"You skinny twat! Saw you downstairs as I transferred from Barcelona but you disappeared outside after what I assume to be that Sprog of yours. I didn't think I was going to make it; there was a BA client junket this weekend in Aspen. I thought at least I would get us some serious skiing though. Chamonix will be better anyway, not!" He pretends to punch me in the stomach as proof of our familiarity. The only punch he has ever pulled.

"I'm skiing demon at the moment. I could still hop out to Aspen on Sunday anyway; I will see how things go. Depends on the totty quotient. Can't think there will be much going on with your track record though, I will have to make the running as usual." Everyone waits for the tide to go out. Robert just goes; any points of issue are seldom challenged by anyone for fear of a further diatribe.

"Good to see you. Thanks for the plane tickets and hotel." I strain to lie and find a new conversation away from him. His idea for a ski weekend coupled with free travel was enough to bulldoze Johnny into cancelling the log cabin he had booked in Scotland. I resented him for making a vulgar offer the group lapped up but Johnny couldn't refuse.

"No sweat. If the marketing director of BA can't get some slummy economy flights to Geneva then what's the point? Anyway I said I would give them some feedback on the state of economy class since I last went on it twenty years ago." He leaves us in no doubt as to his perception that we are privileged to be in his company.

"And you two getting married, I can't see the point of breaking up a good thing myself. Sophia you still look foxy, maybe business class these days though. Give me a snog." Chris and Sophia think this is a compliment on how classy she looks. Johnny and I wince knowing that this Swingers reference suggests considerable growth in the size of my fiancées lovely Italianate behind and her inability to fit into an economy seat. She pecks both cheeks after he had tried a full-frontal kiss assault.

"And here is the Sprog himself." He pats Bepe on the head like a grimacing Tory politician touching the unwashed masses. How dare he touch my son like that?

"Need a java now. I'm off to Cosa Nostra." Finally we get away from being his audience. Having not acknowledged Johnny or my brother, having insulted my fiancée, disregarded my son and embarrassed me, I judge our initial round with Robert to be a fantastic success.

The steam frother of the coffee shop sucks us into Cosa Nostra – The Sicilian coffee company. Their strap line reads YOU KEEPA COMING BACK OR WE BREAKA YOUR LEGS. When did the threat of violence become a customer focused unique selling point? I can see Sophia bristle at the Italian caricature that brings everyone to this vision of underground Italian culture.

"Madonn'," she whispers and crosses herself.

As we queue they continue their Mafia-themed assault. OUR

Barista's are all Made Men, so don't give them lip while you
wait.

We take our drinks to a corner that can also accommodate the three
stags yet to come. The seats defy the pre-requisite and our expectation
of comfort. The sticky grime on the wooden floor and the abandoned
coffee mugs, all betray an establishment that thinks it is so successful
that it doesn't need to care anymore. James Gandolfini gives us that
menacing stare of threatened action, from a black and white photograph
above the sugar collection point. Everyone thinks this a cool place to
spend some time.

The sound of a plastic boy band covering a U2 favourite fills me
with distaste. Bepe bounces on his knees in acknowledgement of the
Muzak. Before today I would probably have stopped him moving to this
monstrosity but I don't feel able to deny him any little enjoyment as he
starts a new chapter of his life.

My iPhone flashes Juliet back into my life. I hastily pick it up from
the table accidentally nudging my green tea-filled cup. After wobbling
twice on its bottom rim, it settles back to terra firma but discharges a
splash of scalding water onto my knee. This minor pain is nothing to
what I have felt already today.

"Yes, Cosa Nostra, opposite the self service check-in desks," I guide
her to me.

"Juliet has just got off her Heathrow flight and is on her way up."
I throw this information to the group but no one reacts. They are the
crew of a pirate ship waiting to spit their disdain at the woman
coming aboard; muttering under their breath that the captain has
cursed the trip.

"I'll just pop to the loo," I leave them to get used to the idea.

I wait for the unisex cubicle to be free. Just after I hear the clicking
noise of the lock, the warm stench of excrement flushed by a wizened-
looking old man in a hoody greets me. I am not deterred from running
in and slumping fully clothed on the covered toilet seat. What if the toy
had dropped in the road? What if he had taken one step less? Why can't
I look after him properly? When was the last time I cried like this? Am

19

I crying for Bepe or me? The rush of emotion subsides quickly when I remember Juliet's impending arrival.

I exit with clammy hands to see Juliet and Sophia in an over-generous embrace, which I know betrays a needlepoint tension. I tense my facial muscles to remove any remnants of my despair. My combined service to womanhood squeezes itself together in one square metre. I cross the coffee shop desperate to hold this fragile alliance together.

There is an aura of serenity around Juliet; she is perpetual grace in motion, warmth emanating from her that all can see. The immaculate girl is now an immaculate lady, a skilled presentation of accessory and cloth to simultaneously suggest control and fashion. Her face is like a fine line drawing, pale blue eye shadow, and lipstick-perfect lips adorn her fine jaw line. I want to watch her from afar before I exit the years of silence. We are starting a new history when the last one was unfulfilled. Our last words, apart from a brief phone call two weeks ago, were in a flat in the Isle of Dogs, in London's old docklands. Her platitudes of friendship were thrown as an inadequate lifebelt to a drowning man. I blush to remember my former access-all-areas pass to her body, which has been long withdrawn. I imagine being able to stroke her chalk-white thighs with my member, but a rising sickness prevents further mental invasion. She constantly replaces her hair behind her ear signalling that she is troubled, although this time I am able to guess what. Was this just a really bad idea? I want to explode towards her with an unbounded embrace.

"Hi babe, so great you could make it." I move slowly towards her with arms down low. Sophia reaches high alert immediately, checking for any residual sign of feeling towards her. My awkward sideways asexual shoulder hug causes Juliet's shoulder bag to finally spill the remaining contents of my teacup. I still feel love so strong.

"Great you're here," I sigh. Everyone's face questions her presence.

"The sexiest looking stag I've ever seen. Come here." Robert returns with his coffee and seizes the etiquette opportunity to impose himself on a woman.

"What are you doing on a stag weekend anyway?" Robert has the balls to ask the question everyone is simultaneously thinking.

"Just wanted to give Dan a good send off like you."

"You are privileged, you'll see a whole different side to mankind this weekend. How delicate and supportive we can be to a man who is about to go through the trauma of marriage." We wait for the punch line and Robert duly delivers.

"How delicately we can shave his balls and how supportive we can be as we encourage his performance in a brothel. What are you going to do in the brothel anyway, give him a threesome?" Robert is so out on a limb, the air is thick with threat and effrontery; the worry for me is that I don't know how much he thinks is a true reflection of the coming four days.

I re-introduce Juliet to a suspicious Chris and a welcoming Johnny.

"I've just offered my congratulations to Sophia and apologised again for not being able to come to your wedding," Juliet informs me. Sophia stands with Bepe on one hip, she looks nervous, her thoughts compromised by the gift of Juliet's expensive tropical spray.

"Thanks for the flowers." Sophia flashes a grimace that undermines her statement.

"It's so good to see you both after so long. How beautiful is Giuseppe?" All said from the heart, but every word tested for secondary meaning by my fiancée.

"We just call him Bepe," Sophia snaps at her and pulls him away back to her seat.

Send in the clowns so my circus can be complete.

"Staggie!" shouts Max from outside the coffee shop. My shoulders droop from the prospect of the further trouble I have invited. The entry of my boss Max and creative team partner Steve divides all the coffee clientele into either gasps or guffaws. They struggle through the tightly packed wooden furniture accompanied by a life-size ginger-haired blow-up doll. The width of both their grins matches the sex toy's gaping mouth.

"Look who we found. It's that old girlfriend you spent years pining over when she dumped you. She is our plastic prozzy on the spot just in case anyone gets desperate." They present me with the rubber doll and slap my back, insisting on a photograph. I am wracked with guttural pain. Like Robert they jovially stab me in the back, walking the fine line between humour and attack.

"You said women weren't allowed Dan. I would have brought a real prostitute for us all to share." Robert starts the one upmanship. He has made no attempt at re-connection with my older brother and Johnny despite us all being at the same primary school, but zeros in on anyone likely to inflict pain on me.

"Max, Steve meet Juliet my ex-girlfriend." They don't skip a beat over their faux pas with the sex doll.

"Here is your stag T-shirt everyone." Steve dishes out his personally designed lime-green T-shirt to everyone, without bothering for introductions. The front reads: STAGS ON TOUR. REVENGE ON GREENHENGE. WEDNESDAY 15TH APRIL 2009 TO SUNDAY 19TH APRIL 2009. The back is adorned with a photograph of me thrown over a toilet bowl at our 2005 Centurion office Christmas party. The mottled green vomit from an absinthe binge is evident on both my blue shirt and forearm. Steve sniggers self-congratulatory.

"Oh and here are some horny horns for the rutting stag. I got small so that they didn't slip off your greasy hair. I'll put them on." Max adds to the embarrassment. I abide sixty seconds of pain over my ears before I can pass them on to Bepe without seeming too ungrateful. Robert rises to these two new additions with a personal introduction.

That's us now, we unhappy few. I am in the full glare of my supposed true men and good, the people who will form the core of my wedding invitees, future big birthday parties and my eventual funeral. Stag status report: Chris dumbstruck; Johnny perturbed; Robert enthused; Juliet abnormally sheepish: Max smug; Steve fulfilled. My fiancée is at boiling point with her pan lid clacking.

The stag has had his antlers rattled. Being the focus of crass humour and potential physical assault for five days will be a trial. I am exposed to an arctic wind not knowing how hard it will blow. I struggle to think of what to do next but my stags don't.

"Let's get this party started right. Let's have a stag photo. Maybe outside in the hallway?" Johnny tries to engage them and wrestle their raucous spirit for me.

"Stag T-shirts on of course," insists Steve.

"Proper stags only though," says Robert. He glances at me, then Juliet, to make sure I exclude her, automatically expecting Sophia to stay in her place as well.

Juliet realises this quickly and meets it with her own purpose. "Could I stay here to catch up with Sophia; we have so much to talk about." Sophia looks shocked.

We move outside the coffee shop where a perplexed passer-by is enlisted to capture this edgy moment on camera. I lock arms with my men as best I can, crouching down a little to stay at their shoulder height. At this moment I do not judge. During the whooping and hollering we find a level male playing field, a half-remembered playground that I hated even then.

CHAPTER 4

Juliet 14.12

"HOW CAN I REACH ACROSS OUR SEVENTEEN YEARS APART?"

Dan shows no immediate signs of ageing. The same overgrown black hair and wiry physique. The same hooded eyelids conceal his striking grey-green eyes. The same trademark thick black-rimmed glasses. He still tries in vain to compress his tall frame by bowing his head, to feel part of the crowd.

However, seventeen more years must have created a man from the boy I went out with. He has a career in advertising, a ruthless shallow industry that would make anyone grow up. He has made a commitment to a wife and child that he would have been incapable of then. The last time I saw him was on the balcony of our flat in the Isle of Dogs when I said goodbye. I crushed his spirit too easily.

Dan will hate the attention of this embarrassing parade of stag photographs. Men are at their most natural in ape-like packs; they are immediate conspirators. I have overheard their speech instantly descend to perversity, cruelty and insult, casting off care or attention. If they withhold boyish laughter or a sly grin at a crucial point it weakens them. I have seen careers wrecked by the pack and decisions to risk millions made by such a board of apes. I am used to being the woman in the boys' club. In order to be tolerated I must make my own rules; know when to be passive and when to attack. The question is how far will this group go to embarrass Dan?

I have been upright, observing the stag pictures for too long. I must try and close the vacuum with Sophia. As I sit down next to her I

24

imagine everyone else's cappuccinos going cold in her frosty presence. She won't look at me.

"Diddy gone, Mummy." The sweet Bepe seems calm that his dad isn't around. Sophia grips him firmly around the chest.

"Not yet. But he is going on a big plane soon," Sophia explains softly.

"You look a radiant bride-to-be." My olive branch is an unwelcome addition to the £120 tropical spray.

"Why are you here Juliet?" Sophia uses our small window for truth, while staring at the mayhem in the corridor. I get a beautiful flash of her Italian lineage.

"I couldn't come to your wedding so called to apologise. I said I would like to see him before he got married and he asked me on his stag weekend. I thought it very odd but didn't want to refuse a second invitation," I reported the truth but not why I wanted to see him.

"But a stag party, it is wrong. Why are you here after all this time?"

"I wanted to recognise your wedding. I just wanted to congratulate him on growing up and settling down. " I fend off her question for a second time.

"You could have just sent flowers." Now I am worried; she is scared of what he might still feel for me.

"I thought it would be great to spend time with him again!" I may have misjudged this completely, just because I have no residual feelings.

"We are just fine, the boat needs no rocking," Sophia spits at me.

"I am not here for that. I was relieved to hear he had finally asked you to marry him."

"Well you know that didn't happen." Sophia looks at me for the first time with panic in her eyes. If I were anyone else it looks like she would break down.

"Juliet, let's get your arse in the picture Juliet." Robert mocks me from the hallway. I just smile and wave him away.

"I thought he might propose when Bepe arrived, but nothing. Two years ago my papa got a Saturday night date from his golf club, Mere Park. Papa told him he had booked for a wedding. Dan smiles and says 'Great babe'. There was no asking. Men don't know their minds anymore. They are babies; they are Peter Pan." Sophia kisses Bepe's head as he sucks a Rusk.

"I thought it would be safe to come now he is committed."

"What do you mean safe? Safe from you?" Sophia looks shocked again.

"No, no. I mean safe from the resentment he might have for me finishing with him."

"You have a high opinion of yourself." She puts Bepe in between us and sips her coffee.

"No. I just know he can be a little idealistic."

"Look here you, I know what this marriage is. I want Bepe to have a father okay; a boy needs a dad. You have a son, doesn't he have a dad?"

"A step-father."

"And where is his real dad?"

"I had a fling immediately after Dan. I brought Ethan up on my own, but we have been living with Scott for five years now. He is a good father."

"Are you sure Ethan isn't Dan's son?" At last she strikes at the core of her suspicions.

"Of course I am." I issue a firm rebuttal

"He only got a third class degree because of you." I left him and college in February 1992 in the middle of our final year. He exhausted me; his indecision left me spent. Nevertheless I shudder to think of his pain.

"Don't you dare upset him again!"

"Get Juliet in the picture!" I hear the strain of Max's shout. I momentarily think it is me they want, but no it is a reminder for Dan to bring the rubber doll into shot. Sophia privately enjoys my ridicule and I look to the floor in embarrassment. Bepe coughs hard flushing his face with blood; catarrh threatens to bring the Rusk back in liquid form.

"Could I hold Bepe for a minute?" Sophia ignores me.

"How is Dan, Sophia?"

"He is infuriating but lovely. Max undervalues and takes advantage of him because they are old school friends. His music keeps him happy but reclusive." In spite of Sophia's hostility to me she opens the floodgates.

"He cannot say what I mean to him. He lives by himself still and has been hopeless at finding a house for us, so is moving into my parents' house. He lets Bepe run riot; he almost got knocked down outside because of him. He is so distant from us sometimes; he is here but not here if you know what I mean. Why does he want me? Perhaps you can find out? I think he wants to marry me but have never heard why from him so who really knows?" She desperately wanted to say that doubt out loud.

"He is a one-off. You can protect him." I don't acknowledge her request, but feel the weight of its expectation.

"Anyway, just think there would be no Bepe without him."

"Madonn'," Sophia crosses herself.

"I hope they behave for him." I point towards the group who are now sitting astride each other as if in a rowing boat. Singing "Oops-upside-your-head" will be crucifying Dan.

"I've met Chris before; he's quiet but okay. Don't know Max and Steve. Johnny seems nice though. As you know Robert is an arsehole..." I sum up the group.

"Johnny is the best of them, his best man. He had arranged a stag weekend in Scotland for them all in log cabin. But Robert decided he would like a ski weekend so paid for it all. The others agreed when they knew it was free," Sofia adds.

"They are a really terrible mix so I will try to keep an eye on them."

With their pictures taken, the group mooch around waiting for another bonding opportunity. Robert shouts over to me: "We are off to load up on porn mags. Fancy a "Men Only" staggette?" He moves off laughing to himself, neither getting nor expecting a reply.

"Look out for him for me. I don't trust you but I trust them less." Sophia has now seen me as less of a threat and a potential advantage of me being here.

"I promise," I square up to her to convey my sincerity.

Dan rushes back, looking for signs of what has gone on between Sophia and I.

"You look after him." She squeezes my hand as Dan sits down

Sophia passes Bepe to me after all. "Lady naughty," he offers for no particular reason.

"What have you two been talking about?" he asks.

"You know us girls Dan, talking wedding dresses!" Why did I say that?

"No prostitutes!" Sophia states firmly with pursed lips, setting out the worst result of Dan's trip that she can imagine.

"Of course babe. You know they will do something embarrassing…" Dan implores and I agree with him.

Is Dan the same? Now next to me his grey hairs at last acknowledge some years have passed. I worry he is sleepwalking into this marriage. But did I choose correctly seventeen years ago?

CHAPTER 5

Dan 14:27

"We better get through security guys…" Johnny decides to take up the mantle of being my best man. The group shuffle back into the coffee shop. Cups are drained, coats are grabbed and bags are strapped.

"Lets give Juliet a ride on the conveyor belt then." Robert is looking at the rubber doll again but enjoying the association with the real person. Max and Steve cackle approval and follow in quick time, latching onto the Alpha male.

I help my wife-to-be and son gather themselves. For once we move silently, to the edge of Departures. The residual smell of the coffee shop lingers on my clothes, adding to the body odour rising from my armpits, caused by both my travel trepidation and parental agitation. The blue ribbons of the airline queue march my stags in a zigzag path towards our destination. More signage affronts me. HOLD BAGGAGE. INSPECTION POINT. Are they giving marks out of ten for the grace with which I can lift my luggage now? Stupid literal clashes of words clatter around my head.

"Can't let him out of your sight hey," Chris says to Sophia, completely misjudging the mood as I we stand outside the security coral. "We will go. Goodbye Sophia." Chris accepts no response from Sophia, using his broad hands and rounded shoulders to usher Juliet and Johnny towards the security inspection. They are keeping a face-saving distance from the others.

"You shouldn't be going now. Have you considered that?" We hang back and Sophia expresses her unease after our scare.

"I don't want to leave you both." I have not really reconsidered making the trip after the Bepe scare. But what would happen to the others? This whole trip would be merciless for Johnny and Juliet. I can't let them down. I start to seek redemption in Sophia's eyes, something that will never be wholly given.

I sweep Bepe up in my right arm; I see the dark stain deep in the crotch of his trousers way too late. He holds his genital area trying to push the wet back in. The warm glow of urine transfers into my micro-corduroy shirt. There is comfort in this familiarity, that we can share anything. Bepe sets about my neck with a bite, then a punch.

Ahead of us Max feebly attempts to carry rubber Juliet past security, but a stern look prompts her deflation; Steve is given the task. Robert and Max move on, letting him struggle to push the sickly rubberised air back out before baggage inspection. They don't think to acknowledge my family.

"That hippy at the back has coke and a shoe bomb guys!" Robert points me out to get a reaction from security. They give even sterner looks as Max doubles up in laughter. The security guards try to give Robert a talking-to but I assume he is bigging up his role at BA in order to escape sanction.

Johnny and Juliet navigate the ribbon slowly, exchanging glances with Chris to keep away from the rubber-doll crew.

"An odd bunch," says Sophia when they are all out of earshot.

"Which ones?" I take a chance to enquire.

"Max and Steve are creeps. Robert is an arrogant shit. Your brother Chris is so un-expressive. Johnny is a good friend I suppose." Sophia sums up the band with a gaping omission.

"They are just a bit boisterous," I meekly suggest.

Sophia sees Bepe's personal relief. "Your shirt will stink on the flight."

"That's the least of my worries. You can change him again on the way out."

"I have so much to do today." She sees a mental list with change our wet son sitting urgently at the top.

"I am sorry, so sorry. You can only do what you can do babe."

"You should have done this trip earlier."

"It's all going to fall into place now, you will see. In ten days we will be standing at the altar." My feeble pep talk is needed and partially lightens her lead-weighted demeanour.

"Do you really want to stand at the altar Dan?

"Weddings aren't really my bag babe. I know you wanted to do it your way."

"It doesn't mean you had to let me do everything. Why do you want to marry me Dan?"

"Oh babe…you know." I redden as I give her the meekest assurance with my exasperated look. Maybe I am waiting for an answer as much as her. What words can I use that wont be severely tested?

"I suppose I am too stressed. My emotions are raging," she admits.

"It's understandable. You will look beautiful. We will be fine babe."

"I will move that table of stags as far away from us as possible," Sophia informs me, although I never knew they were close by.

"That will stop Robert throwing scorn and bread rolls at us."

Bepe is still perched quietly on my right arm, transfixing me with his grin. I recognise the flicker of menace far too late to recoil from the gun brought crashing into my head. Cheap roughly moulded purple plastic gouges my temple.

"Giuseppe!" shouts his mother.

I put him on the floor. I touch my throbbing pulsing wound; a red slash of blood streaks across my fingers. Sophia provides a tissue to stem the flow from the inch-long cut.

"Why do that to Daddy, he is going on the big plane now," Sophia tries to gain his remorse but at last seems to have released me.

"Diddy go home," Bepe proposes again.

"He will miss you, is all," says Sophia.

"He is showing a real wilfulness. I don't know why. He used to be very placid but he's turning." All the party are out of sight, making me even more uncomfortable.

"We do love you, you know, call us to tell us that you do too!"

"Of course and I'll send texts and photos on the new iPhone as well."

I pick Bepe up again to promote a group huddle; Sophia reluctantly moves into the circle. I luxuriate in our combined body warmth, which wafts a wave of heat into my face. To think minutes ago this picture might never have been possible. I take my phone out, with our heads touching together we all face the camera. A "Schick" sound from my phone confirms the moment's capture.

"I have to go. Love you guys. Bye."

For once look forward, Dan.

CHAPTER 6

Dan 14:35

Leaving leaves me drained. I walk head bowed into Departures; away from love and personal contradiction. I am most relieved to relinquish the position of baby security guard to Sophia. I see myself kneeling in unending despair by the taxi, all hope lost from my outstretched arms. In the end Sophia was okay I think, not too fazed by Juliet's presence, the accident or Robert's boorishness.

Where is my boarding... oh there? I cannot believe Juliet is actually here; she still looks great. Can I remember how to ski after all these years? What a selfish loose cannon Robert is. Chris is going to hate all of them. Hope Max didn't get any more work at that meeting with ByeFly yesterday; we would have to do it next week before I disappear to Italy for three weeks. Juliet and Johnny will hate everyone as well. There is hope if they are all here for me I suppose.

Airport security flexes their muscles again at the security area; they have every right to inspect every possession. What is the right look to inspire trust? I think over-friendly comments would bring as much suspicion as being deathly quiet; beaming inanely must be worse of all. My forgotten belt forces squeals of rejection from the full length X-ray machine. I unbuckle it and successfully try again, prompting them to give me a just-in-case skimming with a metal detector wand. I re-gather my possessions and move on. Why do they make me feel so grateful to get to my plane?

I walk at pace, ignoring the wealth of retail fixes on offer. My group is sitting blankly on thin designer chairs cemented to the floor at Departure Gate 33. As I approach their eyes seem to search for me to attempt the impossible, to weld together this heap of my life's scrap metal.

"Here's our man," Johnny tries to rally them. Downcast eyes betray characters who never think of anyone but themselves. It is scary seeing them all together.

"Really sorry guys." My unnecessary apology is unconditional, unspecific and multi-dimensional in the hope that each person will take a different crumb.

"Did I stop anyone boarding?" I see that the exit door behind the gate is open; it squirts the compressed sucking sound of jet engines. Three young families and seven pensioners line up at the desk, taking advantage of their privileged boarding status.

"No, but there are some clucking hens who want to see you before we board," says Max. He had probably felt duty bound to foist himself on them as a stag. I turn to see seven women slumped pensively in pink T-shirts and plastic tiaras. Their hen spirit has evidently gone flat.

"What's the story there?" I ask him.

"They have no hen to fly the coop with them." Blatantly ignoring the flying inability of this bird.

"She had an argument with her intended this morning and is in hospital or something." Their decision to carry on regardless looks a terrible one. I am glad for the advance warning as a disgruntled hen waddles over.

"This is him, is it?" She enquires of Max.

"Not much on him; bloody tall though." She seems immediately oblivious to me and disappointed in my physique. She nonchalantly kisses me good luck relaying the heavy odour of a heavy smoker. Her spittle invasively hangs on my cheek as the outside air cools it. The other hens seem a little cheered to know someone nearby has the prospect of getting married.

"Where are you girls headed to?" I skirt around their loss.

"Staying in Courmayeur in Italy, but fuck knows why. Our Karen has just busted her intended's head open with a video player. She caught him with his trousers down having a wank watching dirty tapes of him shagging his ex. He is in casualty now with two injuries.

"What are those then?" Max pushes his luck.

34

"He needs stitches because he has VCR imprinted on his head and apparently his dick got caught in his zip as he tried to run off. She has stopped taking our calls, but we think she has finished with him. Anyway we are going for a piss up." She takes me right to the heart of the matter. The first block of rows is called and the other hens shuffle towards the exit.

Chris and Juliet stand up to follow them but can only walk two paces.

"How are your children Chris?" Juliet tries to tempt Chris into his first words in her company.

"Great, all five of them."

"Wow, you must have wanted a lot of kids," Juliet says jovially.

Chris looks puzzled as if there was some family planning involved.

"You got any?" he hoped.

"Yes, Ethan, he's sixteen. I am so proud of him. He should be going into sixth form in September to…" Juliet tails off as she realises the detail means nothing to him and Chris has stopped listening to what he perceives as middle-class babble.

"You must be proud of your brother getting married at last." Juliet over emphasises her statement to Chris whilst turning towards me with a collusive smile to acknowledge that this is really her addressing me.

"Suppose." Chris looks puzzled. In his eyes marrying someone two years after you had a child with them doesn't seem that admirable.

From my seated position I detect a faint smell of iron from her, maybe indicating a fading period. Unfortunately from Chris I receive the pungent sweaty aroma of someone who doesn't change his socks regularly enough.

"We are now boarding rows fifteen to thirty," the steward announces.

Johnny, Max, Steve and Robert stand to attention as Chris and Juliet walk forward at last.

The crowd pushes Johnny and Max into a pair. Johnny is ill at ease, he knows the many lies that this particular hypocritical Christian has foisted on me over the years.

"Look what I have got." Max shows Johnny a bag crammed with pornography. Johnny recoils from the partially open mouths and legs spilling from their front covers.

"Where are you working now?" Max enquires, knowing the answer.

"Just doing guitar lessons from home."

"How can you earn a decent living at that?"

"Just something I can do and feel rewarded for." Johnny is undaunted by their different values. However Max seems to be threatened by this worthy world, presumably hoping it would stay away from his.

"What do you think of the new Killers album?" Johnny thinks he is moving the conversation on by generously inviting dialogue, instead Max is privately seething that he doesn't have the ability to comment on something he should.

I stand as the final rows are called. Steve and Robert are another imbalanced pairing.

"Suppose you have been to Chamonix before," Steve gives the floor to Robert.

"Skied it from top to bottom. I climbed Mont Blanc and then skied off-piste down the Vallée Blanche in one day. It's the toughest resort I know. Why do you think I wanted to come here?" Robert doesn't skip a beat in offering his selfish perspective on my weekend.

"Suppose you have a few air miles now." Steve is trying to make it onto Robert's social radar by constantly giving Robert the chance to speak.

"I'm a director at BA, I don't need them. Just what do you do again?" Robert finally asks with clear disdain.

"I work with Dan as part of a creative team. He writes words for my creative visualisation."

"You paint pretty pictures then?" Robert dismisses Steve's work.

"I will be Creative Director before long."

"Oh!" Robert is bored and tries to end his participation in the conversation.

"Where's the stag sitting then?" I tell Robert 32C, gained after my request for an aisle seat. He looks even less interested in me than Steve, but he is trying to shake him off.

"I've got some Charlie for later if you want some," Steve offers.

"I gave it up years ago, it's for losers." Steve's social coffin is nailed with a hammer blow.

"Hi gorgeous, the picture doesn't do me justice does it?" Robert reaches the desk four people ahead of me and glows at the dark-haired flight attendant who lingers over his boarding pass. The world is suspended around him as he makes advances to her; the presence of the queue behind them disappears. Their private amusement is all that matters.

I tail my stags out onto the puddle-ridden tarmac. I cannot carry their collective behaviour for five days; they will all have to work out a way to co-exist. The rush of spring air sears through my heart again. I relive the sheer relief I felt earlier at Bepe's return. Maybe I can just enjoy the fact I have a son re-born to me after this mangled start.

CHAPTER 7

Dan 14:50

I am the last of the party to clank onto the spongy passenger stairs; my trip is confirmed. I pass the final security checkpoint at the airplane door and am ushered humourlessly down the aisle by the flighty flight attendant that was so attentive to Robert.

A mild "Wooorrr…" greets my approach to my seat, a noise cast from different sides of the plane. My height means I always feel restricted on a plane, I keep my head and eyes down hoping the noise will fade away.

"Hello there sexy." Steve, who I now see has an aisle seat behind me, pinches my bottom. I grin and move on, completely non-plussed by his out of character inanity. I work with this man daily, but my stag status gives added piquancy to everything I say and do.

The "Wooorrr…" sound grows as I arrive at my seat to find it already occupied by a partially re-inflated rubber Juliet. The passengers around me are infected by the ridicule this brings. A large man in a dark suit sits next to her and offers me his hand either as congratulations or to show approval of the way I am holding together under this abuse. My mood collapses further under every attack.

"Your girlfriend left these behind." Robert appears from the back of the plane holding up a red lace bra and knickers' set to the rest of the plane.

"Danny is a tranny!" he half sings, using the props as mock evidence. Some others unite behind this anthem.

"Come on, put them on Staggie." I am pressured to put the knickers over my trousers whilst I am torn with rage. I am at the centre point of the whole plane's ridicule now; please let this stop. I cannot risk not responding to these early challenges; for fear of being branded a spoilsport, which will elicit disappointment and the wolf pack will grow hungry for more. If they really knew what I was going through, they would double their efforts.

"Please, back to your seats now." A stewardess firmly points Robert away from me.

"We are going to do you good you know," Robert says menacingly as he walks backwards down the aisle. His eyes dance at the prospect of my future embarrassment.

I settle alone on my needed aisle seat, escaping handicapped kneecaps and the sweaty claustrophobia of a central one. Due to our separate online check-ins and seat preferences this less than magnificent seven are scattered throughout the plane. I retrieve my iPhone from my pocket and attach my earphones, scrolling anxiously through artists, ABC, Associates, Beck, Costello. I click The Clash into action.

Bepe haunts me; he never sensed danger, naively following his nose across the road. An electric shock pulses through me; the power of "what if" makes me squirm in my seat. I would never have recovered from today; never again would I have been at ease. I would have failed in abject manner to discharge my basic duty as a parent. These thoughts make me nauseous; I feel a need to see him to prove to myself he is still alive, but won't see him for five days now. I see a vision of a pregnant church altar awaiting a wedding day couple, but it fades quickly.

My world is in motion, bringing promise of pleasure and pain. Something's coming, something good, is it my fate?

The man in the centre seat next to me stands up and nudges my legs to allow his exit. I tut privately and judge him to have the bladder control of an incontinent ninety-five year old. I stay seated and twist my legs into the aisle.

I smell her perfumed presence before I see her.

"Let me in then," Juliet nudges my knee, toppling my iPhone towards the floor. It dangles painfully from one ear.

"That's awfully kind of you to move," I hear her now and realise that this is her new seat arrangement.

"I had an aisle seat way up at the front so I thought I would let that guy have it. I have never enjoyed flying as you know." I could tell she was making this up.

"That's great." I am happy to give up my flight of solitude.

Max is with Steve a few seats up on the left. Having returned Rubber Juliet to them I see her under-inflated head peeking from above their seats to boyish giggles.

The pilot announces a ten-minute delay to access our runway slot. "While we wait I would just like to congratulate a Stag and Hen that are travelling with us today. Danny and Karen are both getting married next weekend, but not to each other!"

I cringe again in the spotlight. "Danny is in 32C..." A toothy stewardess with a black bun approaches and pushes my reading light on and off. "Karen is in..." He tails off confused by her absence from the flight manifest.

"Like fuck she is," one of the brooding hens shouts towards the flight deck. The brooding Hens are all together on the right side of the plane. The announcement must be more of Robert's work. He is out of sight knowing precisely its effect on both parties.

"Anyway 32C is Danny's bra size," guffaws Steve from up ahead. I have never greeted an in-flight security briefing before; I use the distraction to sneak out of the knickers.

At six minutes past three we are pinned to our seat backs and shoot up the runway: our journey commences, there is no way out. Flight anxiety causes Juliet's left hand to press firmly on my right; I sense the familiar delicacy of each finger. She closes her eyes in prayer for the minutes that the plane climbs steeply. I freeze, not wanting to break this personal space. Does her hand hold anything other than friendship now?

"I hope they just leave you alone now." Juliet has emerged from her take-off trance. "I thought they were going to make you simulate sex with Juliet for a minute." I blush and offer a confused grin until I realise she is talking about her rubber namesake. The prospect alarmingly attracts me; my balls stir a little.

"How is the advertising business?" I realise I have been mute since she sat down.

"So so, but I think it will get better soon. It's funny; we are working on an airline account at the moment. It's ByeFly, the budget airline. It's not quite like flying with this BA lot though. Remember when we went to Madeira? They are really tough as a client. Max says they may review the account." I am gushing. Madeira is an elephant I have let loose on the plane and it is sat on my lap.

"Why didn't you return my calls all those years ago?"

"I can't remember now." I remember exactly. I got a ripping feeling in my stomach at the thought of her. I was sure she had dumped me to go back with her ex-boyfriend so I just backed off. This precipitated a descent into hell for me. There was nothing I could do to bring us back.

"We never resolved anything; you know, made our peace." I had resolved never to speak to her again in the bitterly cold days of early 1992. She handled it so well, putting the prospect of us finishing to me like I had won the pools. We were sat in a semi circular seat by the window of the Hand and Flower pub in Hammersmith, where we had got off the bus after an unsatisfactory trip to Habitat. I originally took her rejection of my suggestion to buy a double futon as evidence of her dislike for anything Oriental. I soon realised it was more fundamental than that. Maybe I accepted her rationale too quickly to save her embarrassment; it wasn't me, it was what she needed. I was speechless, nervously scraping green foil from the top of a bottle of Pils lager. The communally split bag of dry roast peanuts sat accumulating smoke from a Dutch couple that were sharing our booth. Their happiness mocked us. Those feelings were so tangible; I struggle to understand where something so solid could have gone. Does it get lost with time or just put on ice for the day that you can ridiculously re-declare your undying love on a plane? I dare not look at her.

"You seem distant. Not letting these guys get you down are you?"

"No, I am just dealing with a lot babe." The babe is too informal.

The clatter of unclasped metal locks and the hot smell of the first opened meal trolley wafts down the cabin, prompting me to take my leave to go to the toilet at the front of the plane. I shudder at the prospect of more resolution but have decided I must make some. I rise slowly to avoid hurt and turn round to locate my stags; Robert is the only one I can't see but I should keep him in full view from now on.

"Hi mate." I find Johnny sat opposite the toilet door. He greets me with an over full smile to distance himself from the hard time I am being given by the others.

"Listen mate, I have decided to do something important for Bepe. I want to make a playlist, a Top 10, Top 20 sort of thing." We share a religious fervour for our music, but with such diverse tastes have always found this sort of thing alarmingly difficult.

"Sounds awesome mate, but too hard surely." Normally I would agree with him but decide after my day so far I can handle a more selective challenge.

"No, I know, Dan's Magnificent Seven. That's it, I am going to scroll through the tracks on my iPhone and do it this weekend." This is important to me now.

I shuffle into the toilet where I don't breathe nor touch the surfaces. My urine is sucked and freeze-dried out into the airspace. I slowly return to Juliet resolved to move on.

"Those hens are hammered." Juliet informs me when I slump back to my seat.

"It's their only reason for being here now."

"Did Sophia have a hen party?"

"Sort of, she went out with her mum, sister and cousins to the Lowry hotel in Manchester. Just a night out really."

"Are you excited by next Saturday now?" She seems to have a checklist to get through.

"Yes, sure babe."

"How did you propose to her?"

"Oh it was a private thing between us." Not so private if you include her dad. He had asked when the next Saturday night was free at his golf club, where he thought I could marry his daughter at long last. He said I should wake up to my responsibility now that we had a son and it would make a man of me. I smiled at him and Sophia and the deal was done without a single word passing my lips. I have only told Johnny that. I unpeel the cellophane off my rubber looking meal. A shaft of bright warmth pierces the window on my left, illuminating strands of dust which dance and lay germs into my food chain.

"I thought you were going to propose to me at one point. Remember that weekend we went to Kew gardens."

"No I don't think so." I was desperate to tell her I loved her at that point, but clammed up with fear. The prospect of our future relationship together seemed too important to risk for a bungled expression of devotion.

"What's your boy up to now?" I shift us onward.

"He's just finishing sixth form. Bepe is so lovely don't you think?"

"We had a thing with him at the airport." I feel as if I have no answers to anything she says. My marbled chocolate cake turns to a warm mush as I push my spoon into it.

"I know Sophia told me, god forbid, god forbid…" She tails off. It's the first time she has shown any emotion.

"He just ran out of the airport babe."

"He's a gift you have to protect at all cost." She can't help herself barking at me a little.

"Was Ethan's dad around when he was young?"

"No. I brought him up on my own. I had nothing to do with his dad back then. My mum helped as much as she could."

"Was it Tristan's baby?"

"Tristan, why him?" Incredulity forms an L shape frown in between her eyes. She wraps her black hair once more around her left hand and jumps from her seat a little.

"I thought you left me for him."

"Why ever did you think that? You thought I ran back to him?" She looked horrified; trying to imagine the twisted truth I had held all these years.

"Do I know him from college?"

"No. You just don't know him." She never partnered anyone easily, so a one-night stand would not sit easily with her.

"You didn't have to leave college because of me though." As well as being wracked with pain I added a large helping of guilt for seemingly driving her out of college.

"It was for the best. It was the best thing that could have happened to me. I was too confined…" She has no reservation in re-endorsing her self-release despite the implications for me.

Our trays are despatched from whence they came. I stretch a little and push my plastic shelf onto the seat in front.

"Ethan is my boy and my best friend."

"Bepe was wild with mischief when we came out this morning. But at the end he really didn't want me to go." I say with some unexpected pride.

"He just wants his dad." Something I have failed at mentally and physically so far.

"I know but there is something in him I don't understand."

"Don't try to unravel it. You have done your shift. You have probably had poo on your hands at 3.30 in the morning like the rest of us, so he just senses you now." Sophia breast-fed him, which left me comfortable but excluded back in bed. In truth, most of the time he has passed me by. He is shunted from greedy grandparents to a noisy nursery, from a teatime DVD on to a book on his mum's knee at bedtime. Where have I been?

"He just needs to know who you are." There's the rub. I can start to connect with him through music though. It was my first love, even before you Juliet, could I make it his?

"Yeah, I have been thinking about that too." Since you just mentioned it! "I am compiling a playlist for him to start his musical education, the seven tracks that have meant the most to me in my life." I am thinking about this really well on the spot.

"Sounds like an idea. Think about music that he can listen to though, not the usual obscure post-punk acid-house jazz-funk fusion." Juliet has always strained to deliver deadpan humour, as it is so unnatural to her; she forces her mouth to curl downward to hide her smile.

"Listen, I wanted to say that I am really sorry for what happened to us. There is…"

"There is no need to apologise babe. You were probably right. Listen, I am just going to work on this playlist if you don't mind." I can't stand the prospect of raking over her reasons. Juliet reluctantly picks up the in-flight magazine and seems to read intently about paper re-cycling in Norway.

With my headphones re-inserted tenderly, I consider what to call the new playlist and label it "Dan's Magnificent Seven" for now. I scroll down the alphabetically listed tracks. I touch A, the "Affectionate Punch" by the Associates appears first. Doing tracks alphabetically somehow seems fairer than choosing favoured albums and picking the best track. The letter A produces my first choice.

Number 1. "Another Star" by Stevie Wonder.

How apt is this, given the re-appearance of my ex-partner. Released in 1976 on Motown records, the cracking Latin drumbeat precedes an angelic voice that brings the band into heavenly action. Stevie screams his pain that he is blinded by love for another but they cannot see love for him; irony abounds. There is nothing worse than losing a love that remains in you. Having crashed bloodied and bruised at the bottom of a crater somewhere; you can get back onto your feet but each attempt to climb out results in you slipping back into the hole. I remember using this song when Juliet had left, caterwauling its lyrics whilst I had my headphones on. Its amazing how being jilted creates an appeal for so many songs previously discounted. I was convinced I loved her; she didn't love me, the end. However that's the point, when it is someone else's choice there is no choice. It is an end without one. I thought Juliet loved someone else, but she now says she didn't. I convinced myself it was hopeless. Maybe I am growing; I can acknowledge the size of the loss now. I lost that girl but I eventually found a son.

The dark-haired stewardess Robert was chatting up hovers over me. Having failed to retail to the rest of the plane she presents me with a bottle of Moet et Chandon. I think of Freddie Mercury on his piano singing "Killer Queen" as I wave it away.

She taps me on the knee. "It's from Robert. There is a note." She beams back at me, glancing over her shoulder to indicate the direction from whence it came. Juliet and I are as one again. We look with suspicion at the bottle.

The note reads, "Enjoy the bubbly. Why not join the mile high club with Juliet. I just qualified for life membership with this stewardess. Robert".

"He insists you open it." She now has a glass in hand.

I don't know precisely when I remembered. Was it when I felt the shock of ice-cold bubbles in my groin? Was it Juliet's yelp? It was probably when the cork rebounded from the plastic light fitting into my right eye. I must remember from now on, do not trust Robert. My ears pop with a little relief though, nature's way of signalling our rapid descent.

CHAPTER 8

Dan 18:55

The back door of the mini-van slams brutally, confirming the enclosure of all our baggage. The "Mountain drop-offs" driver scrutinises a scruffily folded piece of A4 paper that confirms our impending transfer to Chamonix.

"What the hell did you bring a guitar for?" Max understandably assumes my guitar case isn't the replacement suitcase it actually is. An overhead roar and an unnatural metallic whiff in the air confirm the arrival of another planeload of ski junkies.

"No room in here Staggie!" Robert slams the sliding door shut, leaving the driver's front bench seat as my only place of transportation. A gust of cold air questions the wisdom of me wearing my trusty purple velvet jacket in a ski resort.

"Hi, I'm Dan. When will we get to Chamonix?" I try to start up a travelling companionship.

"Maybe eight, when it's really dark." The initial warmth of an Australasian accent reveals the clipped endings of a New Zealander by the end of his short sentence.

"We can get dinner at eightish, boys!" I shout towards the back to encourage my stags.

"That's great Dan," Juliet responds.

"Dickheads! A bar at eight, shagging by nine," replies Robert.

"What a crew. These guys will be sloshed on the piste tomorrow," I say chummily. The driver stares hard at the dashboard, he holds no truck with their intentions, as he chugs the cold engine to a start. Has he seen too much disrespect of the mountains to find them humorous?

"That's their funeral," he almost spits his disapproval.

GET NATURAL, the swish Swiss tourist board strap line beams from an illuminated billboard as we exit the car park. Our first mile is in heavy traffic, giving us the dubious opportunity to view the brutal architecture that shot up worldwide in the 60s and 70s.

Shunned by the disapproving driver and physically excluded from my stag group for an hour, I have the chance to fulfil my promise to my family. I wince at remembering the developing eye wound I suffered at the hands of the insistent Bepe. I am scrolling furiously through the alphabet but nothing is up to scratch. Through to the letter E and still no second track, on to letter G and nothing stands the test of time. I am getting concerned about the whole process and the inability of songwriters to produce decent songs starting with the first half of the alphabet when at last another great track appears.

Number 2. "Human" by The Human League

Released in 1986 on Virgin Records I think, great track in a bad year. My fellow Sheffielder Phil Oakey drones his excuses that being flesh and blood excuses his bad behaviour. The Human League had betrayed their avant-garde roots to become mainstream pop idols about six years previously. It felt a very serious and personal betrayal at the time, but I now realise they were just finding a new way. I hated the fact I actually loved this as I had resisted their pop onslaught for so long. I remember this track especially as I was still feeling a void from Juliet's disappearance. I suspected she had been "Human" with someone else, but she says not. I lost all trace of her when I moved to Manchester to find work. It was an unsettling time, one I wanted to move past. I regret not being able to enjoy the sheer unpredictability of where my life was going. Today's near accident dialled up a similar feeling of raw exposure to life's fate.

Looking back into the mini-van, Juliet catches my eye as she chats with Johnny. I feel a mini victory in starting to deliver and smile confidently back at her. If you didn't leave me for Tristan then who was it? Did you just leave me?

The journey speeds up and Switzerland starts to deliver on some of its tourist promise. The inviting lights of still villages climb up the hills, highlighting their little lives. Soaring pine forests seem to hold them in place. I just make out a man walking stiffly into a clutch of houses. I create a life for him: seventy-seven-year-old Jean-Baptiste Clermont, a lonely lately reformed opportunist kiddie-fiddler, the internal pain of his perversion hampers every step.

I was just warming to Switzerland when we say goodbye at the French border. My brother Chris looks nervously for his passport. Robert sneers at him and makes his Dan-has-the-cocaine joke again, but with no external audience its potency for embarrassment falls flat. However, it adds to the derision I feel from my driving companion.

The driver physically disengages even more at the prospect of us having drugs. He waves at two border guards, who don't acknowledge him. When do they stop people? Why don't you take some of these men away? What are they there for? The contrast with airport security is stark.

And now we are really climbing. The darkening hillsides are backlit by the sun which is somewhere over the next mountain range refusing to lie down. The mountains start to close their arms around us, the road zigzagging into their chest. Everything is asking us to look up.

The first sighting of a piste-basher brings me mentally back onto the snow. It clings on to a forty-five-degree snow face, pushing and rolling, producing its corduroy for us to ride tomorrow. Its headlights give it the appearance of some alien force devouring the mountain. We keep coming so the machines keep eating the snow. Something in this expended effort makes me consider why we are skiing at all. It seems so childish when we are asking so much.

Thoughts of tomorrow invade my head. Can I remember how to ski? It is a decade now since I went for a disastrous two-week jaunt to California with Donna Hammond and her family. I skied well for a beginner but the bigger disaster was our emerging five-month long relationship: I think I was too needy and maybe she was too greedy. I hear Steve over-claiming his ski prowess from the back.

We zip through short pristine phosphorescent tunnels punched into the rock core. I noticed that the Chamonix ski map claims: "The majesty of the mountains is within us." More like we are within the majesty of the mountains. No one can quibble about the convenience the tunnels bring but you have to sigh at the result.

"Here's Cham!" shouts Robert.

The pretty town centre reveals itself at the foot of the enclosing rock. Signs for Tabac, Cadeaux and Fondue are the first reminders of the language of this foreign clime. The road becomes a single lane past a Bowling Alley roundabout. We snake behind what looks like the main shopping street.

Whenever I arrive at a new place I see promising glimpses of a future history. Will that be our bar of choice? Will I drink too much there? Maybe I will throw up on the steps there? Will we have a big meal out there? Maybe Juliet and I will walk the main shopping street buying postcards? The driver slows as we pass the main SNCF train station on the right, signalling our arrival at the Hotel Genevieve.

"You can all get out here!" The driver spits us and our belongings onto the pavement post haste.

CHAPTER 9

Dan 20.02

Alcohol lubricates the group dynamic. We have a fire to gather around in Le Caveau bar, the hotel's local filling station.

I walk with a sullen Chris and a chirpy Juliet past the empty railway station, a chocolate-box design dwarfed by a soaring mountainous background of blackness. Its sweet appearance but lack of passengers creates a spooky redundant air.

"Just make it a couple eh!" says Chris, putting the reins on the evening without having taken a sip. He is really uncomfortable but I hope to show him they all have good souls.

"You're right, we have to get up and kitted out before ski school." Juliet helps him.

Four lime green T-shirts scream out of the window in the bar ahead. Frost bites at my extremities, but they tingle more at the comforting prospect of warmth. Le Caveau seems to sit with a great aspect on the town's activity from its five-foot high corner window; opposite the train station, Main Street and mountain range. It will have witnessed the craft of wood and leather skis fall to the mass production clatter of metal and resin. It will have witnessed an evolutionary passage of clientele, starting with the aristocratic European adventurer, regressing to the modern good-time-seeking hacker.

Inside, the bar has a comforting resonance after my weary day. Wooden floorboards worn down by ski boot plastic are covered in fresh sawdust for effect and stability.

"We are just planning some mischief." Max brings me into his conversation with Robert and Steve. Juliet has taken my order and arrives back with my Weiss lager causing them to re-evaluate their conversation. Seven lime green T-shirts alert our potential boisterousness to the Caveau drinkers but surprisingly unite us.

"Hey lets have a toast." Robert stands on the footrest of a high wooden bar stool. He clinks a beer glass with his Rolex to get our attention. Steve and Max hand out the champagne he has at the ready.

"A toast to the chicks of Chamonix. May you enjoy having me!" he guffaws. "Oh I suppose we should toast Dan the man as well. Another fool bites the wedding dust. Raise those glasses." I hope this is well intentioned all the same.

"Oh and another thing, I realised before that Chamonix is an anagram for Chix Moan, which is exactly what any lady lucky enough to pull me will be doing later tonight." He extends the warning around the room to insincere laughter. Robert is here for himself; I sense my stag weekend may get in his way.

Max feels his alpha-male status would be questioned unless he adds something: "I would like to propose a toast to Dan's boys. Let's hope we all get a 69 in Cham or should I say a Cham 69. Geddit?" Embarrassed sips are taken. Max is another problem child. Two toasts prompt the rest to think that a round robin toasting tournament is required.

"I would like to toast Dan and Sophia, who are getting married in ten days' time. They are a fantastic couple that deserve to have found each other. I wish you Sophia and Bepe every happiness." Thank goodness Juliet is here for me. She reminds the boys why they are there.

Johnny gets to his feet. "I want to echo Juliet's kind words about this great couple. I just want Dan to have a great time with his best friends. To Dan." A mutter of "To Dan" follows. The sincerity of the last two toasts has been an uneasy antidote to the first two.

Only Steve and Chris remain, neither of who wants to come forward.

Chris intervenes sharply to save being last, "To Bepe". Glasses are charged for the fifth time, although some are raised empty. Chris is on my side just, although his sullen disapproval can cloud this.

"To Rubber Juliet, I hope she lasts long into the night for you Dan.

Just make sure you blow into the right hole!" shouts Steve hurriedly. Steve attracts renewed enthusiasm from Robert and Max. Steve is a spiteful man, able to flick in and out of being a friend depending on the social weather.

"Speech, speech, speech. Come on Dan," the chorus goes up giving me no option. "Dan, Dan, Dan, Dan…"

"Alright, alright, calm down. Thanks for your good wishes. It's great to have every one of you here for me. Thanks for coming. I can't believe anyone wants to marry me to be honest, especially after today. Anyway guys, let's just enjoy each other and this great place." My address makes the group docile. They have been given a dose of reason and are having difficulty swallowing it. The bar re-adjusts, without our toasting distraction.

"Am I the only one here without sprogs?" enquires Robert of me.

"Yes, unless you are hiding any." He probably has a string of them he disowns.

"Any last requests before we start the stag do in earnest?" I mumble something about an ice-skating rink, knowing full well that my request will not be catered for by the rule of the mob.

"Don't worry about what happens here, what goes on tour stays on tour. You can get up to anything you want to. Sophia doesn't need to have her pretty Italian head troubled by it all." Robert goes to the bar with a raised eyebrow.

"Hi mate. Feel like I haven't seen you yet." Johnny arrives at Robert's departure.

"No. It's been hectic hasn't it? We must catch up, I am getting on with that playlist, and it's great fun. I am whittling it down to a magnificent seven."

"Wow mate, what an impossible job." He stops in his tracks, genuinely taken aback about the difficulty of scaling an infinite choice to close to a handful of tracks.

"By the sounds of it the The Clash is in the mix." He instantly sees through my title, and probable choice.

"Maybe the "Tracks of my Tears" by Smokey Robinson?" Johnny keeps the suggestions coming.

"No I don't think Smokey will make it, but you have given me a great idea. "The Tracks of my Years" that is what I will call the playlist. I can explain to Bepe in later life what the tracks meant to me. It will be like a musical tapestry of my life." Some of these may also be tracks of my tears, but I prefer the pun.

"Cool idea mate, but no Smokey Robinson? Bepe will not thank you for that. Must be a Stevie Wonder track then? Talking of tracks, you had better make some!" Johnny backs away as my brother Chris approaches.

"Have you called home Dan?" Chris interrupts us without consideration of interruption. "I did, when you were taking a dump earlier."

"No not had a chance yet. I should probably do it now while I am not too drunk." Johnny doesn't mind the intrusion and I go toward the door.

Juliet is coming back into the bar having presumably also made her call home outside. "Of course I love you, but you will have to wait." We catch eyes as I move past her but she quickly looks away; embarrassed at expressing these words in front of an ex-lover? Maybe it was just a subconscious old flame feeling. Or does it reveal a deeper betrayal? She does seem relaxed and happy talking to Scott. I have no concept of whether she was ever that way with me.

I walk quickly under the heated blower above the door to contact my wife-to-be. I leave Marvin Gaye's 70's soul to soothe the stags.

CHAPTER 10

Dan 22.30

The mountains breathe their chill at me; I seek warmth from my
distant home. I seat myself on a wooden bench bar outside, which is
carved around the courtyard tree. It is designed for après-skiers, who
have probably been enjoying the heat wave of the past few weeks.
However, the current wetness of the bench creates a big chill through
my backside. I get my phone out to call home but can't help searching
for another track for the playlist. I reach the letter K and abandon it
for the night.

"Hi Sophia, hi there babe." She must be able to hear guilt and fear
in my stumbling voice. Guilt on not being there and fear of what the
coming days bring with the largely mad crew inside.

"I'm reading to Bepe in the bedroom. We are late. It is well after his
bedtime."

"Sorry I lost track, should I call back?"

"No." Her no means she will accept the call but I should have called
at a more suitable time.

"I'm just having a beer with everyone." I glance through the window;
they seem solemn, maybe it's less fun without the prime target to aim
at. Everyone is together though, a good sign I think.

"Listen I'm so sorry about earlier. I can't stop thinking about it. Is
Bepe alright?"

"Yes, no thanks to…" Sophia tails off from another blame game.
She is so strident; she often holds an unjustified sense of injustice.

"Why don't you speak to him?" She offers to me gently.

I hear his breath down the phone first; the receiver distorts it into a bubbly rasp and other ripping noises show he is struggling to hold the phone.

"Bepe, it's Daddy! I've been on the big plane haven't I?" I try to stimulate a response by reminding him of our earlier journey, but I still hear nothing but his purest breath. Having a phone conversation with a toddler is semi-futile. You seek some recognition and dialogue but it is a random collection of thought and noise. However, this minimal response is enough to restore him to me this time. I take comfort in every crumb of his response.

"Daddy loves you and misses you so much Bepe." Sophia is the unintended recipient of my pleading as she takes the phone from Bepe.

I hear him now off-cue: "Daddy airplane Mummy, Daddy airplane," he says insistently, demanding the phone back.

"I know darling, Mummy needs to speak to Daddy now." He doesn't return, accepting his lost opportunity.

"What did you get to do with your day after the airport?" I hope she has made some progress to lighten her mood.

"I tied up some loose ends. Dad has his wedding suit and we went to the club to finalise table settings and sample the food. Also you have a ring ready to pick up on Monday when you get back."

"Fantastic babe, you have done everything." I marvel at the synthesis of endless tasks. The event itself is taking over now, it could happen all on its own; I am sure Sophia could get us married even if I didn't turn up.

I hear Bepe bash his toy hammer on something, releasing random comic sounds from its handle.

"I have been thinking about Bepe a lot today. He really scared me."

"What about me? I almost lose my son, my partner flies off on a holiday with his ex-girlfriend and my father's business partner is lost in L'Aquila earthquake."

"Babe, I know. It's been hard on you darling."

"Hard on me, hard on me…" She wants to explode but doesn't have me there to hit. "I don't want argue with you Dan, you just have to wake up…"

"I will, you'll see. I will be there for you both I promise babe."

"Mmmm." This unconvinced noise means the battle is being held for another day. A day when she can shake me, a day when she will feel vindicated.

"Listen, I have started to compile a playlist of my favourite tracks for Bepe."

"What for?"

"It will be like a time capsule for him. His dad's favourite things frozen at the time his mum and dad were married. I started compiling it on my iPhone; it's called the Tracks of my Years. I want him to have something to remember the wedding by as well." The last part is sheer lies from me, unadulterated off-the-hoof brilliance though.

"Maybe a nice idea." Sophia softens. Maybe I have recovered a half brownie point after the 10,000-point loss that was today's accident.

"I have to go. I need to get him to bed." Suddenly a more forgiving Mediterranean chocolate tone sends a pulse of warmth into my hands.

"I will call tomorrow night and let you know how my skiing went."

"Look after yourself. Goodnight." She tails off in a hushed tone. Maybe Bepe has started to drift off without the aid of his bedtime story.

"Bye babe," I feel deep relief at restoring a little goodwill.

I can put my home life on ice for a day. I feel flushed from talking to Bepe; to think we could come so close to losing him so easily. Something so precious wiped away like a table stain.

The stags in the window look far too serious. What the hell has gone on in there? I must get back in.

CHAPTER 11

Juliet 22.30

"HOW DO BOYS GROW UP?"

Dan rushes out of the bar, as I end my call to Scott. We exchange glances but no words. Scott and I have exchanged events but no feelings. The stags are the only people on the move; everyone else frozen in their own nook for the night, drinking and watching football.

"Quick guys, while Dan is out, can we decide what we are going to do for him over the next few days!" All of his friend's sense collusion at the liberation of his absence, but Johnny is trying to guide them. I get a flash back of gangs forged in summer holidays, arguing about whether to allow Bobby from the next street to take their initiation ceremony.

"When is our big night out going to be?" Johnny starts innocuously.

"Every night," sneers Steve.

"I mean we should have one night out in a good restaurant somewhere, where we make it special," Johnny argues.

"I know he loves Italian food, what about going to Courmayeur in Italy, it's only thirty minutes through the tunnel," I propose this as a distraction before more sinister suggestions can arise.

"There is a restaurant at the casino here. Some serious gambling and a black-tie dinner would do the trick." Max foists his own agenda on us.

"Where are you going to get dinner suits from? I haven't packed a ball gown. It's probably horrendously expensive and stuffy. Courmayeur is what he would want." I win round one.

"I will get a blow-up of the group airport photo and we can all sign it for him to take home." Johnny makes a sweet suggestion, bringing silent ridicule.

"That's all okay but when are we going to make him run around town naked or get him a tattoo?" Max enquires anxiously.

"Bollocks to that, he would freeze his knackers off. Also there is no needle going anywhere near our kid," argues Chris.

"We have to get him somehow."

"Just chuck him in the snow after skiing. Anyone who wants to really hurt him will have me to answer to." Chris wins round two through his superior physical presence.

"For fuck's sake is this a stag do we are on or a trip of the Catholic mothers to Lourdes? The guy is handing his freedom over to be pussy-whipped from next weekend; he needs something to hold on to for the rest of his godforsaken married life. When are we getting him laid?" Robert has been biding his time.

"Not a chance," I spit back at him.

"He has to get laid!" Max supports him. Robert stares fervently at every pair of male eyes for approval. The round bar table is deathly quiet. They are all so weak; no one wants to show dissent, even though they may privately find it appalling.

"There is no way he is going to a prostitute. He would be mortified and Sophia said…"

"Sophia has got nothing to do with this. This is a man thing." Robert deliberately abuses the silence of these men, excluding me and condemning Dan. I find myself without a talking ally so look to mitigate the disaster.

"Won't there be a lap dancing place you could all go to?"

"You leave this one up to us boys. If it is a lap dance he is getting one so dirty that he will cream in his pants." The five men chuckle dirtily.

"You don't have to be there unless you want to join in? You could show him everything for old-times sake!" Robert tempers his resolve but tests mine not to hit him.

"Is that it then, a meal out and some saggy tits? I wanted to get him off-piste down the Vallée Blanche glacier. That will be something he will never forget!" says Robert

"That sounds daft." Chris expects nothing but bullshit from Robert.

"It's this easy off-piste run that you take from underneath Mont Blanc up there and down into the village. It's awesome but easy!" Robert points out of the window to the highest mountain profile set against the full grey sky.

"Off-piste, isn't that risky?" Johnny enquires.

"Not if you are with me it's not!"

"We would have to get a guide, surely," insists Johnny.

"I've done it three times now, it's only about fifteen miles long. It's easy, don't you trust me?" Robert knows no one will openly voice a lack of trust.

"But still we should be careful, I am not sure if we can all ski that well!" I interject another voice of reason. This hadn't gone the way Robert had hoped.

"Okay we will get a flaming guide. Let's book it tomorrow so we don't miss out." Max holds Robert's idea up, revealing their collusion. A roar of approval engulfs the bar, some ball has been kicked in some field somewhere.

"Can we ask Dan about this one?" I make a final effort to thwart them.

Men end arguments by giving no response. With such shrugging simplicity the weekend's agenda has been laid out. Great dictators have probably been allowed to flourish by this method: men shrugging their shoulders at the prospect of gas chambers and mass genocide just because they wont step out of the pack. Chris and Johnny may be on my side of reason but they are silent partners now. All of them worry me.

"He's coming back in!" Dan's phone is back in his pocket and he is looking querulously at our huddle. He rubs his hands frantically to revive their warmth. Everyone re-adjusts with the air of conspiracy lifted. No one agrees with all that has been agreed.

"What were you guys talking about?" Dan worriedly asks as he sips flat-headed beer.

"Nothing you need worry yourself about," Steve sneers at him.

"Listen. You want this to be a weekend to remember don't you? We want to take you to see some sights, are you up for it?" Robert asks Dan.

"Sure, whatever you guys want." More silence allows Robert to reclaim the agenda. He pats Dan on the back to seal his fate.

Dan can't settle, shuffling feet reveal his tension. He is deep inside his own thoughts, represented by the frown taking over his forehead. At last he is a man. He was a boy with me and it is great to see. However, he is gulping down beer as fast as he can and even after all these years I know what he is going to say next.

"Listen guys, I'm going to get an early night. There's a lot to do tomorrow before ski school. Anyway I can't stand the music in here and as for the football..." He tails off.

"Anyone want to go back with me?" Dan gestures for me or any other to go back to the hotel with him.

Now I understand the depth of his impending discomfort.

"Sign O' Times" by Prince plays in the bar, competing with the TV. I know he loves this but he is missing out on more than just that. Whatever is paining him now will be the least of his worries in the next few days.

THURSDAY 16TH APRIL 2009

CHAPTER 12

Dan 06.20

The house on the hill waits impatiently for the return of its owner; it is aching to be brought back to life by the presence of Daniel and his family. Slopes of lush green grass tumble improbably away from each external wall. Sited on such a severe hillcrest it has no neighbour.

Daniel strides out the last mile to his home. A series of undulating hills are all that part them. His legs go loose as the gradient takes him downhill, his momentum producing a semi-run. Then his thighs burn as he pushes his hand onto his knee to aid the upward climb.

Mounting the crest of the first hill he counts the shape of at least three more before him and his home. He lets his legs go loose again as he starts to clamber down, knees locking at every stride. He feels a rise in resentment as his brown linen suit is scuffed from a small fall at the valley floor. This is not right. Rising up another hill top his lungs rasp.

The house is now framed in black cloud, which pushes a wild warm wind to swarm around his face. He questions why he is wearing a jumper and suit to go home. Bepe appears on his right hand side; he had been following him all along. Robert waits in the next valley floor; Bepe runs down the hill and reaches him. Robert is carrying an old-fashioned pail, made of gnarled oak with leather straps. All three stand to look at each other. Robert coolly pours the water from his pail onto Daniel's leather brogues. Water splashes off at first but starts to soak his socks and trouser legs. Daniel stares silently at Robert before carrying on up the next hill.

Another hillcrest, the house seems no nearer but surely there are only two to go before he reaches home. One foot squelches forward, accompanied by the singular splat of the first fall of rain. The warm wet wind blows the sopping wet trousers onto his calf. Another singular splat before the noises bunch up.

Daniel raises his face skyward and enjoys the warm rain mixing with the salt-water sweat on his face. He tastes it and moves on. His footing varies, one grassy step is held by sodden leather, whilst the next shoots backwards as it fails to grip.

Robert is at the next valley floor with a full metal bucket of rainwater. He throws this over Dan's feet again. Dan feels his trousers completely wrap around his shins and moves on.

A thunder crack triggers the hairs on the back of Daniel's neck. He sees glistening green ahead of him, with black clouds at the crest. The grass begins to shift; each footstep pulls the carpet of grass further behind him. Bepe is falling behind but Daniel offers no help.

Up and over the next crest, surely only one more hill left to reach the house. The rain is a consistent sheet of shimmering power. It is a body of water as much as any river. Daniel slides onto his bottom from half way down and reaches the cold pool of the valley floor. Bepe tumbles forward onto his chest and flips over, arms flailing without fear. Sitting in seven inches of rain, Robert appears again with a garden hose that weakly trickles water onto Dan's shoes. Bepe is coughing ingested rainwater, struggling to catch his breath, lips trembling blue with cold and fear.

Dan gets up one more time, but the hill rises ahead as a sheet of brown-black mud. The grass carpet has slid away to the valley floor. Dan starts his first footsteps up the hill. The hill gets closer and closer to his face. Bepe gets up and places his first steps on the hillside; somehow he has strength beyond his few years. Daniel is sandwiched between the sheet rain and the mud wall in front of him. His linen jacket is dissolving with the rain; a sleeve falls off his arm.

Then as if he had let go of life himself he knows Bepe has gone. His grip on the hill was poor, falling backward, arms and legs reaching upward towards his dad. Daniel watches him fall forever, never seeing him reach the torrent of water below. Bepe's face is covered in the innocent expectation that he will be saved.

My head hits the wooden bed head, stinging on the edge of a carved flower design. I am sweltering from the combination of a feather-down duvet, what must be the maximum setting on the radiator and my exasperating dream. A snoring Chris brings me back to Chamonix. I cannot tell if the sharp pain has produced a cut. A shaft of light is gloriously released in between the curtains, highlighting leaden socks cast carelessly on the floor. The thump of blood in my head reminds me of the healing gouge. Why would I just plough on regardless of Bepe? I curl my knees into my chest, hoping to relieve the renewed ache of yesterday. I would never let him out of my sight now; I would drown in my own blood before he would be left to walk alone.

My God, I am skiing today, why oh why did I agree to this? I make a naked journey to the toilet, picking up my iPhone from our junk-strewn cabinet top. The sweat on my body dries patchily as I sit astride the toilet. I fight back the only way I have at the moment.

I sit on the toilet and search for another track for Bepe.

"What are you doing in there? Are you crapping yourself about today? Let me in for a piss eh." Chris intervenes after a minute with a clunking fist on the toilet door.

"Just making some work notes." Brother, there's too many of us lying.

"Bollocks to that, it's your flaming stag do. Let's get out into the mountains." Why did I lie to him?

CHAPTER 13

Dan 08.56

I am blinded by the low direct sunlight as I emerge from the ski shop, my head filled with a potpourri of hot wax and sunscreen. The body shapes of my tribe cast black shadows onto the fresh snow in front of me. This soaring fresh new day can't easily lift the heaviness in my soul as I prepare to rediscover fear.

I stumble a little in my new ski boots; the unbound clips tinkle their disapproval as I try to remember how to balance in them again. My skis slide against each other face to face, blade edges catching and scratching. I clasp them together to use them as an expensive walking stick. Ungainly and unnatural acts played out in nature's playground. I stare at the wave logo of O'Neill on my jacket sleeve as a means of mental distraction and focus. What authentic brand heritage, I dare to dream of the campaigns that I could work up for them. I slip on my shades and everything takes on a bronzed but focused life again.

"Have you got everything, Danny Boy?" Robert's smirk means that I don't have everything. He tosses my gloves into my face; he must have swiped them in the ski shop.

"Max and I are going to hit it from the top of Brevent now." He is pointing to the highest peak in view. I see Robert has taken Max under his wing. They are a well suited but dangerous liaison. The rest of us are reluctantly booked into ski school.

"Maybe we can meet later if you want, say one o'clock back here?" All agree to meet up at the restaurant alongside the ski shop with a nod.

"Twenty-five minutes till ski school, what say we grab a drink?" Johnny unites those left behind around a hot beverage. We clatter over to the outdoor Snac Shack bar, needing some warmth and solace for our impending ski-off trial.

"When did you last ski, Juliet?" I ask as we wait for service.

"Two years ago with Scott and Ethan actually, I'm okay, but could do with the lessons."

"*Monsieur, une tasse du thé, s'il vous plait.*" The barman looks painfully at me as I strain for my CSE French. He plonks a glass cup of hot water on the counter; the tea bag spins but releases no tea.

"Au lait?" I create further disdain by requesting milk; this must be the easiest method for a Frenchman to reveal a Brit. I hand over a five Euro note. My waving hand indicates he should take it all. He has seen them all through here before, from the cocky new skier to the outright scared. He looks happy to be tipped two Euros for nothing in particular. We all sit awkwardly on a wooden bench atop packed ice and gathered snow. Steam mills frantically around the top of my glass.

"So what happens at ski school then?" Chris enquires.

"See where those poles are up on the slope. They will get you to ski down to see what ability group you should go into," Juliet informs him.

"What, we ski down that big slope there?" I can see Chris imagining the ten-degree slope as one of the final stages of a slalom race. Any ski gradient intimidates at first, but with a little ability and confidence they can quickly befriend you.

"There are some real hotties round here!" pronounces Steve. He is self consciously trying to keep the lad quotient up now the two alpha males have left. Juliet's presence is dampening this behaviour but not eradicating it.

The line of skiing novices forms early, a colourful patchwork of Europeans in a union of varying ski ability. Europe seems at its most united here at La Flegere.

"It's time to show these foreigners how to ski." Steve stands as we finish our drinks. Chris looks the most obviously disconcerted, although we all look tentative apart from Juliet.

Boot clasps clack into place, zippers are zipped and skis cracked onto feet. I step precisely up the slope ahead of a young girl. Her ponytail sways from under the back of her woolly hat; she has pure unquestioning anticipation on her face. The three ski instructors confer at the head of the small slope, smoking and ignoring the group gathering beside them.

"I am Jean-Paul your instructor. You ski down. We have three groups. Aldo will tell you group at bottom." He stands ten feet below us, skis in a V facing up the hill. Aldo skis down on one ski in a graceful curve, stopping as if he had never started.

After five faltering skiers complete their trial, Juliet is the first of our crew to ski off. She glides in good style, but her lack of weight means she doesn't pick up speed. Aldo waves his pole to his right and she stands alone.

Chris follows, moving inch by inch in contrast. He is stiff, the snow crunching under his weight, moving crab-like down the hill. He is waved to the far left away from Juliet.

Six others follow behind Chris. I try to judge myself against them; surely I am better than that? Ponytail girl comes next, her eagerness to start pressurises me. Surely there should be a kindergarten for her?

"Good luck mate!" Johnny encourages from behind me in the line.

And then there was me. I try to get going without letting any momentum build up. At six foot three I don't know if I was cut out for this. My legs stretch into the widest snowplough possible. My breakfast comes back into my throat but I gulp it back. As I slip around in my first turn I remember loving this when I last did it. I manage another turn before coming in too fast and very close to Aldo. He points at the floor in front of him.

I have made the middle ground and I am proud of it. Without warning the trial has stimulated my weak male competitive edge. Maybe I will teach Bepe how to ski when he has grown up a little. This will be something that the dad and his lad will really enjoy together, a time to get him away from his mum and show him how much I care. I am resolved to learn quickly now. The sun shines again although it had never been away.

Johnny and Steve do better still, but Aldo makes them join me. Johnny and I show we are happy enough. Steve cannot contain his disappointment at not making it into Juliet's top group. He looks disdainfully at the ponytail girl and the big bloke who complete our group.

Juliet is arguing with her instructor. She walks over towards me. He shrugs and makes a sweeping hand gesture behind her back.

"What happened there?" I ask.

"Oh, I just wanted to ski with you but he didn't appreciate the rejection," Juliet laughs.

"Don't go down the cable car at lunchtime Chris. We will meet by the ski shop after the lesson." Juliet shouts to my worried-looking brother as his group are asked to climb this hill again. He signals acknowledgement with a raised pole.

"I am Aldo, I from Cannazei in Dolomites in Italia and I instructor here three years. This English middle beginners group. Maybe we parallel ski in few days no? Ok, so we introduce now. Next please you say name, where you live. We speak English." Aldo commandingly invites our group to expose their identities.

"My friends call me Kronk and I am from Utrecht in the Nederland."

"I am Juliet from London in England."

"My name Mari Elena in Napoli," my ponytailed friend reveals confidently.

"I am Johnny from Sheffield in England."

"My name is Dan and I am also from England, the Roman city of Chester," I elaborately introduce myself to try to affiliate myself with the Italians.

"You live Roma?" Aldo enquires, somewhat confused by the mention of two places.

"No Chester in England." Aldo lets the Roman reference hang in the air without comprehension.

"I am Steve Priestly, I am an art director from Manchester, true capital of England and I am here on his stag weekend." He fluffs my hair and his pole chafes my ear.

You can just be a wanker sometimes Steve. Who are you trying to impress by saying you are an art director? Why did you tell him I was a

71

stag? I bow my head, hoping that he hasn't just got me into more trouble; this is a man who can inflict pain and embarrassment.

"What is stag?" Aldo asks Steve.

"He gets married next week and we are here to get him laid," Steve excitedly informs him.

"Ah, *buona fortuno,* good lucks. He is stag, you all English hooligans, yes?" Aldo typecasts us.

"Okay now we go." My new group waddles behind Aldo over to the nearest ski lift.

CHAPTER 14

Dan 10.30

Our ski-school status allows us to squeeze past the deep ski-lift queue. Juliet and Johnny are either side of me as we are scooped into the air. The safety bar cracks down into position over my head. As we rise the chair bobs over the first main pylon to create a feeling of travel sickness. This is an unnatural high, being suspended 200 feet off the ground by a series of wires and pulleys is surely for the circus. I get some travelling respite for my legs and heart, so get the iPhone out to continue my quest and reach letter M.

Number 3 "Magnificent Seven" by The Clash.

This was released on CBS. When The Clash rocked into view in 1976, I was scared stiff of them at first. They had real edge, spitting at the world from their high moral ground. I remember the local media had us believing punks were going to riot through every town. Within a few years the riots were real and The Clash and others poured multi-cultural fuel on the flames of Brixton and Toxteth. I used to use this track in my late teens to develop some attitude before going out into Sheffield city centre with Johnny. Joe Strummer hisses disdain at anyone working the corporate nine to five. If only my working days were that short. He is basically saying no one is remembered for doing the corporate gig, so asks what do you want to be remembered for? It's all right for you Joe; you found your magnificence in song. I had the same calling, but no breaks; what is the second act if you can't live by performing? I had to earn some dough Joe.

The top station approaches. Johnny pushes the safety bar up early and we travel fifty yards with nothing to hold us in. The tension releases momentarily as the snowy terra firma appears and the three of us slip off the lift inadvertently holding arms.

"Today we make the pizzas yes, you all know this?" We are all nonplussed, but no-one dares asks for explanation. We are standing atop the highest peak I have ever seen, made treacherous by the synthetic planks strapped to our feet. It feels like I would reach Chamonix town centre if I turned my skis downhill.

"We make the skis like the pizza slice to make snowplough downhill. To turn left you weight on right ski. To turn right you weight on left ski. You follow my line one by one. I stop at bottom and wave pole for next one. Okay, Steve Hooligan first, then the stag. Follow one by one." He skis in six effortless arcs to a slight plateau in the slope, having carved a defined snow snake for us to fail to follow. Steve looks pleased with himself once again and skis off first.

"How are you doing mate? They are all giving you a rough ride." Johnny moves beside me; sunglasses shade my eyes and his ability to read the real answer.

"Yeah, holding it together. Just wish Max and Robert would ease up." I wipe my nose in preparation for my run, smelling the distinctive Piz Buin sunscreen on my hand that I inconsistently applied this morning.

I start to let my skis flatten and slide forward. Weight on the right ski I coach myself, sure enough I turn over to the left. I try the same with the left ski but my turn is not so marked. As I coax another turn Robert appears from nowhere, stopping dead in my path.

"What you doing Dan, walking down the hill?" I slide into him completely off balance. He hops away lightly to disentangle us.

"You haven't even got your boots done up properly!" He helpfully leans down and adjusts the top buckle on each of my boots.

"Thanks, I need to ski to the instructor now." Aldo is waving both poles impatiently just out of earshot.

"I wouldn't want to hold you up! See you later lanky." He takes off straight at Aldo. Somehow he whips behind him when it seemed inevitable they would crash.

Unsettled, I start off again, this time forgetting our instruction. Do I understand the thrill of doing this? I probably won't really find it until I can stop when I want to. Whoever dreamt this up? Putting slippery planks on your feet to stand on snow and ice? After two turns I come slowly into Aldo's vocal range.

"No, no, you make more turns where I show you. The weather is nice yes, but you not on the beach, you not on deckchair. Lean forward. Concentrate now. Okay you better next time stag." And with that he waves to Johnny to follow.

I step towards the beaming Steve.

"He's a good bloke that Aldo. Did you see Robert go by? He looked sensational!"

"Yes, he stopped to help me at the top."

"Didn't do much good then! Anyway we need some time to talk about ByeFly; Max says we are in deep do-do."

"I know." I want to give the impression I am fully conversant with whatever situation I haven't been informed about. As usual Max has seen fit to keep me mushroom-like in the dark.

"You knew about the campaign re-pitch presentation next week and didn't tell me? We are up against two London agencies we think, so really in the shit. We are getting the brief from Max later." My rising spirit deflates at the thought I might have to work on my own stag weekend. A re-pitch is loads of work; it's impossible to do it well in the few days before I am off for the wedding and honeymoon. No, that can wait; I am not letting it invade my thoughts.

"Heep to the hill, shoulder to the valley," is Aldo's mantra. Our procession goes through another two instructional ski-offs, each one marginally improving our ability. We group back together where we started.

"You are doing well Dan, making some progress don't you think?" Juliet tries to inspire me as we wait to be honourably discharged.

"I agree. You are a really good skier though Juliet," Johnny offers his encouragement and a chocolate bar for general consumption.

"You could do with turning more, don't drift so much," Juliet advises. She turns to see where Aldo is. "That Aldo is a lecherous pervert,

I caught him looking Mari Elena up and down. She must be twelve!"
Juliet raises her voice so that she will be heard.

"Okay we finish today. We meet ten o'clock at top of lift station tomorrow and we progress well. In two days maybe you start parallel ski, but we must know our limit, yes. You have nice lunch now. Bye bye." Aldo slips backwards down the short hill in front of the ski shop.

Suddenly Aldo is animated again. "Hey stag hooligan boots not closed! You lean back like the beach because boots not closed. Ciao."

I look down to see two undone clasps on the top of each boot. I realise Robert's supposed help is never as straightforward as it appears.

CHAPTER 15

Dan 13.07

"I will wait here for Chris, you go and sort yourselves out with some lunch." Steve and Johnny didn't need to be told twice that they should immediately address their ski-induced under-nourishment.

"I will stay with you Dan." Juliet would need more shaking off.

"Jules, the queues are horrendous, you go and get in line."

"Are you sure? Can I buy yours as well then? What do you fancy?"

The answers are yes, yes and you. "Spag Bol or something like it." I need a big dollop of European-style carbohydrate. "Tell Robert it was un-cool undoing my boots if you see him." I need to get him to back off, but how do I tackle him directly?

I fall back onto the wooden bench outside the ski shop. With just my weight on one end it threatens to tip up. Now that I am through my morning's ordeal I feel able to face the rest of the weekend. I am at the same spot as this morning without the earlier feelings of dread. I probably wouldn't tip the Snac Shack bar owner at all now.

The hopeful blue and gold stars of the European flag flutter high above my head. I try to count the stars but I keep losing count, as the flag is moving and the sun blinding. I don't think any more stars have been added to recognise the outer reaches of Eastern Europe. If I had just joined like Cyprus I would be pissed off if I couldn't have my own star. Maybe they should redesign it and have an inner ring. At least the Yanks have the right number of stars and states. However, by the time they had re-made the flags another ex-communist country would have joined heralding another paranoid outburst of British immigration hysteria, with dire warnings that the country will topple into the sea with the influx of millions of immigrants. Maybe they could just put some stripes on it and copy the Yanks. My country is the real outlier of Europe, so maybe our star should be printed on the back. As Europe prepares to lunch I think I can distinctly see a line separating the drink-driven British against the perceived grace and sophistication of all other Europeans.

My focus drops to the crowds milling around the ski shop and restaurant, busying themselves with their joint purpose, to get up and down these slopes in as much of a hurry as their ability will let them. I feel I have found the epicentre of European Union, a place where potentially cross snow boarders can happily cross borders! I inwardly chuckle. The collective memory that Han's granddad shot Tim's has been groomed out of people's prejudice after years of snow-induced integration. They should place the European parliament here; the whole thing would be a lot more productive.

My union is exactly nine days away now. I will be married into the Italian mob. I don't suspect my father-in-law is connected but they are undoubtedly capable of breaking my legs if their daughter is crossed. I am glad to be out from under the white-hot glare of wedding planning which I only serve to hinder. I am truly guilty that it all falls onto Sophia but I am incapable. She is a great girl, it is right that I am settling down now we have Bepe; he will solidify us. I also know she is angry about what happened yesterday with him, I will have to fix it before we walk up the mock aisle at the Golf Club.

For a moment I regret taking my right glove off, the cold immediately attacks the warmth my hand emanates. I see another navy blue jacket in the distance but it is too slim to contain Chris's bulk. He is twenty minutes late now, where can he be? I fish for my iPhone but am interrupted by Chris's cursing.

"Bloody rubbish, I could only turn one way. I crashed into this girl in the ski school twice. The rest of them fell like dominoes. I have had enough for today." Chris huffs and pants his way through this brutalist appraisal of his morning.

"Let's go for lunch, everyone is in the restaurant, I think."

"Can't say I like your mates, they're a bunch of tossers." He is glad to get this off his chest, but it just gives me a management problem. We make our way across packed ice, through ski racks, over to the gaily-flagged restaurant entrance. I can see my stags on two separated tables outside.

"Johnny and Juliet are good people." I strive to differentiate the wheat from the chaff.

"Aye, maybe, but none of them are my kind of folk."

"Stick with me brother," I plead.

Robert and Juliet are sat alone and stop dead in their conversational tracks. Their mouths drape open as their brains revisit the contents of the last minute's conversation. Both look uneasy, their previous discussion obviously isn't something they wanted me to hear. What were they saying? It could have been an incident from years ago or yesterday. They have both stopped for too long; I know it was about me.

"Thanks for undoing my boots mate!" Robert just grins at me, happy with his latest subterfuge.

"You are a twat Robert. I am off to get food." Chris has patently had enough of his quiet man status.

I take one of the two remaining seats on their bench next to Robert. The frenetic multi-lingual ski hubbub increases as we move into the afternoon. Robert and Juliet are suddenly united in their determination to finish their meals and go.

"It's good to see my two old college mates together again," I try to bring them union but both pairs of eyes avert to their left.

"What did you think of Aldo's class?" Juliet breaks her silence.

"He picked on me a bit, but it's cool. I have had a good morning anyway, felt as if it was coming back to me after such a long time." The air I now inhabit is thick with disdain. I start to eat my overloaded plate of ten-euro Spaghetti Bolognese. The top strands of spaghetti and sauce have been insulating the inner. A pool of olive oil separates from the congealed sauce at the bottom of the plate.

"Can you believe the three of us lived together in that tenement in the Isle of Dogs for a year?" I unwisely prod these unusually dumbstruck lions from their cages.

"Do you remember us swimming in that wartime bomb-crater below your window Robert?" No reply except increasingly frequent bites of a baguette.

"Your room looked like a bomb-site as well," I aim to keep the conversation light.

"My room looked like that for good reason, I was having the time of my life, unlike you two mice playing happy families. Middle-class and middle-aged all before you turned twenty-five!" Robert unconsciously exposes the contents of his mouth as he talks.

"Class is something you never showed you prig," Juliet smiles serenely while she delivers her invective.

"Oh I'm a prick am I? Have you ever managed to get one to fuck you that isn't a lap-dog like him or someone who works for you?" Robert mishears the insult and goes on the attack.

"Grow up you pathetic boy. I have met enough of your sad types in boardrooms, incompetently hanging on to positions given by their ex-public-school mates. From what I have seen already BA should sack you for sexual harassment of your own staff," Juliet spits back at him.

Robert rises slowly from his bench, belying his intent. He winds his right arm backward to deliver a punch or a slap to Juliet, but as he pulls back he unintentionally cuffs me on the ear.

"Whoa guys. Stop it now. For me, stop it now." Robert only sinks slowly back onto the bench when I sit down and tug his arm.

Chris returns unwittingly to the fold with a tray creaking under the weight of a dinner, a sandwich and a dessert. His physical presence is another antidote to Robert's ire.

Max, Steve and Johnny walk over from their table and hover over us all. They don't seem to have picked up on the dispute. "So where are we all going now that you babes are out of nursery for the day?" Max questions the group.

"I don't think we can ski together, we are all different levels?" I point out in the hope that I can separate the feud.

"There is an easy red off to the left of the Ceil Express four-man lift.

We should all go there." Max suggests to everyone. Eyes dance over eyes again testing our collective strength.

"I'm going to my bed!" Chris says with no prospect of re-negotiation, chomping heartily on his ham roll.

"I will walk back with you Chris. I've done enough for my first day. Is that okay with you Dan?" Johnny opts out apologetically

"Okay then everyone else, let's show the stag some real skiing." Max decides for everyone. "That includes you too my precious," he sneers at Juliet

"Thanks lover." Juliet inappropriately feigns familiarity with him.

"That's great chaps." What am I saying? They are reluctantly staying together for me and I hate it. The animosity between Robert and Juliet overloads my woes. So much for my European union, not even the Brits can get on. I am artificially welding them together but the whole thing stinks.

CHAPTER 16

Dan 14.05

The taut steel cord reaches skyward. The padded metal chairs dangle in fixed fashion, and are eaten by the deep grey clouds that are fluffing up ready for snowfall.

I shuffle my skis forward two more inches, my right ski-tip locks under a snowboard; both metal edges momentarily nip each other. Anxiety to re-climb the mountain is etched on most faces. A plastic mock-clock indicates that the last lift is four thirty, over two hours away. I was once told by a Frenchman never to be polite in a European ski-lift queue, but find it hard not to use British queue codes. Two snow-boarders push across my line to the gate, stopping my progression onto the next lift with Juliet. Robert is on the same chair but the boarders keep the antagonists apart. I twist backwards and see Max and Steve close behind. The frozen lift attendant scrapes ice from the footboard with an inverted shovel, producing a metallic scream. His collapsed demeanour shows the weight on his mind; he is in the playground but not allowed on the swings. He must fight not to just get on every chair that passes him and escape his drudgery. My thighs push against the wooden gate that eventually gives way to let me through. No one is that desperate to get up the hill that they want to join the three of us, so the next chair slowly scoops three workmates into the air.

Snow pit-pats on the polyester shell of my coat. Some flakes roll off; some dissolve by touching the imperceptibly higher temperature of the jacket; some stick resolutely looking for others to join them. I zip up to the fullest, to defend my chin against the harshening conditions. As we clank over a pylon, a manufacturer's sign for Wankel Lifts comes into

82

view, which must bring a childish grin to English-speaking passengers. I just perceive it to be poor global branding for a manufacturer who wants to convey absolute trust and security.

"Listen guys, we need to focus." Max interrupts my drifting. "ByeFly are thinking of ditching us. They have set up a three-way pitch for next Wednesday. Essentially they want a fresh above-the-line campaign to run through summer peak. It should ideally have been ready to air this month so we are behind on production already."

"Did they say why they are re-pitching? What do they dislike about what we are doing?" Steve enquires.

"Nothing much, apart from they think our ideas are stale. They can't stand our fucking obsession with waving goodbye in the current campaign. It's trite and it doesn't say anything about their brand. They want to push cheaper prices as well. Oh and they definitely want to reduce the retainer payment."

"Our obsession? We only worked it in because of them. It ruined that campaign we had designed for them." I make a true but futile protest.

"Well the blame is laid at our door now and so are a pack of wolves if we are not careful, so let's fucking drop it. Ideally we would go home tomorrow and work on it this weekend."

"It's going to be awkward to leave my own stag-do guys." No way José am I leaving for this ungrateful git.

"I can look at flights on Saturday I suppose." I weakly hope that logistics will bail me out.

"You don't seem to realise how crucial this is." Max keeps shifting the responsibility back over my head.

"Well, we will have to start work right away no matter where we are." Max raises the bar on both the chair lift and on my stag weekend. As it hits the stanchion the chair swings back a little, momentarily presenting a threat to unload us twenty feet short of any solid ground.

"It will be tight but we are just going to have to." Steve handles his response well, positioning me as the shirker.

"If we don't then the whole agency is fucked. The consequences of not getting the re-pitch are dire. Three months without a retainer fee of their size would close us down. You two got us into this, get me out of it with some magic words and pictures." Like a Catholic about to exit the confessional, Max absolves his guilt simply by uttering the words; he doesn't even have to recite three Hail Marys as penance.

As we level out at the top station, the snow swirls under our feet. The glum male station attendant pretends to be cool from his windowed box, unable to hide the mind-numbing anguish of his job. I feel a sharp jab in my right eye from a hail-like piece of snow. I struggle to pull up my hood with ski gloves on. The weather has taken a nasty turn.

My skis are silenced by the wind as I slide over the few yards towards Juliet and Robert who are at least conversing again. Dead ahead is a massive metallic panelled ski map, its face covered by a frosting of hard blown snow. People are starting to choose their descent carefully now, feeling hesitant at re-taking previous ski route challenges.

"It's too wild. Let's make this the last run of the day," says Juliet. Robert ignores her and pushes onward with Max; they beckon us with their poles. Max skis backwards, shouting something inaudible through my tightened hood. His absolution has perked him up. I know he wants to compete, show me a lesson, but my inexperience means that it's a complete mismatch.

Aldo enters my head, prompting me to stand up on my skis. I slow and turn more smoothly to the left. I stay forward for my next turn and I feel yet more control. I deliver a Spaghetti Bolognese burp and inadvertently breathe in its warmth and smell of decayed flesh. Juliet is thirty yards ahead of me and pulls up to a standstill. I tense up and edge towards her, while Steve overtakes me. Behind the line of her skis the mountain hides; falling away so steeply that she is silhouetted against the Chamonix valley floor. Where did the piste go? As I reach her I see Robert and Max positioned twenty feet below, off to the right.

"Let's do this one turn at a time," she says to Steve and me. Steve decides that further delay will only eat his negligible confidence away and lose him credibility. He pops over the lip of the hill, running straight at Max. With skis distended in front of his body, he makes no turn and hits them side on. Robert pulls away leaving Max to absorb his impact.

Juliet has shuffled further up the ledge. She is turned towards me having picked the flattest entry route. She pushes off crossing the slope away from the others, jumping around one turn to wait for me. I can barely see her tracks as I stand atop the ledge. I forget the awaiting ridicule to my right and focus on Juliet. Hip to the hill, shoulder to the valley, my skis pop over the ledge, pushing my weight backwards, way too fast for comfort. Only when I manage to push my hands forward do I recover some control. I shoot past Juliet; turn now Dan; turn now Dan; turn now Dan. It happens on my third count; for a lifetime I am facing downhill on the biggest mountain I have ever seen.

"Brilliant Dan!" Juliet shouts at me, she effortlessly passes me again to come alongside. Max, Robert and Steve have started to get hazy as snow blows from mounds made by this morning's skiers.

Robert skis towards me, cutting across my line. I vaguely catch some derisory comment about pace. They start to dance on down the mountain, pushing through its core. I turn after my second prompt this time. The slope has reached a comparative level of comfort; I can turn provided I go from piste edge to piste edge.

Juliet stays two turns ahead, escorting me. Max is nowhere to be seen. I have limited mental capacity to deal with his poorly timed brief. Something is rotten. They sounded quite sure about what we were doing on the campaign at our last monthly meeting. Max has a history of blowing these client things out of proportion to work Steve and I like Trojans. Anyway they know they are not the cheapest-priced airline. We can do a better job, but I bet it is him who is the clients' problem. Why do I have to deal with it here though?

Skiing over sheet ice is not something I have done before. The rigid clacking of my skis is an uncomfortable reminder of how hard it would be if I fell. My shoulders hunch up, my bottom goes backward, and my anal sphincter is pursed. The clacking doesn't stop; I feel it in my ankles, the feel of the inflexible ski dropping between hardened ruts. I am running out of piste. Turn now Dan, turn…

I didn't really feel the fall, just ice crystals shooting into my face. It is perversely fun to be moving so fast. Shapes from the slope and sky mix in kaleidoscope fashion as I hurtle headfirst. I can see my skis are still on, I try to brake but gain speed. When will this fall end? My head is exposed now, as my hood is ripped back. I have to turn round. As soon as the slope decreases a little I dig in with my shoulders and my legs carry on under me. I recover a modicum of control and skiing decorum. I flash past Robert who is standing out of my way. I slow to a halt. I have my first skiing adventure, my first battle scar.

"Hey skinny, you look a bit Martini. Shaken and stirred that is." Robert reaches me with poor jest, offering me a hand to help me stand up. "Listen, don't bother trying to turn on ice until you can ski properly you silly twat."

"Are you alright? Did you bang your head?" Juliet arrives in a state of panic as the others gather around as well.

"I feel fine, I was lucky I think." I am strangely buoyant to have survived the spill.

"Not lucky enough to have friends who look after you," Juliet shoots a stare at Max and Robert.

"Hey, this run is easy enough." Max defends his choice.

"Yeah, where is the buzz in this slope?" Robert decries the challenge I have just faced.

From the gloom above us a piste patroller arrives. *"Bonjour. Ca va?"*

"Oui. Thanks. *Très bien.* Okay." I give him a gloved thumbs up.

"I am coming down and see fall." He has detected my Englishness and takes off my beanie hat to search for signs of a wound or blow.

"What kind of skier are you?" Good question I suppose. "What is your ski class?"

"Oh, I am a middle beginner I think."

"You should not be here. This is ice no? This red is skiing black I think. Do not do this for safety no? Who is your leader?" Like the stranded alien in every Star Trek movie he insists on finding out where our point of authority is.

Eyes dance over eyes, we exchange rueful glances, but nobody is going to give up Max for a French roasting.

"Go now. Weather very bad is coming." He leaves us now that we are safely in view of the chair lift. I wish he could stay with us for the weekend; his authority would be welcome.

CHAPTER 17

Dan 16.37

The tree is refracted through the bottom of my dimpled glass tankard. Wheat beer and gas surge down my throat, its distinctive aroma stinging my nostrils; I can't take any more. Above my glass Chamonix station accepts the steady flow of après-ski travellers that I had anticipated sat here last night. Above the station the circling mountains sit with brooding aspect, holding back the weather we have just escaped allowing us to ripen in a soon to disappear sun. Most of my stags stand with me in the courtyard, our tired limbs reverberating with the smooth swing of Erykah Badduh boomed at us from speakers hidden in the tree. Juliet and Chris wobble on high chairs at the outdoor bar besides us; the mental age of some of my stag-mates suggests they would be more comfortable in romper suits strapped obediently into plastic ones. The lowering of my glass prompts a collective moan, another stag challenge I have failed to meet. Yet again I sense my inability to rise to the occasion is wearing them down, maybe they will give up trying soon?

"Surely you can neck one pint Dan! It's your stag do, put some effort in." Chris chides me having seen off his pint in three gulps.

"Your brother has never been able to drink. You used to make an arse of me when we were at college. He was an embarrassment as a man then and remains one." Robert makes his nasty judgement known. I choose not to respond but feel aggrieved. He is always crossing the line between ribbing and outright insult, he reminds me why he makes my blood boil. I don't respond, as it will only give him further cause to insult me.

"And here you are letting me down again. It's called skiing you know Dan, not sliding."

"Hey it was icy, anyone could have fallen," I defend myself.

"But only you did," Max interjects.

"That piste patroller said it was like a black."

"He's just trying to scare you. There is no way it was black. You just have to learn how to ski. It was funny seeing the panic on your face though, you were bricking it." Robert is looking at Max all the while as their collusion deepens. They accept that it is my first war story, but they conceal the fact that their irresponsibility conceived it.

"Maybe he should just take lessons from you. He wouldn't have been so exposed then would he?" Juliet surprisingly intervenes from her bar stool.

"If he jacks in ski school I will show him how it is done in an hour. You just commit to the hill, lean forward and angle those legs. It's like life, the straighter you go the easier it is." Robert picks up her sarcastic challenge, deluding himself that I might actually do it. This latter observation is deep for Robert; who needs Nietzsche?

"I am surprised it would take that long with you teaching him?" Juliet fooled me, her constrained laughter forces a dimple to appear above her brow; revealing her game of ego inflation.

"Let's do it Dan. I won't give up more than an hour though, women to ogle, places to ski!" He genuinely believes I would do it.

"Maybe if I can get my money back mate." I am safe in the knowledge that the ski school is expressly non refundable.

My brain is flooded with light as the sun stands on the horizon. I try to keep looking at its fall, but my shades cannot keep out the piercing rays. They seem compressed into one final burst for the day and then they are gone. A chill falls upon us.

"More drinks guys?" Johnny offers and takes the simple order for beers all round.

"I will give you a hand." I go inside the bar with him, but it is much diminished in daylight. Burgundy walls ooze with the addition of nicotine stains; its rustic wooden floor is pitted beyond repair. It is transformed into a tatty Wild West saloon, the shimmering clink of ski buckles replacing the metallic ring of spurs.

"Are you feeling sore at all?" Johnny asks as we stand at the bar. A swarthy Scandinavian type, hair tousled to the point of distraction, serves the swooning English girls next to us. We smile weakly at them and they ignore us.

"I'm good my man." I lie to him about the frost burn on the back of my neck and the developing warmth in my right knee that talks of a sprain. I know that I have to be careful but am generally energised by my performance. My accident is woven into the developing tapestry of this weekend, something that they can pinpoint as embarrassment, which may quench their thirst for more. I have fallen big time but nothing bad happened, maybe I can let go more now.

"How are your tracks of the years coming along? I know I couldn't do it."

"Coming along, coming along…"

"I'll bet that Prince has made the cut." That gives me an idea.

"Not yet but he will. Which track would you nominate though?"

""Girls and Boys" of course," he states emphatically. "Are you okay mate, you seem distracted."

"Oh nothing that a good night's sleep wouldn't put right." My natural course is to lie about what I feel. I do it so cheerily and well.

"Actually I am feeling a bit raw at the moment, but I just can't let these guys down can I?

"Max and Robert don't give a toss mate, just try and stay clear of them. Juliet hates Robert; I don't know what he has done."

"If I am honest mate I feel a little unsure about the whole wedding thing, I am…" I tail off as the barman approaches. He is less happy to be serving us than his previous customers.

"What do you mean mate?" Johnny knows something is up.

"Oh nothing. You know how it is, just pre gig nerves. Let's get these drinks back to them." Lies, all lies, why is it so important to me to keep the peace? We take our short and overpriced tankards of wheat beer outdoor.

"We can chat another time…"

"Okay, any time. I can't wait to hear the seven tracks mate. Maybe we can play them at the wedding disco." Johnny knows the commitment necessary for me to complete this task and is enthused by my dedication.

Seven pints clunk onto the wooden bar-shelf, glass edges grind as they are squeezed together. These beers bind us for at least another half hour. Tree bark blows into my froth flaked off by a chill wind.

"And anyway it's just another American fear-based scam. There is more chance of a meteorite blowing us away than all the ice melting in Antarctica." Robert is holding court on environmental change on our return.

"What? The Americans are the ones in denial over global warming!" Every sinew in Juliet's face stretches for emphasis as she nervously bunches and re-bunches her hair into a sprouting pineapple sculpture at the back of her head. "I can't believe you. We are heading for a disaster in my boy's lifetime." Juliet is standing now. She has the cuffs of her fleece pulled out from under her jacket, clenching them over her wrists, which reveals her mental turmoil to me. I know this position; she is on measured attack, holding on to feelings to keep logic flowing. God forbid these boys ever see her real depths. In this male company it would be a fatal sign of feminine weakness and she would never recover her credibility.

"The yanks are hyping it up now so that they can get us all to replace the wealth from their declining industrial military complex with some half-baked umbrella to stop the sun." Max chips in with another great American conspiracy theory.

"The planet is warming, people are dying and you guys are looking to the Americans for leadership? Maybe I am just a little girl who doesn't understand these big boy things." She is riled but laughing, hoping to give the conversation a dead end by putting her own views to the sword. All of them mistakenly take her comments at face value.

"Hopefully it's all not as bad as they make it out guys." No one responds to my take on the issue. I feel self-conscious talking about these issues below the mountains. They seem to cross their arms Buddha like, withholding their judgement. I feel we should speak in hushed tones so they don't exact their revenge.

CHAPTER 18

Dan 17.44

In the sun's absence, ice crystals grow on every stone on the gravel pavement; my hard plastic ski boots skid over each one. The weight of the boots makes me imagine I am moon walking. Our hotel is maybe 300 steps from the bar, but each one is filled with this icy treachery. My shins have been released from their clips for two hours but still throb from earlier compression. Juliet and I hold hands when a step becomes a slide. My balance has been further upset by four beers.

"Come on Dan, stand on your own two feet will you," she reprimands me as I hastily grab the sleeve of her jacket. We pass a photography shop, promoting itself with the usual staged beaming of un-photogenic families.

Juliet yelps as one foot slides off the pavement. She grabs me around the waist and laughs, wishing she could retract her previous plea. I get a flashback to previous summer sun; the two of us roller-skating in Battersea Park, her holding my waist for stability and propulsion.

"What's that Max said about meeting at half six?"

"Just some agency stuff we have to do." Bloody writing a new campaign is all.

"You are not working on your stag do are you? That's not on. Does Sophia know? They are pushing you too hard Dan."

"It's all okay babe. I need to ring Sophia actually." Those bastards are going to make my life hell until this pitch next week. Max never accepts any of my ideas are good until after a pitch; faint praise is only given after it has been sold.

"I could stop them. I could ask for a meeting with the stags at half six to discuss your big night out tomorrow."

"I have to do it before next Wednesday babe. Thanks anyway."

The pavement turns into more forgiving tarmac, but even that glints with shards of ice. Our hotel is around one final bend in the road opposite a footbridge over the railway track.

"Listen babe, I am going stay out and make that call cause Chris will be in the room." He had left a pint ago, sick of the posturing in the bar. I need some privacy for my brief call home.

"You are a bit fuzzy Dan, couldn't you do it later?" Damned if I do, damned if I don't.

If I go onto the footbridge I will be out of view of any stags walking home. I clank relatively easily up the ten footbridge steps, although I hadn't really thought what it would be like going down. I pace slowly towards the middle, standing above the dark scars that are the railway tracks. At the end of the bridge, framed by a metal arch I am surprised to see what looks like another train station labelled CHEMIN DE FER DU MONTENVERS. What do they need two stations at the same place for? The grey slate roof and white façade pick the building out from the developing mist.

"Sophia, hi babe it's me." My mobile connects at last.

"Are you drunk?" She smells the alcohol from hundreds of miles away.

"No way babe, just had a couple after skiing."

"It's bath time here. I will call back." The phone clicks off to give me the chance to find another track. R, S, yes there it is, it was Johnny who made me think of it.

Number 4. "Sign O' Times" by Prince

Definitely released in 1987 on Paisley Park records. It seems eons ago that I was listening to this yesterday in Sophia's dad's car on the way to the airport. Prince was the top man, the coolest dude. This track captured the paranoia of the mid-1980s. Everyone scared of an AIDS epidemic; so unsure of what it was, we thought we could catch it like a cold. Natural tragedies seemed to be on the rise as well, hence the reference to Hurricane Annie. There was a feeling that this was all heralding some apocalyptic revenge for the savagery of mankind. But the real tragedy of the times affecting me was man – or should I say woman – made; the savagery of Margaret Thatcher's Britain. She may have been an economic moderniser but she was a cultural and moral wrecking ball. I suppose being in the advertising trade makes me an expert at signs.

My phone eventually rings.

"Hi Sophia, just a quick call to check in. Are you both okay?"

"Yes, we are good." The "we" seems to be verbally underlined.

"It's been great so far. Steve, Juliet, Johnny and I are in the same beginners' class. Our instructor is Italian, he's called Aldo and he thinks I'm too laid back though." Facts are reeled off as I skirt around this afternoon's fall. Better left unsaid, its danger was obvious and now past, but her worry would grow from a distance.

"He is right isn't he? Can you ski now?"

"Sure, I am making progress." Tomorrow I will do a lesson with closed boots. "It's a real thrill," I add unconvincingly but am allowed to move on.

Two snowboarders appear from the hotel side of the bridge. They sludge along with boards strapped to their backs, dragging their attitude behind them. They nudge past me and walk towards the mist.

"Listen, how has your day been?"

"Tiring, Bepe didn't sleep well last night. He must have woken up eight times, sometimes bad dreams, sometimes water. I let him sleep in my bed from five o'clock. He has been asking for you," she tells me through gritted teeth.

"Can I speak to him?"

I look to the far end of the footbridge and see no arch. The foul weather has eaten the station. I see two cigarette butts move magically in the mist. The scene evokes some wartime rendezvous between the French Resistance and an English pilot, the mist drowns the bridge in a thankfully lost world of Hitler and Churchill. A train surges under the bridge. I feel I am riding it as it passes through the grilled metal under my legs.

"Bepe mate. Bepe. Bepe."

"On the plane diddy." He is gabbling but was drowned out by the train.

"Yes, I went on the plane yesterday. Daddy loves you and we will play when I get home I promise. I will be a good daddy for my baby."

"Listen, don't make any more drunken promises to my child." Sophia was back on the phone.

"I promise I will do more with him babe after we are married." I plead.

"You work too much for that. You see Max and ask him to get another copywriter on your pay and for your hours. You ask him because you never see Bepe in the week." Not a good day to ask for less work. I choose to neglect to mention the new ByeFly campaign.

"You worry me sometimes. You don't know what is slipping through your fingers. Listen, enough. I got to go but we haven't agreed on our wedding presents." I wait for Sophia to go further. "Should we say a limit of £200 or have you bought yours?"

I can get through this. "I'm happy with something around that mark babe." I can ask Juliet what she is going on about later. Can't feel my hands; they are frozen onto the metal casing of my phone. I know she suspects my vagueness.

Snow pit-pats on the polyester shell of my coat and this time it sticks instantly.

"I will be better babe, I promise. He really shook me up yesterday."

I hear heavy footsteps releasing in a "Thwooing" noise from the metal bridge.

"I will call tomorrow babe. See you." I end the conversation in haste, without receiving a reply, just in case this has a bad ending.

More steps, heavier and more quickly. I cannot see anyone but the steps are doubled. Why are they running? I sense it may be the snowboarders again. I move quickly to the top of the steps I came up. A man rips past me and after one step down he leaps off them completely, arching his back for effect and spotting the landing with ease.

The snow falls with unrelenting ease.

The second man stops dead in front of me at the top of the steps, watching his friend land so well and escape into the Chamonix town. We are face to face, deep in each other's personal space. He strips his lungs for his next breath. He must be twenty; I smell his tobacco breath. He shows no expression to reveal his next move. I imagine myself faced by Bepe at this age, his frame suddenly bigger than mine, his life suddenly more vital than mine. What answers will I have for him then? He grins at me.

"You fucker!" he screams with complete abandon at his friend across the road, but facing me. He pats me on each cheek with his huge boarding mittens and leaps from the top step holding his snowboard aloft. Savage brutal youth that will out given time.

CHAPTER 19

Dan 18.36

Six minutes late now, what am I to expect? The tiny lift holds me in; a metallic coffin moving at the Zimmer-like speed of a broken Tardis. I fall out of its doors into the hotel lobby, immediately cracking my breastbone into the shoulder of a black waist-coated waiter.

"*Pardon. Pardon Messieurs.*" He is all apologies despite my culpability. He balances his tray superbly, only losing one can of fizzing Red Bull. He disappears behind the bar again.

I am still steadying myself when I spot my Centurion colleagues across the open hallway. Steve is parked legs akimbo on the edge of the low-slung lobby chairs: a modern version of some back-breaking 1960s' design when posture hadn't been invented. The seating area has an adjacent bar and flows one way into the dining room, the other to the reception desks. Max stands arms folded in front of a massive rustic fireplace, all rough-hewn wooden lintels and stone; its flue disappears into a high wood-beamed ceiling. He is flushed, probably from a shower and the unseasonably lit fire; I want to take a run at him and barge him into its flames. He concentrates hard, trying to muster the words to motivate us. He knows he has a big problem, but wants someone else to shoulder it.

"Come on man, come on." Max squeezes these words out, while pushing a flip-chart pen into his top lip. This is the instrument to record our company redemption. I slip into the seat alongside Steve; the laid-back chair frame may suit mine but I feel stupid, almost lying prone with my neck bent at ninety degrees. The waiter I had mown down reappears, his tray replete with Red Bull and a double espresso for each of us.

We await Max's speech. I imagine him stood atop a hay cart like Kenneth Branagh's boyish depiction of Henry V, rallying the troops pre Agincourt.

"I want the big idea now boys. We are going to create iconic work that is going to change brand perceptions of ByeFly. The campaign strap line will be on your gravestone. Let's have some blue-sky thinking about flying now, just give me the big idea for their positioning now boys." He has emptied the advertising cliché drawer in front of us.

Since when would anyone want little ideas? He wanted a big idea on a poster campaign for a sad local gun shop; "shooting stars" became their nonsensical strap line and resulted in us being blamed for the air gun assault of a local celebrity.

He takes one leaping stride towards the flip chart and squeakily carves BIG IDEA onto the first sheet.

"Over to you guys. How do we deliver?" Max throws himself onto the couch and flicks the black marker pen into the air with thumb and forefinger. It tumbles over and over in a looping trajectory. Steve catches it emphatically and takes to his feet. Just what do they want Max?

"I get the brief boss. Thanks for that." That was no brief; it was sweaty desperation. Steve underlines the words with a flourishing squiggle.

"Let's go through some kick-start themes, emotional, rational, surreal, price lead… What ones do you remember Dan?"

"Err. Before we launch into it, can we talk about the problem a bit more?" I meekly seek clarification. We few, we happy few, we haven't got a clue.

"We haven't got time boss." Steve cuts me dead.

"What problem do you want to talk about Dan? How many months I can pay for my M6 convertible without the ByeFly account?"

"Can we at least think about that customer research we got and what it says about their brand?" Max knows I am right; Steve stares at him to see whether I am to be humoured.

"Okay then, a problem statement. The customers know the headline prices are a con, they always end up paying more after taxes and baggage charges. They are mostly single students just going to get pissed to places they have read about in *The Guardian*. They also know that the service is as basic as it can be, but by their standards they think it is the Ritz. They recognise the brand name as a budget airline that offers a squalid service for a depressingly false price. They just want to get on the plane, close their eyes and get off as quickly as possible. The market context for budget airlines is crap; consumers read all about mindless hedonistic stag parties and planes choking the earth to death. Where do you propose we go with that lot?" Max depressingly sums up to move us on quickly.

All clients want a differentiated brand position from which to build recognition, but they are rarely prepared to invest time, money or brain power to get it. That's ByeFly, trying to hoover up dumb flyers that have little choice.

"So the only answer is to go beyond the brand experience to crack this brief?" Silence answers my proposal.

"Where do you propose to go then?" Max cutely sanctions me to take the floor. He suspects I am right but wants me to come up with a solution before he will endorse my thought.

"If we focus on the product and service we just end up screwed by all the other airlines who can deliver on them." This is my version of a motivating rallying call.

Juliet glides through the lobby, observing our petty business theatre. She looks lovely and reminds me there is life outside this cocoon. I picture her from behind, rising naked from our student bed in London; I always waited for her to get up first for this very reason.

"Can we just get on with it?" Steve acts impatient for the benefit of Max.

Max re-takes the pen, has a shot of Red Bull and stands up again.

"A ByeFly on the wall." Steve starts the brainstorm.

"Buzz off to your destination," I add.

"A magic carpet flies you there," Steve follows my theme.

"A fly past – you know, the Red Arrows," Max makes his first contribution as the pen squeals our ideas onto the second flip page. He writes with such vigour, it feels like he is raiding our brains.

"Forget plane travel – Beam me up Scotty," Max adds a tired attempt at a Star Trek link.

"Maybe we could name a cloud after every passenger!" I can't tell if Steve is a genius or not.

"What about "comfort is for wimps"?" I add

"I want to get some price-led ideas as well. If it cost any less you would have to walk." Max focuses on their biggest weakness as a budget airline.

"Or Robin Hood, he steals from the rich to fly for the poor. The people's liberation front of flying." I delve back into Robert Lindsay's feisty depiction of the Che Guevara of Tooting in *Citizen Smith*. I spend my life half-remembering sitcoms of my childhood as a source of inspiration for brands today.

"Maybe we have an anti-brand spokesman. Rather than Richard Branson, we invent a parody Hitler look-alike, like Freddie Starr used to do, who dictates that you should fly with ByeFly." Steve at least goes out on a limb.

"What about emotional blackmail, the staff could be seen pleading, fly with us or we will be sacked." Sometimes you throw in an idea just to keep your numbers up.

"It's not an emotionally based brand." Max commits brainstorm hara-kiri; he judgementally dismisses a theme when no idea is meant to be a bad idea.

"Okay, what about telling a story then? How could we use a story style like a thriller, comedy or action story to depict the brand?" I suggest loosely.

"What about doing a version of *The Office*, with Ricky Gervais playing a dense pilot who thinks he is God's gift?" Max again tries to rely on copying something else.

"What about that customer service guy on the Nationwide adverts who couldn't give a toss about what he tells the customers," Steve continues.

"Problem with that is that ByeFly would be the joke airline," I point out.

"What about a spoof remake on the Airplane films? That would have plenty of scope for some laughs." Max makes a reasonable suggestion; I should have thought of that one.

"What about reprising the end scene in *Casablanca* where they are about to go on the plane, do something all moody and emotional in black and white?"

"Or Strangers on a Plane," I chip in.

"What do you mean?"

"It's a take on *Strangers on a Train*, that 1940s' black-and-white movie. Fly with us and meet the love of your life, to take your mind off the crap service." Would Max dare to take on something more abstract?

"That sounds good, like a pastiche with stiff acting like Harry Enfield did in that Mr Cholmondley-Warner football sketch." Steve likes the idea; he must have forgotten it was mine.

"It would hit the demographic profile of most frequent flyers being single. We could do a PR stunt where we marry a couple that we got together. It would also be funny doing the price message. "Darling, it's positively tragic that other people pay more than £10 for a trip to Athens."" I develop and endorse my own idea, Max thinks about whether he could sell it, Steve waits to be told that Max likes it.

"Why don't you two work that one up and the price-lead Robin Hood one for tomorrow?" Max has made his undemocratic choice.

"Are we going home tomorrow? Did you look at flights Dan?" Max asks knowing that I have hardly been out of his sight and can't possibly have looked. He is such a bastard for pushing, but knows he can dangle my job carrot-like in front of me.

"I haven't had a chance. I could look to go on Saturday if you like, but we have ideas we can sketch out from here can't we guys?" I know Max will keep pushing to go home early.

"Alright, let's stay here till Sunday as planned, but we need these ideas developed and on the plane home with us." Strange, Max must have some confidence in what we have done to agree to that.

"Come on, soup is out guys!" Johnny beckons us around the corner to dinner.

I have earned my corn for today, even though we are on holiday. Max is happy for now, he has raped these ideas from us. He has some intellectual property that he can use to make himself look good in front of the client next week. The problem is moving on, and the drama abates for now.

CHAPTER 20

Juliet 22.01.

WHY DOES DAN PUT UP WITH THESE SO CALLED FRIENDS?

Our group weaves into the Chamonix night traffic. Dan certainly doesn't know the reason for my rejection of him but it cannot stay that way. I am here to let off a time bomb, however inconvenient that is. I picked up this puppy, after I was emotionally mauled by Tristan, how naïve of me to choose either partner. Our unresolved past has subtly affected every relationship I have ever had.

My hand brushes real fur; how many foxes were killed in the making of that coat? The lady pushes a stroller imperiously through the heart of our group. The baby girl is flat out asleep; I would never have dragged Ethan around this late at that age.

The stags hunt for a suitable bar, each with very different visions of success. Some are passed for no good reason, except maybe the absence of under-dressed women. We are getting nowhere. An ornate toyshop stretches their opening hours to take a last sale. The evening promenade of the well-heeled elite is ending. The night shift of youth is starting. Ethan would love to be here now, but not with this jaded crew.

"What about this one? It does cocktails." I suggest somewhere that has a chance, as they will think there will be women in it. Robert has the upper hand, so despite our lunchtime bust-up he must be humoured. We can't really see into the smart looking Chaise-Longue bar as it has its entrance four steps below our feet.

"Okay Jules, I am sure you just want to get your lips wrapped around a Black Russian. Let's see whether the talent is up to scratch in there."

He accepts my suggestion with smug sexual allusion. Shoulders are shrugged all around and I score a petty victory.

We enter the calming presence of the lounge bar. For the first time there is a collective pause for breath. Chris and Johnny are the first to slump in the chairs, awaiting beer. The gloomy bar only holds two couples posted in different corners and a group of three women at the bar. The male faces around me seem confused. Maybe we can take a different path.

I try to extend my influence further while it is becalmed. "Should we put a kitty together to cover our drinks bill, say fifty Euros each?"

"Great idea babe, it will save a lot of messing." Dan is the only rubber stamp I need in this context, he seems glad of something to keep us together. I squeeze the gathered money into a small coin purse I have.

Robert moves behind me, leaning over my shoulder as I await the drinks order. His lips are close to my ear. I feel something stir in his trousers; he holds my right arm. He speaks collusively. "Is that a kitty or a pussy you have there? Maybe I could stroke it later?" I despise this creep.

I turn to face him while he is up close, beaming a false, broad smile. I spit through clenched teeth. "Piss off you pervert. The only thing you will get to stroke later is your own member." I struck a good tone but member was too tame, my mouth would not give him the pleasure of using another word. Max and Steve converse exclusively at the bar so Robert takes his Jack Daniels and Coke towards them. Dan sits next to me opposite the others.

"How is it going babe? I know you have had a tough day with him, but we are alright aren't we?" Dan seeks assurance.

"Of course. It's great to be here with you. I wanted to spend some quality time with you before you were wed." I lie. "We must get a chance to talk properly, get some perspective on the past," I flush with anxiety as I try to set up my needed conversation.

"I would like that, what about now, we could…" Dan tails off as Robert comes back from the bar looking bored. He will allow no-one time off from their duty to entertain him. "I am staying at Mere for the wedding, anyone fancy a night out next Friday?"

"I will meet you there," Steve invites himself.

"No, no, I was thinking of a crowd of us having a night out in Manchester or chasing young fillies around Knutsford. Come on boys." Robert jerkily drinks his whisky in disgust at the lack of a convincing response. Everyone else seems to have a life Robert.

"I will probably be busy mate, but will let you know," Dan skirts the issue. He seems to definitely handle him better than he used to.

"Are you not taking your girlfriend to the wedding? Won't you want to take her out?" I enquire.

"What, Samantha my fuck buddy? No chance. She is staying well away so that the mouse can come out to play." He empties his glass.

"Come on girls, finish your drinks, let's get going to somewhere with some action." For a few moments the group had let go; it held no animosity or desire to shame. But every man now takes his drink and dispenses with it. Tension rises again.

Robert wanders to the bar. "And where are you girls headed?"

The three girls turn their heads to face him, revealing their synchronised straw drinking. All three are beautiful; they have no need to explain themselves to him so no reply is offered.

"Cat got your tongues?" Well-done sisters.

I am the last to step outside. I just see Robert's back as he strides up the street. A pedestrian area opens up ahead and a river gushes underneath us. Robert pulls the group onwards to the main town square. When I catch up they are in a queue of fifteen people, mostly women, trying to get into the Café Blanche. Music and heat escape with each departing group from its ornate pink metal-framed doors.

We shuffle forward. The club thumps. I am in no hurry to get in, although it doesn't take long. Inside my men now seem meek and mild. They seem to be lustily appraising female limbs around us.

I see Robert at the bar with Dan. He is mouthing, "Where's our pussy?" but knows I can't possibly hear him over the intense French rap. He stands on the bar footrest reaching back towards me to get the money. Robert the Supreme Being is back, as he bounces stupidly like an ape.

We ascend the spiral staircase to the source of the music on the first floor. I inadvertently brush my white-wine spritzer onto the midriff of an olive-skinned girl as I reach the top step, causing her to jump. I apologise and she ignores me. The boys are in a semi-circle in front of me: Robert, Max, Dan and Steve all seem to receive a cheap thrill from my contact.

A DJ stands behind a small pedestal, one headphone clutched to an ear, listening to his own re-mix. A sign advertising himself as Josef hangs over his head. A group of about twenty people bump along lazily to his current groove.

I re-imagine old school discos with spotty boys prowling around without the mettle to ask me to dance. I feel the tension of exclusion felt by these even weaker men. They try to project attitude to the feminine beauty in front of them. They try to feign disinterest before they can be disregarded. Four of these boys are married, one is to be betrothed in seven days' time and one is a creepy megalomaniac. Yet all stare with intent at the dance floor, imagining improbable liaisons. There is no approval for them here, the throng boogie on regardless. I feel a trace of pity for them. I am cheapened by my presence here.

Robert must think that to be alpha-male he has to break rank. He must conquer womanhood. He looks for no support; but unleashes himself on the cheapest smuttiest looking pair of girls. They laugh at his first approach, whispering to each other as he dances alone. They can mock so much; his 1980s' haircut, his lack of style. He makes it so easy for them to ridicule him with his dancing. I hope to witness rejection but no, they are straight-faced now and accept his intrusion. The youngest and prettiest one dances with him. The other moves aside. This is not right.

He conquered without a word; he put himself out there, having chosen his prey well. His armoury was confidence and the smell of money. Maybe to gold-diggers he fits an acceptable profile: no style but branded by Gucci loafers and his top-of-the-range Cartier watch. He pushes himself towards her ear as he had done with me earlier, slithering his hands onto her waist. She pushes her chin up to accept his kiss on her neck. I hate this woman; she has kept the merry-go-round turning, offering comfort to the other losers.

I had been staring so hard at Robert that I missed the shift of focus. The other stags are reminded of their libidos. Chris is smiling vacantly just thrilled to be near a woman. Max is thinking, maybe she might succumb. Steve is salivating. Even Johnny seems to have a lump in his trousers. They are seeing me as meat now. They all want something. Is it me or is every eye looking towards my breasts; I feel cheap for having any cleavage on show. Could Ethan be a part of this brotherhood? I feel sick in my throat.

Dan should stand apart. I know he isn't like this but he just looks meekly towards me.

"Would you like to dance?" Max pushes his hand into mine and sneaks an arm over my shoulder. His tone is smooth. I shake my head.

"Come on Jules," he tries again. I look to Dan in obvious discomfort.

Through his inaction I now see no difference for his years. He is strikingly the same; without the means to react, to impose himself. Say something Dan. Show me that you are ready to take this step forward. But I know this face. He looks wistful, dreaming that it will be better tomorrow so that he doesn't have to confront today. How will I be able to reach this boy?

"I have to go, I am not well." I push my glass into Max's expectant hand and turn back towards the staircase to leave alone. I am afraid for Dan.

FRIDAY 17TH APRIL 2009

CHAPTER 21

Dan 06.41

Bepe is running and laughing through verdant hills; giggling prey to his father's mock chase. He runs toward the magic windmill. Each step shudders his body, his young locked knees creating halting progress. He turns his head and squeals as the chase seems to be ending, but every time his father allows him to elude his sweeping capture. The Teletubbies play their part, distracting Dan in this game of "Run Away". Bepe finds La La and hides behind her rotund belly for a few moments, before darting off in another direction. Pollen, wet earth and grass invade Dan's nostrils as he determines to finally make a real capture. "Time for tubby bye-bye, Time for tubby bye-bye" lilts the echoing announcement. Bepe runs towards Po, tripping her up with one foot hooked around her ankle; she cries as she falls. He shoots his Scooby Doo gun at Dipsy and Tinky Winky; they give a Teletubby shriek as they both get jammed trying to escape down the same rabbit hole. Bepe is now pistol-whipping the fallen Po with no remorse as he tries to get to his feet. All four make a desperate escape underground as the baby sun looks down scornfully.

Bepe leads Daniel to a picture-perfect picnic on one of the many hillsides. A tartan blanket is spread out with sandwiches, jelly and cake in abundance. Bepe tucks into the strawberry jelly first, using his hands. Splashes of jelly stick to his face and wobble. Daniel takes egg sandwiches from the platter in front of him. As he chews he gets a shooting pain in his mouth. He looks down to his orange plastic plate and sees two of his own incisors lying on the bread. Blood lines his bite from the sandwich. He takes another bite in defiance but the bread, mayonnaise and hard-boiled egg mix with three molars and two front teeth in his mouth. As he can't swallow safely he spits the bloody contents of his mouth onto the manicured grass; blood spatters onto a nearby daisy. Daniel reaches for Bepe with blood covering his hands, his mouth devoid of teeth and dripping with blood enriched saliva. He starts to wipe the jelly from Bepe's face but only spreads the bloody mess. "Diddy hurt, get plaster," Bepe worryingly observes his father. Dan looks up to see Sophia standing frowning alongside the four Teletubbies, all of them with arms crossed.

Again I am awoken by a frantic dream. Thursday started with a bang on my head, Friday starts with a gasp for air. I am dreaming so vividly but it is not hard to understand why. Bepe looms large in every thought. At the moment I feel so close to him, we are apart.

The room smells rank from my unwashed brother Chris. I look over to see his naked bottom exposed by a single sheet. We never did lower that heating and it is raging again now. I see the half-eaten remains of a McDonalds burger on the cabinet, witness to our hunger on the way home from the bar last night. Robert continued his weekend of my embarrassment by offering me the sexual services of his new partner's friend. I could not tell if they were paid for their services. He looked so camp as he swung his paper burger bag at me and stormed out with a lady on each arm. Why did Juliet leave so early? Why did we all let her leave alone?

I shower with vigour to wash off some of the negativity of the first two days here. I dress eagerly today, in anticipation of enjoying today on the snow. My guitar case is still bulging with the extra clothes I brought, even after I have selected my favourite corduroy shirt to inelegantly accompany my sweaty salopettes.

I open the balcony door handle with an inelegant clunk, but it doesn't wake the reeking Chris; I pray he washes today. This is another chance to further Bepe's list. Further noise accompanies my repositioning of the heavy wooden balcony chair. I am overlooking the railway bridge I called home from last night. With the mystique of the mist removed, I can now see that the second Chamonix train station serves a tram with red carriages that winds up the mountainside. A fresh coolness descends from upon high; today's weather has yet to come over the mountain.

As I flick through the list again I feel liberated and restricted. Liberated to make some positive choices but restricted that these seven are to stand for a life spent listening. Will they collectively mean anything? Will they feel like the spine of my life when they are chosen?

Number 5 "This Charming Man" by the Smiths.

Morrissey seemingly asks on behalf of both of us if nature will make men of us. His apparent bashfulness always made me feel comparatively strong; reminding me that I did have some good qualities, whatever they were. This was my signature tune for the decade, the heavily rotated soundtrack to my first real job, as a copy checker at the *Chester Chronicle*. Max knew someone high up there so got me an interview. Life seemed to be taking shape again on my terms after London and this happy-go-lucky tune fitted perfectly. The lyrics resonated with my previously troubled northern soul.

I had come back north with my tail between my legs. It was as if London just spat me out. My college friends were now scattered back across the country. Having been rejected from numerous jobs in London, I could not live on the state and have a life. In contrast I loved the small city mentality and youthful optimism of Chester, all played out under its Roman walls. It seemed a warming antidote to the harshness of the big city. Why didn't Morrissey have a stitch to wear though? I never understood what he meant about returning the rings; I always assumed that it would just make sense to me one day but it never has. I do hope Bepe and I can live a life of being interested in each other's music. Don't judge your dad's taste too harshly when you listen to them in years to come Bepe; I was a child of my time.

CHAPTER 22

Dan 10.11

The helicopter blades chop insistently at the air above me, releasing a metallic roar into the valley. This unnatural sky-high platform must have heavenly views of the mountain massif, reaching across Italy, France and Switzerland. For a few moments it is the lord of this place; with nothing higher it flaunts its power. What a great vantage point to look into the souls of the people inhabiting the valley.

Juliet doesn't need to stare into my soul from above. She can usually see my truth, the one I always mask. Can she see that I have Sophia's love but it is without passion? I am sure that the flavour of my love would not delight her palate. How to describe it? If my love for Sophia were an ice cream, Juliet's tongue would push expectantly towards the cone, eyes closed, expecting the refreshing flavour burst of lemon sorbet, but getting the confused disappointment of Tutti Frutti.

Our group is gathered but apart. We have no option but to wait as Aldo is ten minutes late at the designated meeting point. Skiers have to squeeze past us, as we are awkwardly accumulated beside the ski lift. Kronk our resident Dutch giant and Mari Elena stand separately away from the four of us.

"Your ski suit is really nice, what make is it?" Juliet reaches across the divide to ease the discomfort of the young girl. How does this generosity of spirit come so easily to women? They dissolve boundaries of age or any chance of competition with a pure well-meant exchange of views on ski suits. A flurry of fashion information allows them to sympathetically climb inside each other's lives.

I stand unsure that I can prove myself again. Will I fall today? Will it matter if I do? I am taken back to my first days working as a copywriter for Max, holed up in a one-room office above a pastry shop on Eastgate Street. Every time he passed on a new client brief to me I would sit frozen over a blank sheet of A4 paper. Thoughts would come quickly, but my perverse desire to write something memorable would make me tragically halt. I would keep clicking my pen top back on just when I thought I had a breakthrough. I would be paralysed for days, clinging on to the comforting smell of sausage rolls from below, hoping that Max stayed away and failed to get more clients that I couldn't write any copy for.

It was my lack of productivity that made Max insist that I started to call anyone I knew who could possibly give us any business. I remembered Sophia, one of Juliet's friends from college, had an Italian family shoe business with shops in Manchester. I called her at home, having plucked up the courage to get the number from their office. She was genuinely pleased I had called and we talked for an hour and a half; I couldn't find the point to interject the real reason for my call without hurting her feelings.

We met in Manchester but it took six more nights out before I could ask without it seeming callous. At last in Henry's bar I asked if I could approach her father to talk business, but she instantly suspected an ulterior motive. Seriousness descended upon her face. I now know that she thought that it was an elaborate way for me to move the relationship on to the next level and meet her family. She respected my apparent directness. On a battered green studded leather couch she leant over to kiss me with a determination I had never felt before. I got the meeting with her dad after a five-course Sunday dinner at her house with every relative they could dig up. Importantly Centurion got its first reasonable client. Suddenly I could write just enough to justify my existence at work. Years later she gets to marry me.

"We move away from here!" Aldo has arrived without apology and signals us away from the ski lift. We line up in front of him further down the run.

"Ciao everybody. We don't have much time but maybe we stop for coffee in an hour so we meet each other. Everyone has good night? Everybody has boots closed?" He looks at me with affection and ridicule smirked across his face.

"Okay today we try more pizzas but start to ski parallel with two skis. We move un-weighted ski in to join weighted ski. Everyone okay? I show you."

And so the procession leads off again leaving me last in line. I wonder if my emergent ski ability will have been erased overnight. I will wait for the first edge to engage before I believe I can still do this. If you think too hard there is no logic to having control on skis. I try to walk through the ski turn in my mind, you can do it, you can do it. Hip to the hill, shoulder to the valley. I attend to the permanent running of my nose, using the integrated nose wiper on my gloves.

Just let me go please. When I am instructed to follow I defy my instincts and push my body forwards towards the snow. I scratch unconvincingly around my first turn. Carving the omnipresent snow crystals, I nervously imagine each one is only a light beam away from extinction. I am sucking in air, flying into space. Growing willpower is defeating my logical fears. However, hypercritical self-judgement follows in my tracks. How fast am I going? How smooth was that turn? How do I look? Leave me in peace to ski.

"Here comes the beach boy," Aldo greets my arrival. "Good stag, you are forward more, we allow the ski to do the work. Skis close to parallel, good, good." I am getting somewhere. Juliet seems much quieter today. After three more practice runs we move on to Aldo's proposed coffee break; I admire his Italian lack of urgency.

Johnny and I take our coffee from a hole in the wall of the on-piste restaurant.

"You really came on there mate," he says with surprise obvious in his voice.

"You are not so bad yourself. I wish we could just keep going now." My praise tries to deflect what I think is true. I can ski.

"How is the track listing coming?"

116

"It's almost signed, sealed and delivered," I confidently pronounce, revealing the five tracks to date like I am presenting an Oscar.

"Great choice, but there are so many essential artists to fit in. What about Kraftwerk, New Order, The Beatles, I could go on." Johnny remains impressed that I can pin down such a mammoth task. He would never do it just in case any of the artists found out about their exclusion.

"Maybe I will start listing some other stuff for him, things I have done, places I have been and so on. I am going to make him proud of me one day." I speculate.

"I have been meaning to tell you something exciting. I think I am close to getting a record deal. Would you believe it, Rough Trade is interested?" I had been so wrapped up in my drama that we had not even talked about him in the two days we have been here.

"They are still going strong, with Arcade Fire and Jarvis Cocker and such like." He continues in unnecessary justification of their impeccable pedigree.

"That's fantastic mate, after all these years it might happen for you." Johnny has written songs all his life and they have kept his dream alive. I can't stop a pang of raw jealousy that he might step out of our shared world of fandom.

"I will find out next week I think. You can be my road manager if you want."

"Maybe mate, but I probably have to hold down the nine to five grind now I am getting married." I keep falling into the middle-class plot that Joe Strummer so openly exposed.

Fourteen ski boots click clack back into their skis, prefacing our return to the lesson. I make sure I stick closer to Aldo, as the plateau becomes a slope again.

"Don't get too big for those boots Dan." Juliet smacks my bottom gently with her ski pole and gracefully slides by to where Aldo has stopped. This is the top of the run I fell down, but with sun on the slopes and my ability on the rise I look forward to taking the test again.

"This is red slope, but we can all do this no? Keep behind my line and we will be okay." That means we must stay away from the ice. Aldo skis over the lip Juliet had paused at yesterday and I follow them both this time. Push forward, weight on one ski. The danger is much reduced as my edges bite the snow and I can see well. The point of my fall is now acknowledged as a danger spot, guarded by two crossed poles dug into the snow. This is yet more vindication that the conditions, not my ability, defeated me twenty-four hours ago. The three of us stop with the lift in sight.

Further up the slope, Johnny is tailing Mari Elena whose salopettes are covered in snow. She is moving so slowly that it is very hard for him to stay behind her; she seemed so confident yesterday.

"What happened there?" I ask Johnny when they finally join us.

"She was just about to ski off at the top when you cut across her and she fell. She has been a nervous wreck on the way down."

"Stag no beach bum now, he Franz Klammer." Aldo lauds me, unperturbed by her accident.

Everyone is here except Kronk, who stands still as a tree at our point of departure.

"Come on Kronk you can do it, it's easy," I find myself shouting in vain to him. The pecking order in the group has changed and on my reckoning I am at the top with Juliet now.

"Come on Kronk, we want to get some skiing done. He looks like a ski Bambi." Steve shouts and laughs at him. "Come on you lummox."

"Maybe Dutch no good at skiing as they never see hill." Aldo joins in out of Kronk's earshot. Eventually he pushes off going as flat across the slope as possible. At the point of the turn he sits down on the snow, flops his skis around and gets up to traverse in the opposite direction. His legs are so far apart in a snowplough that he is in danger of being ripped in two. With the next turn he gathers some speed and heads straight at us.

"What are you doing?" He hits Steve hard at the top of our line and apologetically gets back to his feet.

"Okay it is easy run to lift now. We stop at lift and finish today. You follow now." Aldo falls away with superb grace. I jump the gun on everyone else to follow him. This is great; I love this now, the sense of achievement rushes through my veins. I have never been so fast; my cheeks start to feel icy with the increased wind friction.

"My stag man, you start to ski parallel now." Aldo gives me the approval I crave. I have beaten Juliet down for the first time. Maybe I can get something right for a change.

CHAPTER 23

Dan 13.46

"Go left everyone," Robert shouts directions to the group at the top of La Flegere.

"Go right Dan," Juliet whispers as we move in the opposite direction.

"Dan, I said go left you fool," Robert's ungracious squeal fails to affect me as he disappears from view.

"Let's hope they never find us." Juliet proposed at lunch that we break away and ski alone together, which I secretly jumped at. The chance to ski with her and hone my skills away from the pressure of the stags was too good to be true. The oily Spaghetti Bolognaise well may have been re-heated at lunchtime but there was no evidence of leftovers from the group. Spring sunshine finally seemed to thaw the atmosphere of them all.

I move slowly down the slope while trying to re-fit my right glove as we go. My hopes on this Friday afternoon were to kick back before the onslaught of my stag party tonight.

"Can I help you Dan?" Juliet comes alongside.

"With what?"

"To ski of course; I can help you or we can just ski for fun." I am a little taken aback. Wasn't I the fastest down the hill before lunch? What can she teach me?

"That would be great babe." My refusal now may lead to embarrassment later.

"Going faster can delude you into thinking you have control." Maybe she viewed my run prior to lunch not as successfully as I did. I feel equally ashamed and relieved that someone cared.

"When you think you are leaning forward, lean forward even more. It's all about commitment, skiing is so much easier the straighter you go. Follow me. Don't forget to smile though Dan." She sets off and I concentrate on the path of her bob of brown hair. I double my effort to lean forward, which has such an incredible braking effect that I almost tumble over my ski tips. I ease off to find a compromise position, but my turns feel more secure.

The Brit quotient is turned up in the afternoon; they dutifully force themselves out to bash the piste from morning to last light to make the most of this scarce mountainous resource. Our mainland European cousins have mountains on their doorsteps and use the afternoon for lounging in deckchairs. Brits have the afternoon to practise the barked orders from the morning's ski school, to seek out the Holy Grail of the parallel turn. The rest of Europe taught their children to ski every Saturday afternoon. British kids were inside hiding from the rain, making papier-mâché mountains out of old Littlewoods catalogues.

"That's better; you committed more. You didn't force it; your ski worked for you." Someone I trust knows the route and I am happy to be taken for a ride.

"Let's loosen your legs up now." I follow her in trust as I have always done. Juliet is heading for the very edge of a blue run, where the snow is churned up and hard. She leads me outside the blue marker pole onto uneven snow for the first time; I am unnerved by it and quickly dart back onto the piste for security. She turns and waves an arm to tempt me back onto the road less travelled. I follow her again and am instantly re-cast back as complete novice. My skis cut into the lumps, which completely cover my boots. As I rise out of the snow I go faster again; I am concentrating so hard on my feet and leaning forward that I missed the fact that Juliet was skiing across my path up ahead.

"Hey Juliet," my feeble announcement arrives just as I crash into her side, pushing the legs from underneath her. I contort myself to fall backwards, away from her, and splash softly into the un-bashed snow. My skis snap off in response to their contradictory directions. All my limbs are packed snugly into the snow, like a spread hand pushed into fresh dough.

I delight at Juliet's girlish squeal as she falls onto my chest. It instantly takes years from her, revealing the young woman not the mother.

"My legs are really loose now, babe."

She buries her face in the front of my ski jacket; she convulses with laughter, but hides it away so I cannot luxuriate in it. Why is she so scared of being different in front of me? A deep intake of air accompanies her head rising. Her elbows prise open the space between my third and fourth ribs; I dare not complain in fear of losing the moment.

"See, it's all about control." She attempts to resume her teaching role but realises she had been complicit in our harmless accident; her face is buried again until her laughter can be tamed.

"Do you remember ice skating in Streatham?" She rediscovers her poise. Our closeness brings her back to mothballed memories that I no longer let out for fear of their pain. Of course I remember. I remember it all.

"I don't know which one of us was worse at it. You fell over and couldn't get up because you were afraid of getting your hands cut off." I remind her of her stupidity and her face is back in my ski jacket. We went home on the bus eating a mountain of popcorn, spilling it into the wooden floor slats. I feel the release from our frantic girl-on-top sex on the sofa afterwards. My stomach always turned at seeing the murky brown foam peering through the threadbare cushions. Spiky spilt popcorn kernels pressed into my face. I have framed the look of imploring ecstasy that carried her to orgasm. Does she feel these things now?

"You know there is trouble ahead?" A sharp intake of thin mountain air allows her to recover composure. She is happy to stay perched on me, but my ribs are going numb.

"Am I going to get my head dunked in the toilets?"

"I mean it Dan. Robert is a nasty sod. You will need a clear head tomorrow."

"A clear head? I am going to be force-fed beer on my stag night but still need a clear head in the morning? What are we doing?"

"Just prepare for intense skiing." I was invincible with her at my side; maybe she can be there again.

"Do you think Sophia would like to ski?" She incisively drops us back into our reality. I can't answer for her anymore so don't.

"Are you missing Bepe?" Her eyes are puffed from laughter, but because she uses so little make-up her face is still in place.

"I miss him so." Bepe has never possessed me like he does now. He is becoming present in each action and reaction. Is she testing my commitment? He was snatched from me when I had never been so close. At least my stag trials are distracting me from this heartache.

"Can we go down to shop in Chamonix? We can have a coffee and catch up." Juliet has a plan.

"That's possible babe." Of course it is, I would like nothing more.

"Listen, I just wanted to say that…" She looks at me solemnly and tenderly. Oh my lord.

"Let's go then babe." I don't think I am ready for what she has to say. My head is spinning and I need to think about Sophia and Bepe. If I don't go through with the wedding what would happen?

The snow that I have displaced is dying in the afternoon sun, but anything I fell onto is thriving with a confident shimmer. I have suffered her digging elbows long enough. I push upwards for both of us, breaking the spell of our closeness. We reassemble our equipment and ourselves.

"Where to now babe?" I ask.

"Let's finish this run. We will stay on-piste now, but keep going straighter down the hill," she says insistently.

And so I ski on in a heady state with Juliet in my sight. I try to displace the tonne of lead I feel in my heart at the fleeting thought of losing Bepe. Maybe this will be a new best memory in my life. My mental journey is now accompanied by the sweeping orchestral themes of John Barry. Skiing broadens the scale of our little lives; the grand mountains bring hopeful immensity.

"Last one to the bottom gets the coffee!" I scream straight down the hill past the unsuspecting Juliet. I don't know how to stop at such speed but it isn't an issue now.

CHAPTER 24

Juliet 15.05

"WHY DON'T MEN SEE THE SIGNS?"

"Attention Messieurs, attention!" the French van driver knows Dan is in danger

Dan is unwittingly window shopping and in danger of being carried through it. The high-sided metal-framed trolley overloaded with clothes is heading straight at him. The driver lost control as he closed the van door and it rolls speedily down the steep top of the avenue.

His hopes rely on either the driver catching it or in him waking up to the danger in the next twenty seconds. I am standing twenty yards away perusing the postcards on display outside a tobacconist. He had seemed so relaxed this afternoon, so happy with his lot. He crouches slightly under the awning of the record shop, which is also probably shielding the noise.

Ten seconds maybe; the van driver is over fifty but he is making good progress hampered by tight fitting jeans. All is lost then. The rest of the break will be visiting Dan in a hospital bed. He will be slashed from head to toe with window glass and maybe suffer a broken right arm from the impact. It will certainly ruin my shopping expedition and my chance to set our record straight. My eyes narrow to shield my view of the accident.

Two seconds left. I only realised that the trolley had missed Dan when it started to head towards me. The van driver hurled himself at the cage to deflect it away from Dan, only for its new trajectory to be this bookshop. I take the necessary two steps backwards into the road, and stand between two parked cars. The cage is eventually halted by the display of postcards I had been viewing. Then the second-hand books on a low wooden shelf take a beating. Display on display topples over, but no glass is shattered and no human hit.

"Juliet babe, are you okay?" Dan had run behind the cars and put his arm on my shoulder. "You were in real danger there babe." He has no hint of what was to befall him. I am speechless at the change of fortune.

The dumpy bald bookshop owner has clambered over his scattered displays and knocked the van driver on the ground. He instantly regrets it as the driver rises to show his physical presence. They push each other and seethe in French.

"Typical French, losing it over some clothes and books." Dan still doesn't register his potential part in the piece.

"Let's go in that sports shop," I suggest as we cross the street.

"I can deal with that. Let's get a baseball bat in case things turn really nasty." He is so empty of his own agenda and open to mine.

The carved wood and glass door shuts with a swish enclosing the smell of new cotton. The staff seems to avoid us as I scour the printed T-shirts for a present for Ethan. I feel closer to him again. I picture hastily unpacking the top of my suitcase on Sunday night, giving him a present as a token for my time away.

"Ouch." I look up to see that Dan has walked into a wooden snowboarding sign hanging from the ceiling at a height that threatens none but the very tall.

"Are you shopping for Ethan?" Still rubbing his head; it's the first time he has mentioned my boy.

"Yes. He is a medium, so if you see anything…"

"What about this, this looks cool." Dan holds up an orange 1960s' retro-style ski jacket, with Chamonix lettering sewn into the front.

"Would you have worn that in your teens?" Dan seems delighted that I remember his taste. He was so light-hearted, child-like in everything except his height. I know he loved me but it was surely the love of an over-eager puppy dog. I don't know maybe the jacket might work. I pay sixty crisp Euros to the snooty owner. One present down, one more to go.

Walking out of the shop, the scene from which we escaped has been fast forwarded. The clothes, van and its driver are nowhere to be seen. The bookshop owner cradles his forehead, sitting on one of his upended displays, as his assistant picks up books.

"There is a really good book store at the bottom of the street, can we go there?" Dan's acquiescence is both charming and unsettling. The whitewashed buildings of Chamonix are covered in low sun. Dan walks behind me. I turn around to see him superimposed on the backdrop of the mountains.

We take a step into the bookshop but Dan sees his brother Chris at the window of McDonalds. He walks towards the window but retreats. Maybe Chris wouldn't want him to witness him eating himself silly. My next intended gift is to get Scott a book about the mountains.

"*Bonsoir, Mademoiselle. Ca va?*" Do bookshop owners work harder than sports shop owners?

"*Oui. Avez vous la grande photographique livre cette Montagne?*" I give him enough to provoke a reaction. He guides me to a huge table covered in just what I am looking for.

"Chamonix, Mont Blanc, Vallée Blanche?" he asks. My head jumps at the mention of the destination of tomorrow's expedition. I glance at Dan to see if I have unwittingly revealed anything, but he is naturally oblivious. All of the books are breathtaking. I study the Vallée Blanche book but it is in French. I find a photo of a door marked with the word "Attention" in many languages. The word "guide" is mentioned numerous times. It gives a chilling perspective on where we are aiming to ski tomorrow. The inside back page seems to be a dedication to those who have lost their lives on the mountain. I must get Robert to cancel this foolhardy trip. I pay for a book on Mont Blanc without opening a page.

"Hi Chris. See you back at the hotel." Dan exaggerates his speech so that Chris can lip-read from inside McDonalds. Chris gives a thumbs up while pushing his plastic tray with empty burger wrappers away with his elbow.

"It's been really nice spending time together today. Should we get a coffee before we head back?" I make a final request.

"Great babe let's do that. It's been great for me too! Can I get a postcard to send home?" Why is he asking my permission? He worries me with his knowing looks.

We select a postcard each from the next shop we see; I choose Chamonix town against Mont Blanc, he chooses Mickey Mouse on skis.

"Keep a look out for runaway trolleys," he shouts as he goes inside to pay.

We cross the paved river bridge to find an outdoor café in the buzzing square. The café is nearly full with relaxing après-skiers and well-heeled Europeans.

"You get the table. I will get the drinks, what do you want?" I instantly regret my offer as I see a queue at least fifteen long. It's time now; we have re-established a faded friendship but he must know why I left him. I apply lip salve; I don't want to dry up. The queue goes slowly.

"*Deux cappuccino, aussi une l'eau naturelle, s'il vous plaît.*"

Dan is finishing his postcard with a flourish as I return. He grabs the coffees before I have chance to drop the water bottle under my arm. I regret the choice of location as it lacks much-needed privacy should he be distressed.

"It's ten past four, what time are we going out?" Dan enquires, being the stag in the dark. I have less than ten minutes to talk.

"We are meeting at about six in the lobby, but I have to get back to meet the others in a bit." Robert insisted we all meet at four thirty in the hotel lobby to, as he put it, discuss "Stag tactics".

"I am desperate for the loo babe, I will drink up quick when I get back." He goes inside and I think the opportunity is lost. It needs to be right.

Dan knocks the table as he leaves; my water splashes his newly written postcard. The gel pen ink has smudged in three places. I retrieve a tissue from my pocket to damp the wet patches. I find myself obtrusively reading it.

Hi Sophia and Bepe.

Daddy misses you so much Bepe. Mickey Mouse will cheer you up till I come home. I will take you and Mickey skiing one day. Sophia, sorry about Wednesday, it hit me hard. We need to talk as I struggle sometimes. Skiing brilliantly now thanks to Juliet.

Dan.

He cannot send that to a woman eight days away from her marriage, he sounds like he isn't going through with it. Why has he got cold feet? He doesn't think anything is happening with us does he? Heaven forbid. Does he think I came on this trip to stop him getting married? How much is he going to hate me when he knows the truth? What does he think I have been doing all these years?

"Hi babe, are we ready to rock and roll?" He remains standing to gulp his coffee. The last draught takes an age as he waits for the froth to descend from the bottom of the cup. I slip the postcard back on the table, as he looks skyward.

I gather my things.

"Sorry, we have to go but I am really worried about these bastards Dan." I never swear.

"Let them play their games, I can handle it." Dan says as we cross the square again. "Don't get me wrong; I hate all the macho bullshit, but they are harmless. They have come away just for me haven't they, so they deserve some fun. They don't worry me anymore." So what does worry you now Dan?

"I think I know a shortcut to the back of the hotel from here." I propose a new route.

"Okay babe I will always follow you." He smirks at me as if we are on the same page. I think the man still loves me. We are in deep trouble.

CHAPTER 25

Juliet 16.29

"WHY CAN'T MEN DEAL WITH AN EMOTIONAL TRUTH?"

I walk at city pace, too fast for conversation. I stride beyond my natural gait expertly weaving around human obstacles. This is a pace used after a pressured lunch break or en-route to my next mode of transport. My walking boots provide necessary grip, but my right heel rubs and threatens to blister.

Dan lopes alongside, beside or behind me, grinning, as the pace does not exert him. Our innocent shopping amble through Chamonix feels long gone. I am going to be late anyway, but have to get to the stag meeting before it is too late.

We re-cross the pathway over the river, it gushes with grey swirling mountain water.

"We can cut through behind the Alpine Museum." Dan shrugs and smiles at my directions. He doesn't realise why I am in such a hurry to meet his stags. I am also propelled by the growing confusion between us.

"When we get to the lobby, it's best you go straight up to your room." He doesn't need to hear more nastiness. He accepts the instruction.

We cross a half-filled car park. Locals sit in the boots of their 4x4s changing back into normal footwear. Skis are in danger of toppling at the side of their cars. I rise over a dirty snow mound churned up by the successive parkers. Not far from the hotel.

We enter a narrow cobbled passageway, the Avenue du Temple. Our footsteps echo from the church to our left, which hides the low sun. We can barely manage to walk single file; my shopping bags brush the tight conifer bushes on our right.

First we hear a burst of laughter ahead. Then "Donatella!" is shouted for all to hear. Three young men burst out from a bend in the pathway. All early twenties, I immediately assume they are Italian. They are so wrapped up in their own teasing that the first man cannot stop in time, he shoulder-barges me and his legs tangle with the sports bag. Ethan's top spills out onto the cobbles.

"Watch out will you! Look what you have done." I turn angrily to recover the bag, but am pinned against the bushes.

"*Inglese Buffone.*" My assailant has detected my nationality and is angry as well. His hair is coal black in ridiculously tight curls. He presses his left forearm across my throat to keep me still. His friends see the spilt bag and pick up Ethan's jacket.

"*Molto bene.* Kappa." They immediately start to argue over the destination of the top.

"Hey guys let's give it back to the lady," Dan implores them to return it. They offer it to him then snatch it away when he lays his hand on it. Dan smiles patiently and tries their game again unsuccessfully.

"Come on guys." He stands without urgency, hands imploring by his side. His long hair and glasses mark him out as an English eccentric. They know they have his mark; the two jostle and tease Dan as I am held.

"Sexy lady want jiggy jiggy?" The cliché would be laughable but I can't judge his strength of purpose. He licks his index finger longingly and plunges it towards my crotch. One finger is forcibly pushed into my covered vagina, as if it could pierce my jeans. It is a naive attempt to persuade me of his sexual prowess.

"You want?" He thinks he is getting somewhere.

I deliver a punch below his ribs. It makes an impact but his snowboard jacket softens the blow. He makes a move to grasp my right breast but I swing the Chamonix book at his head. He uses the left forearm across my throat to push me further back into the bushes. I am momentarily stuck in them; hair entangled. He runs off past his friends who are still taunting Dan. I recover my balance and pull myself out.

"Guys, guys." Dan has shut down; his hooded eyes try to cover his embarrassment. He hopes it will all disappear. A second Italian runs off. As a final insult the last guy drops the jacket on the floor, unzips his trousers and urinates on it.

"Yeehah!" He cackles at his insult and shakes his penis in our direction. Re-zipped he in turn takes off, running towards where we came across the car park.

This sickening insult is over in a flash; the only material evidence is my soaked present. Although I am in a state of high indignation, I am also relieved that it stopped where it did. I can make no real sense of this violation.

"You okay babe?"

"I have just been half-strangled, threatened and touched up by strangers. Okay doesn't really cover it."

"They were just in high spirits." Daniel tries to re-make the scene into something more benign.

"High spirits! Don't be such a walk-over all your life Dan." How does this man exist? How could he ever look after anyone else? So charming and self-effacing, I see something sinister in my ex-partner for the first time. He is completely without conviction.

"Hey, that's not fair."

"Let's just get out of here Dan." A cold surge is wafting down this besmirched passageway.

"I will get the jacket for you."

"Do you think I am going to give that to Ethan now you idiot?" I was going too far but I had to express my outrage. He hadn't asked for this to happen.

"Just put it in the bag, we can dump it at the hotel, but hurry will you." He picks up an untainted sleeve and drops it into the partially ripped paper bag. I am fifteen minutes late already; I don't even know if they will still be there. We chase on down the rest of the passageway with even more urgency. Behind the hotel, we pass under an enclosed wooden footbridge that joins its two wings. At the front of the hotel I hear whispered voices above me.

"Take that Staggie." Max and Steve shout from a window on the footbridge. Chris empties a full bucket of snow from on high. Dan's hair is swallowed, his glasses knocked to the ground. All of the group look down on him from above. Some snow splashes onto my face. I instantly regret my shortness with him. He is under attack from every angle and needs help. A second bucket of snow misses its target as we dash inside. I hold out no real hope for him.

CHAPTER 26

Juliet 16.44

"HOW DO MEN MANAGE TO LEAD?"

"Snow man how goes it?" Max is the first to arrive in the lobby from upstairs, but the others come running and laughing just behind.

"Snow way! Is that Dan I see before me?" Johnny contributes.

"Is it snowing again outside?" Steve asks him.

"Very funny guys, I should have expected another prank today." Dan accepts his plight in good grace. He shakes his jacket and litters clumps of snow on the rustic tiled floor in front of a silent receptionist. They have probably seen worse.

"As for you Chris, you are meant to be looking after me bro," Dan protests.

"It's better than stripping you naked and dumping you in a snow bank which they wanted," Chris replies.

"Anyway there is snow chance of you coming to this meeting Staggie so piss off upstairs," Robert directs him to the lift.

"Look at the state of you. You look like you have been dragged through a hedge backwards. Did you two love birds just have a shag for old time's sake somewhere?" Robert turns his attention to me.

"Hey, leave her man; we have just had an incident with some Italians." Dan belatedly stands up for me.

"Is Juliet thirsting for some foreign cock then?" Robert is alive, warming his negligible charm up for the main event. I ignore him. I don't ever expect his sympathy.

"Let's get this over and done with. Grab those seats over there by the

133

fireplace. Go and piss off lanky. Does your ex-girlfriend want to go and hose you down you while the boys sort out the main event?" With me out of the way Robert knows he would have the whip hand.

"Thanks but I would be delighted to hear what you boys have to say." I am sure Robert never expected me to leave but it was worth a try. Dan catches a lift, not knowing how I intend to rescue him.

"Jules babe, would you be a doll and use the kitty to get a round in while we kick off?" Max is also trying to exclude me. The barman is busy. As everyone settles into a seat I wave and attract his attention. He mercifully comes over.

"*Cinq bierre, une l'eau naturelle, si'l vous plait.*" Robert and Max exchange disappointed glances as I get water.

"Alright then, it's almost five now thanks to the late arrivals. We have three things to discuss; tonight's party, tonight's after-dinner entertainment and tomorrow's skiing." Robert kicks off a rehearsed agenda.

"What's happening for dinner Johnny?"

"I have booked us into an Italian restaurant in Courmayeur, called the Tunnel at seven o'clock. We should be back over here for about eleven. They know a stag do is coming so are sticking us out the way. I have booked two cabs to pick us up from reception at six."

"Hang on isn't Courmayeur in Italy?" Steve tests his geography.

"Yes, that's what's special about it. He loves everything Italian. It's a short trip though the Mont Blanc tunnel. Oh by the way I have had the airport photograph blown up as promised. Can you all sign it so we can present it to him tonight?" I am sure his love for Italy is not at its highest at the moment.

"Okay, okay, is that settled, get down here for six? Can people just think of some things that will embarrass the shit out of him?" Robert tries to move on quickly.

"Do we need liras or will they take Euros?" Steve laughs out loud at Chris's travel ignorance.

"Max and I have been seeking out the ladies of the night around here! They all gather round the back of the casino, so we will take pot luck when we get back into town." They all grin but some are straining.

"No chance. A stripper maybe but you cannot expect him to have sex. He won't do it anyway." My moment of intervention has arrived.

"Look girly; we have been through this. We are all going to put fifty Euros each into a kitty to get him some action."

"I refuse to go along with it. You are not getting a cent off me."

"I don't think I could get it up if it was me." Johnny tests to see if there are any chinks in Robert's armour.

"Frankly I couldn't give a fuck. Well I could and I can actually." Robert becomes aware of the eighteen-year-old waitress standing in earshot by the dining room.

"Don't get involved, this is a man thing," he lowers his tone. I can't win but Dan will probably be falling over by midnight so that should get him off the hook. I will stay close.

"Money in the kitty now please!" Everyone seems to be complying. I go to the toilet to escape this detestable man.

"... by twelve o'clock we will be fine." Robert finishes a sentence on my return.

"Do what by twelve o'clock?" I ask.

"Gone up the Aiguille du Midi cable car as planned," Robert snaps back.

"You are not still planning to take four novice skiers off-piste still are you? Have you told them that they are expected to take climbing gear to avoid falling to their death off the first ridge? Or maybe you have just prepared them to ski half-drunk in deep powder, which they have never done before. Probably you told them there is no piste patrol to look out for them when they have to pick their way down the crevasses to reach the valley floor. And of course I bet you have got that guide booked. You prize idiot." It needed strong intervention.

For the second time on our trip Robert slowly raises out of his seat, prefacing an attack on me. This time it is Chris who intervenes.

"I am not going on that, you can fuck off, and I don't think our kid should go either," Chris tells him. The only man here with discernable balls.

"Have you got a guide then?" I ask Robert again.

"I made an enquiry, but I know my way down without one."

"Why don't you and me call him now and see if he can make it?" As usual the others stay out of the argument, either primed to agree with Robert or too timid to challenge him.

Robert waits for the number to pick up as we stand by the bar. "*Parlez* English?" he asks, obviously receiving some sort of yes as he continues in his native tongue.

"Can you guide a party of six down the Vallée Blanche tomorrow? I see. Great!" His eyes flash up at mine. "No nothing like that. Yes, it's a great adventure isn't it? The weather is cold at the top though."

"Can I speak to him Robert?" He moves away from me shaking his head. He places both elbows on the bar.

"Okay then, about twelve o'clock at the bottom of the Aguille then. *Bonne nuit.*" Robert ends his call.

"Are you sure he is okay with it?"

"Back off will you. You are lucky to be here lady. In fact why are you here? No-one would have missed you." Dan would have.

We return to the group. "That's sorted then. We are meeting Jean-Baptiste our guide, at twelve at the bottom of the lift station." Robert informs them.

"Why don't we ask Dan later if he wants to go?" I think surely he will say no.

"Ask away if you like, but we are skiing the Vallée Blanche tomorrow. It's for Dan for Christ's sake. Where's the buzz in his weekend if we don't do something for him to remember? See you all in about an hour for the Italian job." Robert has his success for now.

"Don't forget to sign his card," Johnny encourages them as they disband. Beers are drained with gusto. Battle orders are prepared.

CHAPTER 27

Dan 16.56

Peace at a price. I lie awake on my harshly sprung bed, forearms crossed over forehead. My calves are pressed painfully into the bed frame, from the weight of my over-hanging feet. Hot water gushes into the cavernous bath, fanning waves of scalding heat back into my bedroom. The stale stink of festering clothes soaked with body odour hits me like smelling salts.

I am trying to assimilate today. I press uncomfortable bulging thoughts back into my head; but it feels as uncomfortable as manipulating newly formed piles back into my anus. Why didn't I protect Juliet better? How dare they push me around like that? Would Leslie Nielson do an *Airplane* spoof for the ByeFly campaign? Does Juliet still love me? Why does Robert give me such a hard time? Can I parallel ski now? What would I be feeling if Bepe had been run over? Do I really want a paisley waistcoat? Will the reception have stamps for my postcard? Will enough young people remember *Strangers on a Train*? How can I love both Juliet and Sophia so differently? What about listing the seven best places I have ever visited for Bepe? What are they going to do to me tonight?

I turn onto my front and pull the pillow under my chest to sketch out some advert headlines for ByeFly. I will need to pass them on to Steve tonight for him to visualise.

"Fall in love at 35,000 feet. Don't be Strangers on a Plane with ByeFly."

"Join the Mile-High Love Club. Fly ByeFly."

"It's ripping, prices are so hideously low. Let's ByeFly darling."

I write more variations on the theme. Each one seems anti-climactic, a betrayal of the idea, they are not strong enough I fear. The *Airplane* idea is particularly hard to develop as it is so visual, I will need to work with Steve on those.

The bathwater is a solid mass now; the noise of gushing water is swallowed as it has less distance to fall. I strip and look into the misted mirror. I wipe a hole in it to temporarily spy my face before the condensation takes over again. In the blurred facial image I see through to my soul; fear, confusion and disappointment dance within. Hell I look like I am about to cry. I avoid any angle where I can see my body; its lankiness mocks me and reminds me of my fragility. I pull the plug to let some hot water out while mixing cold water in.

Stepping into the bath a shooting pain rises up both shins from today's compression and over exertion. Bubbles rise and froth like thin cappuccino, some spill onto the tiled floor. I hyperventilate a little when my bottom rests on the enamel; panting like a dog to introduce some cold air quickly into my body. Somehow I get accustomed to the heat and a feeling of weightless bliss arises as I fully recline. My head bobs above the surface of the completely full bath. "This Charming Man" chimes its jangly chords in my head again. After five minutes a sharp intake of breath allows me to immerse myself fully, setting my long hair free to float on the surface. I can't stay under for long.

I had purposely tried to keep thoughts of my impending marriage away. As I prepare to go on my stag night I know my marriage is a coming of age. I feel grown up beyond my mental years. This rite of passage must be entered into soberly, as it prefaces a real union. The bones in the back of my skull rest painfully on the bath lip. I close my eyes to shut out the warring voices in my head, relaxation at last claims me.

I stand at a marbled island in the centre of a gleaming modern kitchen, dressed in a blue apron. The kitchen exudes money from every marbled surface and each solid Birchwood door. I slice red onions and peppers for a Moroccan Gordon Ramsay dish; I don't cry although his sullen craggy image intimidates me from the front of his book. It is my house and Miles Davis trumpets it out loud via Sketches of Spain. A key click opens a lock; well-

heeled shoes clack down a wooden hallway towards me. A woman approaches me from behind but I don't turn around. I feel my hair swept off my shoulder and a kiss hits the nape of my neck. The pressure of Juliet's lips is firm, insistent, rewarding. I hear a toilet flush back in the hallway and realise he is with her. Juliet continues to hug me from behind, resting a warm cheek on my thin summer shirt. I move to pick up the vegetable knife again as more footsteps come from down the hall. They are more definite and heavy this time. My wet finger slips from the knife handle and nicks the bottom of the blade, releasing my thumb and a pure purple patch of blood onto the chopping board. Ethan strides into the room looking for his mother...

I sit up suddenly in the bath. I massage my impacted calves and thighs that are so weary that they don't feel attached anymore. What about that idea of listing my seven wonders of the world. Maybe I could design the ultimate father and son road trip.

So where would we start? Fly into Vancouver first I think, a city in the great outdoors. I am at my most comfortable in these places at the edge of the world. We could hop over to Vancouver Island on the ferry and stay in Tofino to go bear watching. Then we could go down to San Francisco. It's just cool, a city of the world rather than America. I remember a great day on a hired bike cycling Golden Gate Park, from hippy Haight Ashbury through the Japanese Gardens and on to the soaring Pacific Ocean. I was transported to a more loving time in the mythical 1960s, when I imagine people accepted each other more for who they were, but who ever knows the truth? Our third stop would be just a three-hour drive inland in Yosemite. It's immense, too big for just two eyes. Searing waterfalls and giant Redwood trees reduce you to nothingness. I wished I had stayed there. It was so peaceful at the bottom of the valley; like nature's cathedral.

Travelling to destination four. Maybe a few days exploring the ruins around Chichen Itza in Mexico. I was obsessed with the Mayans when I came back. I have never been somewhere so sinister; play football or lose your head; be a young woman and lose your head; look funny at someone in a big hat and lose your head. They must have bred like rabbits to keep up with the bloodshed. The Pyramid of Kulkulcan is freaky; it is a giant calendar that turns into a snake at certain times of year, which is all too much for me.

Flying further south to Havana, Cuba, the rawest most authentic place, a complete one-off in a time capsule. The place does everything differently from anywhere else. It's like one of those films where Charlton Heston walks around a corner to discover the land that time forgot. Its buildings are so elegant and decrepit. You can imagine fables of the botched CIA plot to kill Fidel Castro. You know you have travelled when you go there; you have been exposed to a raw place where a wrong turn can end badly.

Maybe too much time in the Americas. Fly back to Europe for number six then. It must be Rome. I like Venice and most Italian cities but Rome has that jaw-dropping moment when you see the Forum for the first time and think what the hell happened here? You can see the age-old importance of somewhere that is irrelevant today. The Parthenon and the really old buildings just ask why.

Fly where to our last destination? Maybe back to England and just the Lake District, but it doesn't have the oomph of the others. Maybe even Chamonix. Maybe…

What is the time? I leave number seven for now, a tough decision. The body of water sloops back into place as I pull myself out of the bath. I step onto the cold wet towel I discarded this morning, if only Chris would use one. I had relaxed with my seven wonders road trip, but a wicked tension hangs in the air again. I am naked in the face of their plans. My fingertips have become withered prunes, over emphasising the whorls of my fingerprints. I raise one foot onto the bath edge so that I can easily dry underneath. What is the time? Almost six o'clock. I dress for the stag-night gallows, socks first. What can I wear to look okay but protect myself from any further physical assault? I select the thickest socks I have as Chris enters. An air battle rages near the door, my steam-assisted bath fragrances against his skiing sweat and burgers.

"You okay Chris?" Chris harrumphs a non-verbal but sarcastic reply to the negative.

"Are you getting a bath?" I hope.

"I will change me shirt."

"What's been going on down there? You have been over an hour." Socks and underwear are donned.

"Oh just arguments. That Robert is a prick, why did you invite him? Juliet is trying to stop him but no-one else helps." What are they arguing over? Maybe I am the only one who can sort them out. Every item of clothing donned carries me further into certain uncertainty. Buttoning my shirt feels like an ultimatum; are you ready for marriage?

"Listen, they want to take you off skiing in a big valley somewhere tomorrow. It sounds like some serious skiing. When they ask you later tell them to bog off, I just did."

"I am not worried about skiing tomorrow, more about humiliation tonight." I want to ski with them all to show them my progression. Even Robert must concede it; I won't be an embarrassment any more.

"If you want me to I can sort this Robert lad out. You know, scare him off for you."

"No Chris, he is hard work but just leave him be." Chris has revealed his bare chest; his shirt goes on without any cleansing.

"Do what you want, not what that prick wants," he re-affirms to me.

"What are you going to do tomorrow then?"

"I can amuse myself for one day if you are fool enough to follow him." I can see he is imagining a burger fest.

I sit on the bed waiting for Chris to change his trousers. Underpants that have just skied Chamonix are ready to carry on into the night! I get a whiff of fresh fruit but don't associate it with anything. I see a red scar on my pillow. I pull back the covers to see berries placed there this afternoon coagulated under my bed sheets. I must have squashed it all into a smoothie when I lay on the bed before.

"That weren't my idea bro." Not his idea but he is an accomplice none the less. I peel off the bed sheets and throw them in the bath. A strawberry drops into the curve at the front of my scooped black shoes.

I notice that my breath is shortening again: altitude, fear or both? I must let everyone know how I feel.

CHAPTER 28

Dan 18.05

My mobile phone radiates a patch of wasted light into the night. Its sleek black plastic lines and silver edging contain communication and entertainment technology beyond comprehension a few years ago. Does anyone even remember how a delayed journey could often not be communicated, leaving one party in semi-indignation or the purgatory of being stood up or genuine concern for the absentee. A crow flying my call home would need days to do it; soaring over Mont Blanc, over Geneva from whence we came, over Paris, skirting London and Birmingham and finally on to Manchester. What simplicity could propel a message so accurately so far? I feel the radio waves buzzing into the side of my head; it must be that physical to produce something this powerful. I step off the top step at the front of the hotel as Sophia answers.

"Hi there, all okay with you?" I picture her reclining on her dad's sofa. Bepe will be kneeling on the floor absorbed in a CBeebies programme. His blue duck will be tucked under one arm, maybe a warm milk bottle held precariously in the other hand. He will be grasping a dummy with his teeth, sucking it for imagined sustenance, the noise growing louder as he gets sleepier. Improbably he has fallen asleep in this position before.

"Hi Dan." There is tiredness in her reply. A waft of evening dinner smells blow down the steps from the hotel, as the door opens. Juliet has arrived; she stays under cover sitting next to Chris on the bench outside. I walk away across the car park to maintain some privacy. Pulling my scarf tighter around my neck, I try to position it so that no cold air can hit my chest directly.

"You a bit tired babe?" I am not sure what her flatness indicates yet.

"Yes, but I am not feeling great either. I have sorted so much out today. Briefed the video man and disco as to what I want."

"Can I have a say in the music playlist?" At last something I could do. Maybe I can save our union from a foreboding start in disco hell.

"If you insist, ring him up next week. But I warn you, make sure that people can dance to it. I've also been to the florist to see their table arrangement. The wedding cars we wanted have broken down, so Dad's made them upgrade us for no charge. I was in town so I even went by the jewellers and picked your ring up. I think I can take the weekend off. I have organised this wedding on my own."

"Yeah, you have done great. That's saved me a trip on Monday." I cannot disagree. "Hey, I am being taken out for my main stag do tonight. We are going to Italy for dinner would you believe?"

"What nonsense. How are you getting there?"

"By taxi, takes half an hour apparently to go to Courmayeur. I am not meant to know but Chris has told me."

"Make sure there are no women involved tonight." A warning that is too vague. Juliet is getting Chris to talk more than one syllable answers.

"Of course. I don't know what they are planning but I won't go near any women. I promise. Hey, I can parallel ski now."

"How could you possibly learn so quickly?"

"Oh, I have just had good instructors. I really enjoyed today." I stand with one foot raised on a hard packed mound of ice, blackened with mud and gravel, at the furthest point from the hotel. I can stop pacing if I am in this position. I need to make myself heard.

"Only a day and a bit till I am home. I have missed Bepe so much. I have been carrying on with my time capsule thing for him. I am planning a road trip for us. Can I speak to him?" I detect the phone being transferred by a series of scratching noises, probably from his dummy.

"Bepe, Bepe, it's Daddy." Nothing.

"Bepe, Daddy misses you loads and is coming home on the big plane to see you very soon." I hear the confirmatory sound of suckling.

"Bepe, Daddy has made some music for you son. We can listen to it when I get home. You look after Mummy for me."

"I can't get that dummy out of his mouth. He is watching *Charlie and Lola* so you won't get anything out of him. I miss you too you stupid man. I am still cross with you over Bepe's accident. What time am I picking you up on Sunday?" She wants to sulk more, but it is too straining to keep up at a distance.

"Six thirty in the evening I think. I can't do anything about the accident now babe. It wasn't my entire fault, he just ran."

"Diddy I got plane. Diddy I got plane. No plane Diddy." His little voice is briefly insistent and then disappears as quickly as it came.

"Aaah. He went and got his toy plane and brought it back to the phone to show you. How precious is that?" I hear her plant a series of kisses on him. An increased hubbub rises behind me at the hotel steps. My stag group is present and correct. Oh my god, Rubber Juliet is with us; fully pumped up and being tossed around once more.

"Listen I forgot to mention, Juliet was attacked by a bunch of Italian lads this afternoon."

"What? What do you mean attacked? Is she in hospital?"

"No, it was just some lads coming on to her, she is okay." Robert is making his way over to me. The taxis are ten minutes late now.

"She has six men with her. For god's sake who was looking after her?" Her logical question goes begging, lest I incriminate myself.

"Let me speak to the condemned woman." For the first time Robert arrives at an opportune moment. I pass him the phone.

"Sophia, you sexy beast. Just wanted to ask, you do have travel insurance for this one don't you? He has been an animal on the piste and off for the last few days; you don't know what he has been up to. Thank goodness what goes on tour stays on tour. Thankfully I am here to look out for him and Hoover up the women for him." I am only grateful that he has been so over the top that she knows it isn't true. Two taxis are at last turning into the car park, with yellow neon banner signs atop them.

"Sorry about that, you know what he is like."

"Yes and I know what you are like too. Be very careful with him; don't let him push you around."

Johnny, Chris and the real Juliet drive off.

"Danny is a tranny, Danny is a tranny, nah nah nah nah nah." Max, Steve and Robert resurrect the stupid chorus from the airport and get in the second taxi waiting for me to get in the front. Rubber Juliet gets a ride in the boot.

"I must go now, the taxis are here. I do love you, you know."

"It sounds like that was in doubt at some point Dan."

"No babe, you know what I mean. I know I am not the man you want me to be, but I try, I do try, honest babe."

"Well we love you too. Listen I might have some news when you get back."

The taxi horn is sounded loudly.

"I think I am feeling crap for a reason. I don't know yet, but maybe number two is on the way."

"You what?"

"I might be pregnant again you fool," she whispers, presumably because her parents are in the house not because of Bepe. I open the passenger door and hold it open.

"That's amazing. I can't talk. I have to go now."

"Tell her you love her Dan. Go on." I sit down, as the three of them chide me to end my call appropriately. It also looks like I have another impatient driver to deal with.

"See you soon babe." They think I bottled it in front of them. In reality I just defied them for the first time in three days. It feels like I have a chance now.

CHAPTER 29

Dan 18.30

We fizz through the Mont Blanc tunnel, ripping through the wounded mountain. Our increasing speed is marked by the strobe effect of the tunnel ceiling lights through the front window. I try to imagine the immensity of rock and snow overhead, destabilised by this underground cavern. My three fellow travellers mutter of unknown plots in the back seats, while I again sit uncomfortably upfront alongside an uncommunicative local.

"You have enjoyed your skiing Dan haven't you? You can ski better as well can't you?" Robert gives me an unexpectedly rosy two-day progress report; I can feel myself being painted into a corner.

"Yeah I can parallel now I think."

"Well I have something special lined up for you tomorrow, we are skiing the Vallée Blanche. Most of it is piss-easy. You will have something truly memorable to tell the brat. Of course if you are not up to it I can cancel the booking with the guide and the special lift tickets, it's only more money for me to lose. No pressure but it's a yes right?" I don't answer him now, I want to ski but I don't want to openly succumb to his bullying.

"Just tell me as soon as Dan." He lets me mull it over.

"Have you developed those ByeFly concepts yet Dan? Steve says he hasn't got anything to draw up from you," Max enquires. I can imagine Steve grinning profusely in the back having blown me up to the boss.

"I have some strap lines here that I can to pass on to him." It shuts them both up.

I ate too little today, I try to hasten the cab to my dinner. I can see light at the end of the tunnel, or should I say night at the end of the tunnel. We exit the toll both at the Italian end, passing under a grand arch. We emerge into the ubiquitous nighttime urban phosphorescent glow; a subtle choice of light to underplay the environmental rape we have just witnessed. That was the easiest border crossing I ever had. The taxi climbs a hill into Courmayeur, as it reaches a bend in the road he stops to let us out. We are near the end of a cobbled street that I assume is the main shopping area. I take an instant liking to the more homely alpine small-town atmosphere contrasted to the chic ski resort that is Chamonix.

Over the road is the Tunnel restaurant, where I presume the others are already stationed. The logo for "*du tunnel*" is printed on a yellow metal sign outside. It is meant to depict a brick oven with a fire burning beneath the tunnel. However, it is so ill drawn it is grossly insensitive as it looks like the fireball that engulfed the Mont Blanc tunnel seven years ago, killing thirty-nine people. A new logo and strap line could be written and visualised over dinner if they give Centurion the brief. Every seat is taken inside; this place has a reputation or a captive audience.

"Dan, I knew you were used to Italian food so I arranged to come to this place." Johnny is happy to have pulled his plan off, as he greets me at the door.

"Yeah, it's great man, really authentic." In different ways I owe all my stags gratitude.

"Here is to the first of many!" Juliet has got a round in as we squeeze together at a small bar near the door. Italian men sitting either side of her at the bar talk at her. She looks panicked after her ordeal before.

"Let me help you Jules." I grab three beers from the bar, but as I hand them out I find myself encircled, and spin around to clink with each stag. The waiters pass by happy that we are sober, offering me congratulations. We are under a watching brief; they have taken a chance on an English stag party, concentrating on the likelihood of an inflated drinks bill. They have taken the precautions; we are isolated up a flight of wooden stairs to a balcony overlooking the whole restaurant. The rustic walls are peppered with dusty arrangements of dried flowers, old enamel ski posters and ancient ski equipment. We are strung out on one long bench seat, all over looking the balcony. Another round of seven beers hits the table before we sit down. To my immediate left is Robert, with Max and Steve beyond him. To my immediate right is Juliet, with Chris and Johnny beyond her. An order of garlic bread all round thankfully arrives, while we decide what to order.

I get to my feet. "Can I just say I am so grateful that you are all here for me. I have had a smashing time so far. I am buying the wine with the meal tonight to say thanks." I break up some garlic bread and pass it down the table. I should have eaten before drinking anything.

Steve has sat rubber Juliet at the end of the table; garlic bread hangs comically from her extra wide mouth. For the first time I think of her fondly, she was intended to embarrass maybe but she is comical all the same. He made an effort with that and the T-shirts that we all wear again tonight. The seven pictures along the table of me being sick don't deter me from wolfing more garlic bread. I order two carafes of red wine to try to slow the drinking pace.

"Let's talk about the women we would shag." Max starts the evening's bravado.

"Uma Thurman." Johnny surprises me by making the first entry.

"Posh Spice." Chris amazes me even more.

"Posh Spice? You would split her in two!" Max retorts.

"I would take Kelly Brook up the shitter any day of the week." Robert inevitably lowers the tone. "What about you Juliet? Which woman would you go to bed with?" He is pushing her too far again.

"I always thought Liz Hurley was very sensual, but I think in bed with Madonna would be fun." She covers her mouth having surprised herself and sloshes wine onto the gingham patterned plastic tablecloth.

"Way to go girl. What a threesome that would be." Robert applauds her choice.

Pizza from the rustic oven sizzles onto the table on black platters, cheese spits menacingly at me stinging my cheek. Seven pizzas only just squeeze onto the table. We all rip into our meals; I order more wine for lubrication. Very quickly my jaw aches from chewing so fast. I start to slow down, my movements become more vague; everything and everyone softens. I enter the good drunk zone; I cannot hide my condition and have enough control to say roughly what I mean. My stomach can detect neither hunger nor fullness despite possessing most of my Quatro Stagioni now.

"Dan. Everyone. Dan." Johnny stands for attention. "Before I get too far gone I just want to say a few words about my best mate Dan. He may be a bit scatty and laid back but I love him. He has had faith in me when others... Anyway, in a week's time we will all be in England getting pissed again at his wedding... raise those glasses to Dan and Sophia." Everyone thrusts them high but remain seated.

"Oh and here is a little something from us all mate." Johnny hands me a signed copy of the photograph we took in airport departures. I hug him across Juliet and stay on my feet.

"Thanks a lot guys, I will treasure this. Just to say, thanks for coming all this way for me. I know we have had our moments, but it's not easy. I thank you all. Chris, you have been a great big brother to me, but lighten up bro. Max, you have kept me in a job for years now, so I thank you for that. Steve, we have been creative partners for so long, too long for some, but we work okay despite the bullshit. Johnny you are my soul mate, you are the best a man can get. Juliet, you were once my girlfriend and though you dropped me from a great height I still love and respect you. Who is left, the little fellow, yes Robert that's you. Thanks for the free tickets from our official stag sponsor BA; much appreciated. I just hope your ego can cope after being roasted by my skiing tomorrow." I have nudged everyone's truth; they all have their cards marked. I can't and don't want to remember what I said to them all. All I know is that for the first time in three days they are together in laughter.

"Even if one of you lets me down, I still love you guys. Enough, more wines Signori. " I slump back into my seat and breathe more easily.

"You have come to life. I didn't think you had a pulse in that lanky body of yours." Robert leans in to speak to me over the growing noise.

"Let's have some more fun shall we. Everyone has done truth or dare haven't they? Well let's make it truth or truth; everyone has to tell us something scandalous about Dan that we don't know. Dan you are first up." Robert insists on party games.

Back on my feet the room is swimming a little. "Thanks Robert. Err a truth about me that I don't know is very hard. What I can reveal is that I am in love with…err… I love without question… The Smiths…err."

"Not good enough, something fucking interesting you lanky shit." Robert decrees I must try again. I am my own lie detector; I may as well have a buzzer and neon light attached to my head. I can't take my eyes off Juliet. Be bold Dan, be bold…

"No, I love without question my son. I don't think I told you all but he almost got run down at the airport on Wednesday. It was my fault for err… not being quick enough. Anyway, he is all right but I thought I had lost him. I can't bear it to be honest. Err, Johnny you go next." It was a sober truth that even Robert didn't dare question.

"Well I am about to release my first album at the end of the year and the truth is I am going to dedicate it to my best mate Dan." He sits down and I just smile at him, I know my power of sentence construction is fast disappearing. Silent appreciation is more apt.

"Come on boys, tell us something interesting will you for Christ's sake." Robert tries to change the tone.

"Err, Dan. You remember you got whacked for spending your first-edition decimal coin set. Dad hit you so hard, you had a massive welt on your leg, it didn't go for two weeks and you couldn't sit down. Well it was me who spent it and I didn't say a thing." Chris confirms what I always suspected but couldn't prove. It was a real trauma for me at the time; a lethal combination of injustice and physical pain.

"Dan, I have never liked you. You have always got on my nerves; I don't know how we have worked together for so long. Let's split up. I don't mean this nastily; I just think it's about time." Steve confirms something that I have always known. It will be great to see him sink without me to blame.

Max is completely gone; he leans into the table unable to stand, a vengeful pose on his face. "I have got one for you Dan. ByeFly have flown the nest. They have taken off for pastures new. Their business is terminal. This is a dead account. The account is dead. It is a dead account." He pathetically slaps the table with the paper I gave him with strap line suggestions, in a take on the Monty Python dead parrot sketch.

"Why have you had me working on my stag weekend you bastard?"

"I just thought we could have one last shot …" He slumps back unapologetically.

"Dan, I am sorry I let you down years ago. Things were very black and white then. Maybe I could have given you a chance to stay with me and…" Juliet is in full drunken flow when Robert has heard enough.

"Come on, lighten this up guys. The lad has had enough of this, it's his stag do, let's have a laugh. It's meant to be things like I just shagged that waitress in the toilet. That's true by the way; she's got massive brown nips. I also had that woman I copped off with last night and her mate; my dick is on fire." He throws a dried slice of pepperoni pizza over the balcony for effect. I agree with Robert; it had all got a bit heavy. I am not sure what to believe about his sexual antics.

"Juliet that was rubbish, you have to do my dare as a forfeit. Swap underwear with Dan while you stay in this room." She luckily has a skirt on and squirms to releases her knickers; her bra is snapped off under her Lycra cardigan. I suddenly have no shame. I flick my shoes off, stand to unbutton my trousers and pull down jeans and a clean pair of underpants. Not one man dares to comment on the size or shape of my genitals, as I'm a shower not a grower. Two waiters run to the top of the stairs in time for my nakedness. They frown and confer running away quickly to get help. Juliet's knickers are at least cotton, however brief they are. I dress again and am made to hook the bra up under my shirt.

"More wine for the whiner's Signori." I am genuinely enjoying this now. Everything has shifted here; at last some unearthed truths rather than the lies that have bound everyone around me.

"Downstairs now Signor, we clean up." Four waiters appear behind the man who has drawn the short straw to tell us to go.

"I wish the eyeties would stop smoking so much, it's disgusting. The dirty bastards." Max offers inappropriate commentary as the waiters hover. We all amble at our own pace downstairs, to an empty restaurant.

They allow me my last request; we huddle around the small bar slurping our last carafe. I settle for the four rounds of wine, we all give in thirty Euros for the food.

"You married? *Salute.*" The bar owner offers me premature congratulations and a Lemoncino as I rest on the bar. I raise my glass and smirk. He is probably thinking Juliet is my wife. Waiters sit down at empty tables waiting for a fight they will not get.

The taxis are fifteen minutes late, having promised a midnight pick up. I have suspended comprehension of what has just happened. Nothing hurts me through my thick skin of alcohol. Italy has been a blast.

Saturday 18th April 2009

CHAPTER 30

Juliet 00.22

"WHY DO MEN HAVE SUCH LACK OF RESPECT FOR WOMEN?"

Johnny and Dan sing from The Smiths' songbook as we exit the cab. They fail to shut the door three times, until I remove a seat belt from the doorjamb. They laugh hard at the aptness of their song; creasing themselves forward with arms across each other's shoulders. No more apologies for us Dan, they stand swaying with their foreheads pushed together, uniting their sweaty fringes.

"The casino is across the square so the club must be underneath." I prompt them. Robert has insisted we go to a disco called Wheelers. The human traffic is against us again; even the hardened revellers are dispersing to catch rest before their skiing. The roar of water is all around, with the river flowing underneath our feet and the forceful spray from the decorative fountain in front of us.

"Ambush!" Max and Steve are running at us from around the fountain, Robert comes from the other direction. Indians aiming to capture the cowboys. Legs heavy with drink, they could not catch a sober person, but Dan is easily pulled backwards. Max grabs his feet, the others his shoulders. They try to throw him into the fountain, but Dan's bottom crumples to the floor, making him impossible to lift.

"Idiots! We will never get him into a club soaking wet!" Chris shouts at them. They know it is true and they let him go to the sound of their own groans. Max decides to wake himself up with a face wash in the fountain. The semi-ice water and freezing air make him wince. A fully

155

immersed human would be only minutes away from an icy death, another good reason not to dunk Dan.

"Thanks for letting me go guys." Dan picks himself up from the slush at the foot of the rounded fountain wall.

"Oh Dan, look at you." I brush snow and mud from his elbows, bum and knees.

"Thanks Jules, you're a star. Boys will be boys hey babe?" Dan perches on the fountain edge giving his assailants far too much respect, far too much leeway.

"Let's just calm down gentlemen if you want to get in the club." Although set against the whole venture, part of me hopes we can just get a chance to dance.

The bouncer stands squarely across the door, hands in front of his groin. He is running a risk appraisal of the group. He probably thinks, seven people, one of whom is a woman so it isn't a stag do. Already drunk so they are probably English or Scandinavian. None of them looks hard, just that fat one but I can take him. Yes they will do, they will drink loads and make fools of themselves. He steps aside for Robert who proceeds to pay for us all.

Beyond two draped velvet curtains we descend three decades down a flight of stairs into the 1970s. The interior designer has caught itself coming back. It could easily be the stage set for an early James Bond film. The stairs give perspective onto a circular dance floor marked out as a roulette wheel, made whole by a huge glitter ball. A grinning hostess greets us with no hint of embarrassment at her outfit. Her bra cups are two enlarged poker chips, while her mini skirt is made from six of them. She shows us to a booth. The stags are dumb struck at being this close to female flesh. The clientele is strictly old European. The men are all older than Dan; the women are all younger than me. Some of the girls would be too young for Ethan. I would dread seeing what his hormones might do to his rational sensibility. Surely he would not react to this, he is a different generation?

She takes our drinks order as we are standing; Max and Steve huddle around her so that her only exit is towards Dan. Once turned, they half-push her and she stumbles towards him. Dan's left hand clinches a buttock while the right hand pushes under her fifty-dollar poker-chip bra.

"Your lucky number is up Dan," shouts Max as she extricates herself. The tray she holds makes it impossible to slap anyone. She must play her part in this time-warped hellhole. Robert slips a fifty-euro note into her mini skirt from behind; he thinks it buys him the right to stroke her bum cheek. She moves away and takes the money as solace for the degradation.

Sister Sledge sings about their family; the song is at an inclusive pace that allows anyone to dance. Some of my sisters are letting it all hang out at the bar across the dance floor. They are maximising their income potential by pouring wine provocatively, while their young breasts bounce eagerly. It's strange to be given licence to look at someone's breasts; they usually spend their lives airlessly trussed up. I am proud to see the beautiful pert shape of a young woman, but repulsed by what she is using it for.

"Look Robert, you have got what you wanted. Let's take Dan over there and let him ogle some young girl."

"You have to know what I wanted don't you." He makes no sense. "It's never enough don't you see? There is always more to do, more to see, more to have. I am off to see a man about some pussy." He pushes out of the booth without letting Johnny stand up so stumbles onto the gigantic roulette wheel. I step out of the booth to help him recover.

"What are you mumbling about? Just leave things alone for once will you. He has seen some breasts let's go home." I implore him.

"Leave it alone? What the fuck are you doing here anyway? We know what needs to be done." He staggers away towards the back of the room.

"Come and dance girl," Max offers his hand. I surprise myself and take it in the spirit of the stag party. He tries hard to dance but his body makes no sense of the rhythm.

"You are alright really you know." He damns me with faint praise for not refusing him. There is a freedom in music.

Sister Sledge fade and Stevie Wonder segues in. Max doesn't notice, he continues his shape-shifting as before. As I smile lightly at his efforts he feels encouraged to try something adventurous. He tries to body pop but stumbles backwards. He plants a leg in time not to fall.

"May I have the pleasure of your dancing Mademoiselle?" Dan has cut in from behind. "Butt-out Max, it's my turn." He tries to push him away. Dan takes my hands and leads me in a mock tango across the floor. We whip around smartly and whoop at the end of each turn. He lets go and spreads his arms skywards and sings.

This is curious, he pointedly never used to like Stevie Wonder.

Dan drops to his knees and covers his heart. He mimes every word of Stevie Wonder's cry for an ex-lover to take him seriously. He sits back on his feet, reaching skyward with over sized arms. This is no longer a sing-a-long; he is singing his heart out to me. He loses control of his voice and just caterwauls. He finds my right hand and presses it to his cheek. You don't really mean this. I see the other stags stand up from the booth; cheering at his loss of inhibition. He is singing and sobbing. I cover my mouth in shock. I never had to witness what I did to him as I left him so quickly. The truth pours forth. He has hidden this for years; his current life is a diversion.

"Come on up mate, it's getting late now." Johnny tries to rescue his friend by grabbing his hand. Dan's face is strewn with tears, and he sobs convulsively. He casts Johnny's hand away; he doesn't want release. At last they guess why he is on his knees and the mood turns darker.

I kneel down to his level. "You are just drunk and emotional Dan. This means nothing."

"Not to you it doesn't. You are everything…"

"Get the fuck up Dan." Chris now tries to save his brother from shame. Dan resists him by refusing his hand.

"Why could you never say this all those years ago?" It probably wouldn't have mattered as I had resolved to get him out of my life.

"I felt it. It was obvious. Is that it, you left because I didn't say it?" He puts forward another inaccurate reason for my leaving.

"I am not that shallow."

"I love you, I love you, I love you. There, three times for the ones I missed."

"It's gone Dan, it's all gone now."

"It can't be, please Jules." I have ruined him; he has lived with this hope for so long that it won't be dashed now.

He cannot let it go, so I must. I run out of the club, leaving the boy I left before, not the man I came here to see.

I run back towards the fountain and sit down to catch my breath. It spits mountain water from the mouths of cast-iron fishes and mermaids. What is the boy going to do? He is heading towards a marriage he cannot commit to. He is as lost as when I left him. I broaden my chest to gulp the wintry air. Hot tears of pity for Dan drip into the icy fountain water.

CHAPTER 31

Dan 01.30

The tracks of my tears have dried and shrunken my facial skin; they have expressed their misguided love. My reddened eyes are refreshed having let loose years of loss It is better out than in. We can all be fools, but at least I can say I am a brave one now. I have somewhat sobered up. My immediate physical concern was the loss of strength in my right knee. Having slid dramatically across the dance floor towards Juliet, it caught on each panelled edge of the giant roulette wheel. Half way through my singing I realised I had landed on Red 7, which I deemed a lucky spin of the wheel. Juliet stood impervious on zero, covering her mouth in shock.

We all stand in lewd proximity to the host of breasts at the bar, observing them discreetly but as often as possible. We are all storing this free pornographic material on our hard drives, accessible for downloading as future masturbation stimulus; a multi-sensory collection of smells, curves, shoulders, hair, pert nipples, tiny goose bumps and downy hair. Look, remember but don't touch.

"What the fuck were you doing you fool?" Robert is incensed that any man he knows has laid his soul so bare. "You are clearly besotted with the bitch that left you years ago. Don't you know the law? Don't ever go back for seconds, especially not on your knees and crying like a blithering idiot." I admire myself for once. A mistake most probably, but time will tell. I see it is half one now; I hope Juliet gets back to the hotel okay. The night feels young in this antiquated discotheque.

"Where you from?" A softly spoken black woman, no more than twenty-five, had snuck up behind me. Observing naked ladies is less violating than talking to them. My eyes now accustomed to flesh drew up from slender hips up to her youthful breasts; nature holds them in suspense, there is no need for any anti-gravitational devices or surgery to make these stand to attention. Too perfect somehow, she lacks the worn-in character of years to come. They seem to be a computer generated graphic drawing of breasts. I try to fix my eyes on the orbs I can legitimately look at, her black brown eyes.

"I'm Dan from England." I don't get too specific in case it tests her geography.

"England, I have always wanted to go. I am Mirabel from Senegal. You here long?"

"No, just till Sunday. Are you a long way from home?" I have asked a semi-intelligent question so don't feel as bad taking another full look at her naked upper body. My cock hardens a little and gets squashed in Juliet's panties, creating yet further stimulation.

"Not so far. I live Paris for long time. Will you buy me drink?" Her lips are improbable plump cushions, which part infrequently as she speaks. I move for my wallet but hear a metal bucket of ice crash onto the bar top. A hand reaches over her shoulder towards me.

"Compliments of the lads." Robert has rounded up a new kitty and is beaming at my involvement with Mirabel.

"You are kind men. Do you come for skiing or business?" She sips the champagne. The others seem to be fighting off advances behind her. Robert is getting more champagne for himself and a brunette waiting beside him.

"I am getting married next week."

"Oh my congratulations. I am in delight. I sing you wedding song from where I come from? She closes her eyes to hum the introduction. She claps her hands slowly to pick up the beat. I imagine the setting for the authentic use of this song in a clichéd dusty African village. Its fragile refrain sends hope to newly-weds. I try but cannot picture Sophia. Mirabel's song and breasts have sapped me of words, I grin approval but conversing with a semi-naked woman about my wedding doesn't wash.

161

"It's time to move on mate." Robert is the only stag mate left; the others have read a script that this actor is yet to see. I overheard Robert say that we were following on in a minute, but I am still surprised they just left us. I am more surprised that Robert has called me mate. He nods acceptance of the extortionate bill to the barman and we take our last spin across the roulette wheel. I grin some more as I leave Mirabel; she walks away from the bar to pursue her evening's seduction elsewhere. Robert leads me to a curtained door at the very back of the club.

We have done it, we have negotiated my stag do and we are heading home. The door leads up three steps and into an altogether different room. The expanse of scarlet carpet and the smell of money hit me first.

"Just let me have a quick spin and we can get off," Robert asks.

"Okay mate, it's getting late though."

Robert schemes as best he can in his state. He looks at a small neon board that shows the outcome of the last few spins. An Asian man stands across the table, caging a deck of chips with his fingers; he drops each chip with a clunk into the palm of his other hand. He doesn't look up; he is in the losing zone. Robert has lost his first bet lightly; he is not fazed by the prospect of losing more. He knows that in his demeanour lies his status in this room.

"Red 7 mate. Bet on Red 7," I implore him.

"For you on your stag night, anything you say you lanky fuck-up." He smiles sweetly to cover up the disrespect he is giving me. He is constantly looking around the room to see who is watching us.

"Hey can I have less of your aggression."

"Calm down, you know it is only a ... well fuck me."

I have just instructed my first winning bet, except for a Grand National sweep and that bonus ball lottery syndicate we had at the agency. I was surprised that Steve actually paid out.

"Maybe I could clean up if I had trusted you. Have you got any other sensational hunches?" The croupier looks at Robert knowingly; a gamble that wasn't followed through with conviction means a great night for the house.

"Sir, your drinks are ready at the bar through the billiards room. That way." A gloved waiter instructs Robert.

"What? Oh the drinks at the bar. Come on Dan I have arranged a nightcap for us." Robert throws a chip to the croupier who hands it back.

He cashes his chips in. "Three hundred smackers for ten minutes work, that's the way I do it." He congratulates himself again. "Follow me Dan." We walk past three more roulette wheels and tables for poker and pontoon. Most men are in black tie suits to intimidate each other. I am feeling more sober, but still manage to bump into the last table I pass; I can feel a grazed welt develop on my right thigh. I am so busy trying to right myself that I am through yet another curtained door and into the night before I enquire about the nightcap.

"Robert, I thought we had another drink. Not that I mind if you want to go back now…" There at the bottom of the stairs is a clothed Mirabel. She is the first woman since my mother that I had experienced mostly naked before I saw her clothed. Her brown leather bomber jacket and knee length skirt don't suit or seem to fit her; they are someone else's.

"I am so delighted you are to have another drink with me. We walk, not far away." We are behind the casino; there are no heavy-handed streetlights illuminating this side of the square. We are soon turning into a narrow road of well-kept houses.

"Great, so you are from Senegal. That's west coast of Africa isn't it?" I chivvy our walk along with some geography.

"Yes I think so. I have not been for long time." I am uneasy about her sketchiness. She doesn't exactly offer a flood of information about the geo-political system in modern Africa.

"Isn't Dakar the capital? Have you seen the Rally?"

"Stop boring the girl, she will fall asleep on the kerb in a minute." Robert calls for less chatter.

"It is the next house on the right." She runs ahead slightly to open a black metal gate that is as high as her six-foot frame.

I hold Robert back a little. "What's happening here? We are just having a drink." I whisper so much I don't think either of them heard me. I suspect what is happening; so weak Daniel, how utterly stupid.

From minute one Robert has wanted this. This is the ultimate test of my bravado. But I will play his game, I will go along with it and when I am in the bedroom alone with her I will slip her a few Euros to say I was the best shag since Casanova.

We enter her ground level flat. She lights some tall candles by the door to provide just enough light for our safe entry. Maybe she wants to save the planet as well. I hate the smell of sulphur; a deathly smell but a warm vanilla fragrance subsumes it soon enough.

"I am not sure I can…" Robert hears me waver as we close the door. Mirabel readies herself in another room.

"Stop Dan. This is it, your last chance to dip your wick in some tasty honey. Sophia is still shaggable I know, but you will be having her for years to come. You have to do the business for the guys. They all chipped in for you, you can't let them down. Just imagine that po-faced Johnny's gob when you tell him. Just imagine how jealous that sad fucker of a boss of yours will be. We will all have something to bring us together after this, you have to…"

Mirabel returns in a basque. She walks straight to me and pushes those sensational lip pillows onto my cheek. I shiver as she holds my hand and leads me to a small bathroom.

"Clean yourself underneath and then we have beautiful time together. Here paper towels and a bin." The dinginess is too much; I have to put a light on in here. Unfortunately at the wash basin, I see what others have been looking at for hours; my long hair matted ridiculously at each side of my face. I drop my trousers and push my hips forward to take a leak, holding a straight arm on the wall for steadiness. The pizza repeats on me; a little bit of vomit escapes onto my tongue. It burns my throat. I wash my hands; I have no need to wash any other body parts as they are going to stay in my trousers.

She comes to meet me outside the toilet; she puts a hand over my penis. "You super clean boy now?" I flush a little at lying to her. Robert must be in the kitchen as there is a light on at the other end of the hallway. More candles in the bedroom; a gothic arrangement either side of the bed throws scant light onto a cushion strewn mattress on the floor.

Her wiry hair is fixed close to her head in braids; I wonder how different it would look unleashed. A presence moves across the far side of the room, obscured by the streaming of the candlelight. It is a trap, we are going to be beaten and robbed.

"Robert!" I shout to see if he is still conscious in the kitchen, as I take two slow steps back to the door.

"Not so loud old boy," he answers back from three yards away. "Hey, now dont get intimidated by my prowess."

"What do you mean?

"We have paid for a double header." As he steps across the minimal light from the far set of candles I see he is stripped to his underpants. Too much flesh surrounds me.

"You don't mean a threesome do you?"

"No chance you gay bastard. We just both take turns for a ride. You can have first go if you really want but I would prefer not to have sloppy seconds." Mirabel is plumping cushions; cocooned in cheap home furnishings, waiting for insertion. Her breasts barely move as she takes her basque off; they have a different quality now that they are touchable. I am a few feet away from touching my first black breast, but they have lost their allure now I know we have paid for access. Her facial features are hardened by the transaction; she knows she has to deliver as well. She has seamlessly moved from innocent enticement to hard-nosed naked businesswoman. There was something girlish about her in the club; she has betrayed that falsehood now.

"I'm not sure if I'm ready. Why don't you go first Robert?" Maybe I can slip out while he is in flagrante delicto. Maybe I can say I don't fancy going second. Maybe I can claim brewers droop.

Robert jumps onto the bed straight onto his knees. While he is airborne he slips his underpants from his crotch to his calves and throws them at the wall behind him. He holds his cock and pumps himself a few times to maximise his hardness.

"Can I get a suck first?" he enquires.

"Pay extra yes?" Robert stays kneeling while those perfect pillows slip over and up his cock; they are innocence violated. He controls her rhythm by holding the back of her head.

"No more, I will come. I want to fuck doggy-style now." He reaches for and applies a condom from a box on the floor with one hand. He flips her over and pulls her hips back onto him. He smacks her right buttock and she responds with a moan. He smacks her again and frantically pulls her hips back and forth like she is a masturbation machine. Again a smack but this time it produces a whelping noise from her.

"No hard please," she asks in between breaths.

Again a slap but this time he changes angle and hits her outer thigh. Robert comes like an apology; a short ohh greets his end. He grabs her breasts as a last thrill for his money as he pulls himself out.

"Your turn Dan, I am just going to put the spunk in the toilet. I need a dump as well." He walks out proudly displaying a semi-erect penis.

This is my chance; I sit on the bed while she turns around. "I am sorry about my friend, Mirabel. He is rough with you."

"He is not first. You will come now?"

"No. I can't do this; it is not right for me."

"I am not right for you." The smell of the candles is intense now; I waft it away and point my nose towards the back of the bed to get respite.

"No, no. We got on well in the club. But I can't have sex with anyone other than who I choose. I mean, just say to Robert that we had a quickie, you sucked me and I came…

"Dan, let's see you ready for action then." Robert is back.

"I think I can't get it up with all the drink."

"Get it out and give the girl a ride you prick. Or should I say get your prick out and give the girl a ride." I unbutton my cuffs and pull my shirt over my head, revealing Juliet's un-filled bra. Why do I have to be here? My top button on my well-worn jeans pop open with much ease and fall to bind my ankles. I feel the goading presence of the bully behind me. Mirabel props herself up again with the cushions and lies with her legs open and knees in the air. I get that primal urge that you always get from the certainty and thrill that soon you will enter a vagina;

a warm glow from my loin that I struggle to hold back. I imagine holding onto my boy at the airport, I will never let him go; this image of purity starts to combat my animal.

"Look it isn't happening down there." I only have Juliet's knickers left as a barrier.

"Get on with it man. Get your knickers off you pervert." He must be luxuriating in this farcical image.

What would this girl's father have wanted for her? Maybe he wanted a small family, or for her to get a job in a new factory unlike her homebound mother. Not great dreams, not asking much. The man's beautiful daughter is laid before me opening her deep charcoal black vulva with two fingers. This doesn't fit into a father's life of dreams. I bow my head to him, I am sorry for my part in this man's torn life and degradation.

I crawl onto the bed, with her crotch directly below my nose. The smell of other people's sex turns my stomach. It is an act I didn't want to witness and certainly don't want to smell. My nose catches a hint of rubber from the used condom and I can't hold back. It is not so much vomit but a spray hose of watered down wine that saves me. I bow my head slightly to direct it away from her stomach and onto the whitish sheets. A violet red patch forms easily; leaving pools and eddies like when the tide goes out. She squeals as I inevitably splash her inner thighs; she holds her hands together over her mouth, wrapped in disgust. This conjures a vivid picture for me. I did not have such a clear view of Bepe's delivery but I imagine him emerging from this mess. My bottom lip quivers as I remember the vaguely green coating he had all over his body. I had not really expected a baby to appear; we were there so long I had forgotten what we were there for. I think I have been in shock ever since. Bepe's arrival should have provoked what Wednesday's re-birth eventually did. I can feel him in my bones now; there is no truer feeling, no scarier thought than losing him.

"You bastard Robert. You pushed me to this. All the way you push me." I wipe vomit from my hand as I stand to confront him. "No more now. I have had enough now." He has no retort to the shock of this gruesome scene.

"You finish off for me if you can work round the vomit. I've had enough of your little man shit. I am off." This has given me the excuse to disappear with a high moral tone.

I need to change in more ways than one. Vomit on Juliet's knickers reminds me how close I came to violating my principles. It looks as if I am bleeding from a chopped off emasculated penis but I can start by getting out of here fast. My shirt and trousers slip on in indignation over Juliet's bra and knickers.

"I can't be with you Robert. Mirabel I am sorry." I walk away with some pride. Saved by the sick maybe but I am proud of not prostituting myself.

I am most proud of where my Bepe is in my heart. I leave the front door with a stagger; I am not out of the grip of alcohol yet. I slam the metal gate shut behind me. The phosphorescent hue of the centre of town is ahead. I need to repent my soul; I need a wee.

CHAPTER 32

Dan 02.10

Thump-thump, thumpety-thump. My heartbeat explodes in my skin; seemingly seeking a weak point for exit. It normally beats incongruously, but now shows its power. I thank it for its continuance without demanding my conscious effort. It is only revealed because it is working hard, but why now? Water pours beside me; incessant, demanding, flowing, commanding. Its constancy leads me to suspect a natural source, although a hosepipe might do it. No, it is a natural source and I feel carried along with it.

Salt water kisses my lips. I had felt water on my face but now I can smell and taste it, the rest of my body is temporarily unknown to me. There is a sweet warm smell in the air that I cannot locate. I want to go back to sleep, circumstances have worn me out. Without opening my eyes fully I sense light above me, but I am largely in the dark. I don't think I am moving but the water force might be carrying me along; maybe I am a twig buffeted on a stream. I want to stop the water, turn it off now. I gingerly lift my head to scan my prone body, although it is still truncated from feeling. I am intact but my penis pokes curiously from my trousers; a mole sniffing the air before departing his burrow. I pop him back in but he is shrivelled to a bump; why have I no underpants on? I was once asked what I did for a living while a nurse stared intently at my member for any sign of sexual disease; I waited for my dick to reply. Why am I unzipped now?

Thump-thump, thumpety-thump. A nearby club plays trance tunes that echo in the space around me. I drop my head back onto hard ground; rocks and a little vegetation cradle it. It is difficult to rest it without sharpness in the back of my cranium. The jet-black sky is littered with stars. I look to my left and see my arm draped in a river; the force of which powers a foot away from my head.

I remember now I needed to pee in the middle of town. I found some metal steps leading down to the river and thought it might be discreet. I wanted to get to the riverside before unleashing myself but found a locked metal stepladder at the far end of the platform blocked my way. Six feet or more above me is the metal platform I stood on to wee, from which I must have fallen. The sweet smell is the result of my core body warmth heating up the urine puddle I must be lying in. The last thing I remember from up there was the expansive splash that my wee made on the rocks below from a height. I can move all my limbs but the night air numbs them. I touch my face on the left side, it leaving small traces of either blood or mud on my fingers. My left shoulder has taken a beating. My physical preoccupation is to escape, bruised and battered. How long have I been here?

Last night will be judged as the worst of times. I sit up and water drips from the sleeve of my jacket back into the river. That bastard Max, stringing us along about ByeFly. A prostitute for Christ sakes; I was a glass of wine away from suffering irreparable damage to my marriage. I couldn't have managed it with Bepe on my mind. Bepe, I can't wait to see you at the airport again; hug your little frame. Can't imagine Robert stayed amongst the wine-induced vomit. Steve is a little shit. I can't feel whether I have really damaged my left arm or it is just frozen in the cold. A woman shouts "*Merde.*" in the street above me, followed by the rapid clatter of her accelerating high heels.

"Oh my god," I say out loud to no-one.

"Oh, my god." I don't really have a god but I am asking any one to sponsor me now and erase time for me. My left knee still hurts. A surge of energy springs me to my feet; it is the feeling of complete embarrassment that does it. I need to get back to my life to repair any damage. Juliet sleeps with the thought that I am a love-sick teenager who never recovered from her. Okay, it may be my truth in some ways but I have accommodated it for years. That loss is part of my DNA and I was not looking to alter it. I select Another Star from "the Tracks of My Years" as soundtrack to this ultimate embarrassment; I will never be able to listen to it properly again. Exposing this truth amongst the others might mean trouble. I have to be Bepe's real father; now nothing can come between us. How am I ever going to get out and up to the platform again?

I jump with no real conviction to grab the platform above me. It is only now that I realise the loss of strength in my left arm. I could never have reached it anyway. I was lucky that the riverbank was uncovered, despite the spring thaw. I upturn my jacket collar and button each button for warmth, while trying to wring out some of the water from my left sleeve. A boulder stands in close attendance to the river wall; one roll and I could use it to climb up. Initially I don't get low enough to push it, so I get on my knees and push with my right shoulder. It rolls over once, scraping moss onto the top of my sleeve, but coming to rest near where I needed it. Stepping onto it and with one hoist I pull myself onto the top rung of the locked ladder and back up to the suspended platform.

I re-orient myself on the pavement back in town square; the casino and club off to the right, the hotel will be left. Just imagine if I had fallen into the river; the knockout blow would have drowned me. This has to stop, days and years of self-neglect, but it's not about me anymore.

A couple walk arm in arm towards me, but edge away in fear when they get close.

"Are you all right?" the girl asks hesitantly, unsure of whether she wants to be drawn into my drama. She discharges the potential guilt of not helping an injured soul.

"Never better." I say with blood on my face, smelling of piss and alcohol, my jacket and hair soaked. I must tackle this head on.

CHAPTER 33

Dan 02.53

"Jules," I speak in an insistent whisper as I walk the third floor corridor. I am trying to selectively rouse just her so I strike an apologetic tone. I know she is here somewhere as I called her room yesterday before we left for the restaurant, it was 32 something.

"Juliet," I step unknowingly onto a used room-service dinner tray. The weighty cutlery drums out a shrieking beat onto the crockery. The whole tray slides under my foot, but I manage not to skateboard too far down the hall. I fall onto my backside and get carpet burn from the tight acrylic pile. All my consideration for the hotel guests at this early hour has been betrayed. The noise stops and I cringe at the clatter but no one seems to notice. I use their cardboard door hanger to scrape soggy baguette and coleslaw from underneath my shoe back onto the tray. I notice too late that the guest who had this light evening snack has also placed a breakfast order on this card. I try to shake off the coleslaw that has obliterated their order for scrambled eggs. The standard seemingly innocent breakfast form is a painful multi-choice questionnaire that defies logic at the late hour that anyone fills it in. Can I have scrambled eggs and porridge as they are in the same section? Can I have water and orange juice? But I don't want toast with my selection of pastries; it is bound to be heart-breakingly cold. Consumer choice clashes with bossy cost management. My stomach churns at the foodstuffs I am immersed in. I try to push myself off the floor but my hand is in something ill advised. I smell mustard from my fingers now.

A chain and lock unhook a room door, throwing sharper light at the hall wall in front of me. The light would accuse anyone in its path of inconsiderate behaviour so I shrink from it.

"Daniel, what the hell..." And then her head pops out of the doorway.

I can't really imagine what Juliet must have thought I was doing; maybe scavenging a pathetic late-night feast at someone else's expense? Maybe I have been driven to make a wall painting using discarded food? I sense her shock although I cannot see the expression on her sharply backlit face. Luckily she doesn't judge me too harshly.

"Just get inside will you. You scared me sitting there." She offers me a hand that I splash with food as she pulls me up.

"I'm so sorry for it all," I plead vaguely to this immaculate cross woman. She is wrapped in a blue silk robe which reveals a Chinese dragon embroidered on its back as she walks inside. She seems untouched by sleep; there is no crumpling of her body, hair or demeanour by being so brashly awoken. She is the only one who gets me, even after all these years.

"You are shivering, your arm is soaked, and you are cut there. What the hell did they do to you?" She takes the duvet from the unused second single bed in her room and wraps me in it.

"Ask not what my stag mates have done for me, ask only what I have done to the stag." A pompous way of saying it was my fault. It didn't help her at all.

"I am so sorry to drag you into all this."

"I am a big girl, I chose to come. What did they do?"

"Max got me a prostitute. She was called Mirabel, she came from Senegal but..."

"I don't want to know about that tart, what did you do?"

"We went to her house at the back of the casino. Robert had sex with her first but I..."

"My god you both did it. You idiot Dan. Why couldn't you just say no? You don't know what you will have caught from her or that bastard Robert."

"I didn't do anything; I threw up on her before I got the chance."

"Thank god Dan. Sophia would be history if you had done anything. Why are you wet?"

"I fell into the river and passed out for a bit."

"Your shivering is getting worse; you need to warm up. Get undressed and I will run a bath for you." She disappeared to start the water thundering. I cannot detect the prime source of my shakes; being left out in the cold, my proximity to illicit sex; my drunkenness or being close to a woman I really loved?

"Get undressed then. I have seen it all before." I start to unpeel discoloured and misshapen items of clothing in the bathroom. My jeans stand all by themselves.

My jaw chatters in waves of panic. It binds together as I try to speak, obstructing the passage of truth. "I think I still love you Jules." I utter this softly as the knickers hit the floor.

"At least we can swop our underwear back," she smirks, initially ignoring my comment.

She continues to parcel my clothes together without looking at me. "No you don't. You love someone from seventeen years ago. She didn't love you enough then so doesn't deserve you now. Listen, it has been great seeing you again but love isn't the reason I am here. I will get changed into something else and you can use my robe." There is gravity in her statements but she has not taken me seriously.

"Get in the bath will you," she says as she leaves the room taking off her robe as she exits the bathroom.

I have taken so many blows over the past few days that this latest one seems inevitable, even though it is an important one. I view disappointment as a comfortable friend, an ally against the outside world. The water scalds me; Juliet scolds me. Just how does she know my truth? I try to put some cold water in the bath but cannot turn the tap. I sit down and my body fizzes against the bubbles. I cannot feel anything in my left arm. I close my eyes and submerge myself, sucking the water over me as a veil. The pain from the graze on my face brings me back up in haste. I have moved too quickly and water sloshes onto the floor. She comes back in fully clothed.

"I'm sorry, I must have embarrassed you tonight."

"No, no, I am fine. It has been great spending time with you, but we can't go back. Your future has never looked better, you are about to be married…"

"…Because Sophia's dad arranged it for me. I was invited to my own wedding." I finish her sentence. "Yes it's fabulous being Daniel Greenhenge. I have probably lost my job if Max is telling the truth. Most of my friends are arseholes. To cap it all I almost killed my son three days ago." My blood is boiling twice over from the bath.

"I've got to get out of here." I mean the bath but she thinks I mean her company.

"There is no hurry; I just want to set you straight before you leave. I have not been completely honest with you."

I see a chink in her armour at last. What does she feel? "What do you mean babe?"

"Dry yourself off and we can talk in the bedroom." I hop out of the bath and grab her already sodden towel. The towel is moving water around my body but not removing it. Her robe clings to me in the middle of my back; I hadn't dried sufficiently between my shoulder blades. When I exit the bathroom I see her sitting cross-legged on the only chair, tugging at her hair, knotting it and re-knotting her bunch.

"I did come here to tell you something. You have a right to know. Dan you are a father. I mean you are Ethan's father."

"But you said…" All alcohol is drained from my system.

"Forget that, I lied to you years ago and on the plane; it wasn't really the place to tell you."

"Are you sure, you said…"

"Positive, I never got back with Tristan. I said it at the time to give you someone else to hate when I told you we were splitting up. Anyway, I am telling you because he is sixteen and wants to meet you. In fact he is coming to the airport tomorrow with Scott to pick me up and he wanted to just say hello. Just for now that is. He has a right you know."

"Woahh babe. So you dumped me when you knew you were carrying my child."

"Yes, but I knew we weren't right and I didn't want to trap you into staying."

175

"That's not fair; you never gave me a chance. You never gave me a chance to be a dad."

"But you are a dad now."

"That's hardly the point babe. You denied me…" I stop reacting to assess how I feel. My head is stuffed with anger, joy, denial and excitement. How will Sophia react to this?

"Did you want to blow the wedding apart or something?"

"Of course not, I just wanted to let you know about your son before you got married so that you could start married life honestly." That's my son, that's Ethan, another joy in my life. What if he doesn't like me?

"Hang on; he is my son when you decide he is. Was he my son when he came out of the womb? Was he my son when he went on his first bike ride or on his first day at school? What gives you the right to say when he is my son?" I have never felt so angry so quickly. She is no different to the others; they fill me with scorn from their disrespect. My own flesh and blood is an adult I would pass in the street. What will he want from me?

"Do you want to meet him tomorrow or not?"

"Hey, don't be like that. You have just dropped the biggest bombshell of my life on me and you are getting shirty. Too much babe, way too much. Are you sure he is…" I ask again because I couldn't take the heartache of more false hope.

"We don't need a DNA test; there was no-one else at the time. I went back to my mum when I left you and …"

"No more now, I am wrecked. Let me get out of here."

"But Dan…"

"See you tomorrow."

On the way out I see a mug on the tray I had tripped over. Without breaking stride I kick it cleanly; it lifts off the tray and arcs down the corridor. It bounces on carpet and stays intact; but hitting the wall creates an atmosphere shattering smash. I have two sons. I bound down the one flight of stairs in the ridiculous robe that hardly covers my genitals. Juliet has all my belongings but what the hell. I thump on the door to wake Chris.

"What the hell?". Chris greets me as I walk past him into our room. "You look like a poof…"

"I look like a dad," I answer quizzically.

"You smell like a brothel."

"I might well do, no thanks to you and my spineless chums. Just go back to sleep will you, I need to think."

I have moved from having one son to almost none, then to two in the space of three days.

I grab my iPhone thirstily as I need an appropriate soundtrack to the darkness lifting into light outside. I want to block the world out to let me process this; my son Ethan is almost a man for Christ sakes. He must know I never had a chance to be his dad.

Pavarotti will make me soar with the song of not sleeping.

CHAPTER 34

Dan 09.45

My cheek rests heavily on my pillow; my alcohol-laced saliva has dribbled into the collective body fluids festering inside the casing. My watch stares me out from the cabinet; it is annoyed that almost ten hours of the day have already past. Having said that, I was awake for the first four of them. The warm bed tries to pull me back to waste some more. However, it is a ski day and the loss of time provokes instant anxiety in me. Others have been cutting into the groomed slopes for an hour and I probably won't be able to join them for yet another hour myself unless I speed up. From the hallway I hear the distinctive click-clack of ski boots and the rubbing of ski-suit nylon from some over-plump thighs. I roll onto my back, peeling my wet cheek from the soaked pillow; a cobweb of spittle keeps us joined for a few seconds. Alcohol-polluted blood thumps through the nape of my neck, pounding my pillow with its over-exertion. My ears still ring in this noise vacuum after the musical abuse from last night's bars; they have etched their bland symphony of supposed atonal happiness into my head. I have condoned these hapless musical choices by my attendance. A duvet covers my nakedness; today I needed it as Chris turned the heating off. Chris's growling snore hurts my head as well. My penis is gorged with blood and pushes a mini mountain into the duvet. I imagine myself skiing the left-hand edge of the duvet creases, I spy a few ledges that I could rest up on; I could get down that one but there is no chance of surviving the sheer cotton rock face to my right. My legs feel the motion of moving down a slope. The ringing intensifies into a shrillness that wasn't present before, there is nothing natural about it; it is the unnatural call to action that is a telephone.

"Wake up Dan." The phone clicks off without a chance for reply. Robert has brought me around; I detest you, you creep.

"Fuck me I have got a son," I utter out loud. I am not one for swearing but fuck me life is different. The noise halts Chris's latest snore, causing it to rip into a grunt.

"What? What's the time Dan?" Chris asks me without having control of his mouth yet. He breathes a putrid cloud of alcohol and decay into the room, which I can't avoid to get past his bed to the bathroom.

"Ten and I need breakfast. Get up, get up, I've got a son!" I shout at him without elaboration. Although this news makes my heart soar, I am dragged back to the events of last night that caused me to find out. I step into the shower, but my right foot slips to remind me that I am still under the influence of alcohol. The sharp light of my new life does battle with the darkness of my old one. With shampoo in my hair I turn around and arch my neck to allow the soapy water to drain away. My stance recalls clichéd advertising images of the next best greatest shampoo ever, which will invigorate your life. I scrub my genitals like I have herpes; I pull my foreskin back to wash inside. At its closest it was probably three feet away from Mirabel, but I feel as if I entered her with my whole body; the potential of the whole act repulses me so much. It would have been a betrayal I could not repair with Sophia, but most of all to me. The image of red-wine vomit sloshing between her cast open naked legs makes my nose twitch. I rub myself down hastily with the corner of my towel that is still dry.

Because Chris slept in his clothes we leave the room as soon as I am dressed. I am an exhilarated semi-drunk; I move with purpose to press the lift call button but miss it all the same. We both lean on the wall while our feet remember how to support us. Chris hasn't questioned my declaration about having a son; he assumes it is some drunken habit that I shout out known parts of my life when I wake up. The lift seems to shake with the thump of my heart. I must have such disrespect for my body to get here; but my so-called friends have shown me even more. Last night's celebration of my marriage was more like a dissection of my life. Chris and I bump shoulders as we exit the lift. We must attract tuts

179

from the tail end of today's skiers, who are fully dressed by the door waiting to depart. We scurry through the lobby with heads down.

The dining room is long abandoned, scattered with a dusting of breadcrumbs, tea spillage and waste cereal packets. Juliet, Johnny and Steve are sitting on tall chairs near the ceiling-high window at the far end. They stop eating as I arrive; their half-told manipulated reports of last night will have to wait now that I am here. I am struck by the gaping view up the mountainside as I sit at the head of the table. A small wooden slide in the garden outside reminds me of my younger son. I am disgusted by yet more Muzak; a trip-hop beat with some someone rapping "*Je ne regret Rien.*" Why can't people leave these things alone? Keep your ears covered Edith Piaf.

"The pastries were great Dan but they are all gone," Steve uselessly informs me.

"Just like our jobs at Centurion then." Steve looks away hastily, unable to hold my gaze after last night's revelations. If it is a quick closure I might never have to work with him again.

"*Café, thé, Messieurs?* A young waitress with buckteeth nervously enquires of me; aptly she looks like she is caught in my headlights. She clearly doesn't relish serving us for some reason. I order tea with milk to keep up my English image.

"Where are the other two?" I enquire about the absence of Robert and Max from the group.

"They are over there in the lobby on those bloody awful seats," Steve replies.

"An interesting night don't you think?" I keep my conversation vague to flush out anything I might have missed.

"You were off your trolley mate," Johnny reminds me, "I have never seen you so drunk."

"I suppose it was my stag night." I am disappointed in him especially; he could have helped more as he is my best man.

I join Chris at the buffet and grab a few slices of cheese and ham before he cleans up. The remaining bread is just baguette ends, all hard rounded edges. I choose some and prize them open to take a bite of the more succulent bread inside. I seem to be the last diner. On my return to the table Juliet and Steve have left to see Robert.

"You seem a bit sharp this morning." Johnny tries to get eye contact from me to bring his usual Dan back.

"I'm just coming to terms with what happened last night. You know the abuse, the lost friends, the prostitutes, that kind of stuff." Johnny and Chris stop eating hoping that I am going to explain all this to them.

"But the biggest discovery is that I have a son."

"You said that when you woke up you dickhead. Of course you have a son, he's two years..." Chris chastises me.

"No a second son, he's sixteen actually." This conversation will be good for Chris's waistline judging by his inability to eat, chewing is at a dead stop now.

"But who told you...?" Johnny hasn't caught up.

"Juliet of course, her son Ethan is mine. She broke up with me so that I wouldn't be trapped or maybe she wouldn't, I can't quite remember the line. Whatever, he wants to meet me, which is great, the sooner the better." I see an image of me beaming at him as we meet outside arrivals. He will be tall like me I think, although a more confident rounded me having been in Juliet's charge. A third even harder baguette end is too much; I polish off the cheese, which is a cue for Chris to resume eating. I throw my napkin down on my plate and slurp the milky tea I made.

"Let's find out what plan these brilliant mates of mine have in store for today."

"It's that bloody Valley thing I told you about; I ain't going near it. You can all play silly beggars off-piste if you like but I ain't skiing no glacier. Don't take any more shit from them Dan." Chris withdraws himself neatly.

"I think I have had enough myself bro."

Johnny and I walk towards the lobby where I had the meeting with Max and Steve the other evening. The ghosts of our wasted energy still haunt the chairs.

"Here is the sex machine now. He certainly knows how to show a woman a good time. You must be gay after all Dan, one look at a pussy and you throw up." Robert expects some laughs but this is a private joke.

"Robert my friend, so good to see you. We went a bit off-piste last night didn't we? Did you finish off the evening with the shy and retiring prostitute you picked up? Ladies of the night don't count as girlfriends you know." No intervention from anyone. I feel elevated.

"So then my faithful stags, remind me what we are doing to add to such an unforgettable trip? Just don't leave me behind like last night hey?" Most are looking chastened.

"All sorted, we are going to the Vallée Blanche. The guide is meeting us at the lift at twelve so let's meet here in half an hour." Max says his first words to me since revealing his great lie about ByeFly.

"Bring it on I say. It will be interesting to see how you all ski with such sore heads and heavy hearts." No one reacts again; they all have their reasons to feel as if they have let me down.

"Hi Jules, did you sleep okay?" I question her willingness and ability to sleep, but she just grimaces.

"I was woken by someone falling over a tray outside my room." I lie to her in front of the group. "It's beautiful days like this that make you proud to be alive don't you think?"

"I don't like your tone Dan," she protests.

"I'm sorry, I'm just a bit shaken." I leave the group with no explanation of events. Twenty minutes to get out and show them what I am made of.

CHAPTER 35

Dan 11.20

The automatic glass doors rip apart, withdrawing the multi-lingual plastic Welcome sign hung in reverse. I stand on the steps of the hotel with only Chris for company. If they were that interested in welcoming you someone could be on the door to do it. It's not the worst hotel in the world, but like so many others it offers plastic gestures to cover up its lack of genuine warmth and civility. I pick up my skis from the dank concrete locker room under the front steps. "You must leave the locker key at reception; you must not take skis into the hotel." In other words you must act and behave exactly as I say. Rules and curt practices spill from the walls trying to keep their guests in line. We are manageable units in a cost-efficient low-service environment. When did the world get so bloody bossy? My inner ski boot instantly wets my freshly laundered sock, but the warmth from my legs is bringing it up to an acceptable temperature. I throw my skis onto my shoulder. I am almost sad to feel the biting metallic weight of the ski binding on this, the last ski day of our trip.

Max, Steve and Robert burst through the door as I try to exit. As they get past me I allow the flat side of my ski to whack Max on the head.

"Sorry, I must be more careful." Max cannot detect sarcasm from me, as he never usually receives it.

The ten steps up to the front of the hotel are tortuous. After what I have put them through my muscles just don't want to stretch.

"Okay, I will come up the ski lift with you but that's it." A reluctant Chris has been persuaded to take a ride in the lift by Juliet.

"Dan, will you wait here while I get my stuff?" Juliet is the last to descend into the ski room. My over-riding feeling of being cheated is competing with my enduring affection for her.

"Let's all wait for Juliet please," I command the group to wait and set off together. We pass our favoured bar with the almost midday sun stroking our necks. We go past the bookshop torn asunder by the runaway crate; it seems to have fully recovered its charm.

"What did you do with that soiled jacket?" Juliet is right to be unconvinced I got rid of it.

"I dumped it like you asked." At about three this morning when I got back to my room something compelled me to wash it in the bath. It is now hanging over a wooden chair on my balcony, drying out with its price ticket chattering in the breeze. However misguided, it was the first act of kindness I was able to do for Ethan. I am not sure if I will give it to him yet, but it just felt real to do it. He will really appreciate the "Tracks of My Years"; but what if he is into this trip-hop nonsense or even worse some plastic cover band? How can I help him recover from that fate, having had no real dad to put him on the straight and narrow? Maybe he will need some more intelligent fatherly words of wisdom? But what can I offer yet? My brain is not prepared for adult advice, as I am a generation away from having to give it.

As we pass under the railway bridge my inattention causes a man walking towards us to step into the road. A driver beeps a warning at him. It feels great that it is some other man for a change. We pass through the short flag-lined avenue that leads to the grandly named *Telepherique de l'Aiguille du Midi* cable car. An improbable cable soars out of the station into the sky above. I cover my eyes to try to see the end of it but it fades into the snow line on the mountain in front of us. The atmosphere in front of the ticket office seems very serious; people are breathing heavily down here but even more effort will be needed when the air thins out at the top. There is a mixture of climbers, skiers and viewers. The climbers are encumbered, they break the silence with the metallic clinking of ice picks and crampons strapped onto backpacks. The skiers have their usual gear but most have additional rucksacks as well; what are they carrying? The viewers however are a mixed bag of ski tourists and fur-coated Russians. "Wow. That's some climb hey?" Johnny shares my awe.

"That has to be the most sheer lift in the world," I speculate.

"Ten past twelve, that guide is late. I asked for him at the office but they haven't seen him." Robert had hurried ahead and stands outside the wooden ticket office with seven lift tickets in hand.

"Bugger him we will go without him," he says impatiently.

"No we will not. We were ten minutes late, give him a chance will you," Juliet counters.

"Alright, five more minutes and we are off."

"Why don't you just call the man?"

"I can guide us down, we don't need him."

"He said twelve at the latest; we don't need to call him," Max butts in.

"Call him Robert," I interject.

"Do you really want these guys to have any more expense on your stag weekend. Don't you think they have paid enough?" Robert turns the weekend on me when it was all his doing.

"Since when did you care about anyone else's money? I know your game, you haven't got a guide have you?" Juliet accuses him, smelling a rat.

"Listen. I don't need to answer to you. The guy isn't here; we can go."

"That's why you wouldn't let me speak to him. You never called that number I gave you, did you? You little shit Robert, it's serious you prick."

"Well, did you call him you arsehole? Did you?" Chris tries to bring it to a head.

"There was no need to; I can take you down the VB. We are committed; I have the tickets. It's spectacular up there. Listen, I seem to be the only person trying to give Dan a good time. It's simple, let's get on with it, what do you say Dan?"

"Why not finish this tragic weekend off in style boys." Damned if I do, damned if I don't. I am sick of the bickering. I am surrounded by opinionated jerks, foisting their views on me. I snatch a ticket from Robert's perforated roll and walk to the turnstile, leaving any dissent behind. Sometimes you have to take responsibility for your life, before it takes care of you. Maybe I have got something to say to Ethan after all. We all clunk onto a metallic platform, waiting for the huge cable car to glide alongside us.

"This is all very James Bond isn't it." Robert states the obvious. This is probably the first inclusive comment I have heard from him all weekend. I can feel the end. As soon as I am back I am into the wedding zone. But so much more as well, I have another son in my life now.

"Which Bond was it that climbed out of the cable car?" Max asks.

"It was Roger Moore in an all-in-one wasn't it?" Juliet half remembers.

"We were going to nick your salopettes at some point Dan, but thought it counter productive as you would never have gone out." Max informs me.

"That was another stupid plot I foiled." Chris tells me.

As everyone finishes departing from the other side of the car, a metal safety rail is slammed backwards to allow us to enter. Shuffling and pushing ensues as the first entrants look for a piece of window space from which to view the climb. As it fills, the body of people is conjoined, steadying each other with brushed shoulders.

"I just saw a sign that this thing climbs about three thousand metres in less than ten minutes; so pop those ears guys," Johnny informs us. The scent of cigarettes fuses with climber sweat and expensive perfume. The rich tourist and the true adventurer hate occupying the space together. With one huge lurch some invisible giant grabs the cable car skyward; we are on the way to Europe's rooftop. In an instant the car is hanging over the sprawl of the Chamonix valley floor. I think I can make out the pink exterior of the casino but am not sure. Life looks so different from up here; I can look upwards now. The car pushes through a thin layer of cloud within seconds.

"What would Ethan make of this trip Juliet?" She looks shocked as she remembers that she doesn't hold her secret anymore.

"He would have been excited but apprehensive. Just like his dad I think." There is further shock for both of us as these words are released. I can't wait to see Bepe and meet Ethan tomorrow. Maybe Juliet refused to come to the wedding until I knew about Ethan. Maybe they can both come?

"I hope I can make him proud of me." I know how I can start. I am creating a playlist for two now and as I approach the end of the alphabet I find just the right epic accompaniment to our climb.

Number 6 "Unfinished Sympathy" by Massive Attack

How can you have a day without a night? Well I just have. This track reminds me of working in Max's advertising agency. Released in 1991 on Wild Bunch records. Things felt freer then, every project seemed interesting, and we were on the same side. This had a great video of Shara Nelson pacing down a London Street chanting while the world passes her by. I didn't know I had something missing from my life till now. This is a great track to give you a sense of purpose and strength. Only one more track to go, but only V to Z to find it in.

Grass and rock have been fighting for prominence all the way up our climb, but rock has won. Huge swathes of scree settle uneasily below us. Only a fragile pact with gravity keeps it from abandoning such a precarious lookout. My ears need to be popped. I try not to concentrate on the skyward pull of the car and let go of my grip on the barrier pole. If we were to fall then so be it, I can't help by holding on tight. I let the ingenuity and hard work of my fellow man to build this thing safely take responsibility for the climb.

At a mid station we have to swap into a second cable car to get right to the top. The jostling for position settles down as we are swept over snow that takes over the rock below. The mountain is transformed from friend to foe, no longer does this feel like leisure. Like the first slope I ever skied, there is more danger than pleasure afoot; it is all out of my control now. A huge outcrop of rock and ice appears, a severed left eye disjoints its face-like features. Over its flatter head we start to slow as we reach the summit. A collection of buildings cling unnaturally to the top, coloured like the rock so that they seem almost hewn from it. The car is noiseless now; awe fills the space between all passengers. We reach a swinging stop. As the doors fly back the chill wind seeks out warm cheeks. The metal bridge at this height is iced over.

"There's a terrace to have a drink before we go down." Robert advises us. We all follow him out onto it to try and grasp the opportunity of this vantage point. I keep thinking I have seen this view somewhere before and realise it is from the plane.

"It would be worth just sitting here all afternoon," I suggest.

"Too bloody right," Chris agrees.

"You wait till you get down there in amongst it." Robert disagrees. It is thrilling to be here, but every positive thought is followed by a nagging self-doubt.

"I'm getting some food anyway." Chris is true to form and goes back inside to get in line for a meal.

"Just get a snack, we need to get on our way." Robert makes the skiers hurry up. The snow sweeps gently below us. It is a worrying mystery as to how we reach the flat snow so far below from this perch without skiing a vertical incline. I buy a Snickers, a chicken roll and water for the trip. Something is stirring inside my bowels.

Chris sits alone on the terrace munching away at another continental burger. I can see he has been happy to eat on this extended break if nothing else.

"Chris, we are heading off now. I will see you at the bottom."

"See you bro. Take care now." He barely lifts his head as he chews.

I delay the group further. "I need the loo."

"Look it's ten to one now children, I suggest we all meet up at the locker room at one to get this show on the road." Robert is getting sick of herding us. I wait desperately for a cubicle. The only vacated one is humming with the stench of alcohol and excrement. I push my ski pants down hard onto the top of my boots, but this inflexibility binds my legs together. My bum cheeks only spread wide enough to emit a series of exasperated farts. At this altitude I have also changed sex; my willy has shrivelled into a clitoris. I channel all my thoughts inward, hoping to focus on the excitement of the ski rather than the danger.

I enter the locker room from the adjacent toilets. A huge metal door is sucking people out into the unknown. The travelling six gather around Robert.

"Okay then, let's go. It's an easy ski, most of it is somewhere between a red and a blue, but there is a technical bit in the middle that he have to pick carefully down. Remember to stay close together; we will have to keep stopping for the snails like Dan and Johnny. At the end of this ice tunnel there is a ridge to walk down so keep your skis off for now. We will ski to a lift and get the Montenvers train that fortunately drops us off outside the hotel. Let's hit the Caveau by four. Last one to the bar pays. Any questions? No."

We walk to the metal piste exit door. Johnny and I hesitate at the bleak warnings on it. It does exactly what it should do; guard the innocent and foolhardy like us from walking down the tunnel of ice that leads onto the Vallée.

"Skiers Beware. No groomed runs. No avalanche control. No trail markers. No ski patrols. You are now going on your own responsability." The sic misspelling inadvertently highlights two components: your response to events around you and your personal ability.

"You don't have to do this you two. Go and have lunch with Chris and go down on the cable car. Let the others make fools of themselves," Juliet warns me.

"I can't back out now." I could back out but what will I learn? I can't spend all of my life walking away from risk. I have to think about the kind of man I will be for my boys. I bash the metal sign with my gloved hand as I pass it, dismissing its foreboding.

CHAPTER 36

Dan 13.01

I see the light at the end of the tunnel and I am sucked towards the promise of its sun. Cocooned in the ice walls of the walkway, crystals glint mischievously inside this under-exposed cave. Carefully I place each clunking step towards the blindingly lit arched exit. I feel my core chilled by the effects of this over sized icebox, but I can smell the sun ferociously burning the thin air a few metres away.

My heart bursts as I exit the tomb. I am desperate to see how I get onto the glacier. I cannot see any mountain peaks yet through the wall of backs lined up to consume the view. The uneasy melange of jean-clad sightseers and ice adventurers jostle at the edge. Non-participants shuffle uncomfortably, judged incapable of meeting this ski challenge and soon to be benignly carried back down to earth by the cable car. However, most participants are anxious to start their journey, bristling at the challenge of commanding this unbounded environment, like astronauts ready for blast off. I look over the shoulders of the shortest man I can find, despite being repulsed by his lime green and pink all-in-one jump suit. He must wear this as a badge of authenticity that he was around in the 60s. If he could stop spouting superlatives at the view, he would hear my heart belting my inside jacket pocket, straining to work at this altitude.

The view is at once clear and confusing. The clarity is the contrast between the blue sky that appears to be both above and below us, set against the white peaks stretching on and on for miles around. The confusion is the sheer immensity of this vantage point, my eye cannot settle on any one thing.

This epic view requires an epic tune. I must choose something appropriate, maybe classical or techno? It is either violins or unearthly sounds to accompany me down. John Barry is the man to paint a soundscape for this vista. I select "You Only Live Twice" with its opening cascade of violins. Perfect choice, I have lived my life but have somehow held onto an unrealistic dream life with Juliet at the same time. What have I been doing? The dream life hasn't been even a remote possibility but I have let it puncture reality. She has been an imaginary measuring stick for any prospective partner for years. But no one could come close because the measurement isn't real. I never even believed it was going to happen. I pity Sophia; this has been a real problem in my head. The voice of Nancy Sinatra glides through the song and the guitar line provides a sharp edge to my self-discovery. I hope I can recover myself before a two-year-old and a sixteen-year-old discover who I really am.

I catch my first breathless glimpse of the ridge we have to walk down before we start skiing.

"Let's get through this load of posers Dan." Robert's skis push into my back.

"We have to walk down a ridge first guys."

"I know that lame brain." Robert spits at me.

"Is it steep Dan?" Juliet asks for a report as she struggles to see.

"It's not the walk so much as the drop either side."

"Just don't fall off it or it is goodnight Vienna. This is the only tricky bit, just get down this and it's plain sailing. Are you just up here for a look-see like all these other losers or have you the balls to ski? I will even go first and hold your little hand if you want. Sorry I didn't wipe your arse in the locker room for you as well." Robert lays the humiliation on thick, suspecting I need to be bullied to go.

"Hey, back off man or I'll…"

"What. What have you got to say for yourself now big daddy?" His eyes swell with false bravado but he looks frightened. He always steps over the line with me, carelessly stomping my ego. I am refusing to drink from the trough of ridicule anymore and it scares him. He wants me to fight back so that he gets legitimacy for his behaviour. The first time I feel I could legitimately stand toe to toe with him and I feel only sympathy.

"I will lead us down; I was just trying to get through the crowd." I lie well enough for him to not reply. The crowd dissolves at the edge as I step forward to lead my stags for the first time. This stupidity is on my terms now. I look to see we are all together. Skis locked on my right shoulder I grab the guide rope with my left hand, extending my left leg decisively onto the ridge to start the sideways walk down. The heel of my boot sticks hard into the fresh snow at the edge of the ridge, as a gust of Alpine wind whips though me and pushes my head back.

"Be careful now Dan." Juliet is the last thing I hear before I set off.

I match the rhythm of the words to each step. I dare to look up to see Juliet and the others. The snow tunnel evaporates behind them with each step, another twenty or so and I am off the ridge. I count them down, looking only for the safest foothold on the broken ice and snow below me. The rough safety rope rips the palm of my glove with every step. Seventeen left; it must have ripped a stitch in my glove as a pinprick of icy air hits my forefinger. Nine left; we are the last group visible on the ridge. Four more steps; even now a fall would be fatal. As I reach the end I step backwards onto the glacier and fall on my backside a safe distance away; having held my breath for most of the walk I am entitled to squeeze some air into my lungs.

"I thought I was over a couple of times there." Juliet joins me in my prayer. We laugh together for the first time since I knew a child joins us. We are a broken family who never got a chance.

Max and Robert calmly appear, but Steve is gripped with fear. He sits away from us to recover some composure and lies prone on the snow.

"Steve, Steve," Robert shouts up to him. "Listen you idiots, get your skis on quick. You don't know what is below the snow. You have a better chance with the skis as a platform. That goes for you two as well." We follow the sound advice.

Gargantuan sheets of snow stretch before us. They eat up as much of the rock-scape as they can cling to.

"Seeing as we are carrying a few passengers we will head down the easy way. Keep right with me, and go under those cable cars as we head towards Italy. We will turn left behind that rock outcrop to the narrow bit, then it's straight down to the Montenvers train. We should be in Cham for four as planned."

"This narrow bit, are you sure Dan and Steve can ski it?" Juliet interrupts Robert's belittling of the journey ahead.

"Of course, they're men aren't they? Come on then big daddy let's be having you."

"It's not about sex; it's about ability."

"Well I am confident of my sexual ability, what about you?" Robert casts a sharp glance at me; we share something too now, I am the only one here to have seen him in the sex act.

"What are you staring at? Lost your bottle like last night?"

"I am happy to follow you Robert if you say you can be trusted." The end to the sentence is seen aggressively.

"What do you mean, trusted? I am trusted to run a multi-million pound company aren't I? I was the one trusted to organise your stag weekend for free rather than your busking best man wasn't I?"

"You also said you had organised a guide for us. You also said you wouldn't embarrass Dan last night…" Juliet is having none of it.

"I don't think he meant it like that." Johnny tries to defuse Robert.

"I said I could lead this group from the start and I will. I've done this numerous times; it's the best buzz. Something a stag will never forget!" By bringing it round to me he has won the reluctant acceptance of all.

"Let's go do the VB then staggie."

"Sure, in for a euro in for a pound. It is a stunning place mate so I suppose I should say thanks." I converse with him.

"Keep about ten yards apart and follow me. Juliet, since you are so worried, you take up the rear-end position that you love so much." Robert's insult draws a few titters.

Robert's skis draw a line outside the arc of any of today's skiers. I follow him, knee deep in a carpet of snow. My skis are held in perfect parallel lines by the trough of snow we are skiing. I try to move my ankles outward to get an inside edge but they are locked. I am alarmed; this isn't skiing, its more like being on a conveyor belt. Without control of my skis, the terrain sets the speed, altering my pace through imperceptible changes in gradient underfoot. To prove my point Robert stops for us to re-group; I strain to move my invisible skis into a snowplough. I use every muscle to slow me down but only halt by travelling over the back of Robert's skis.

"Magnificent lark hey? Look it's Mont Blanc up there." He points out a snow-capped rounded hummock starting a few hundred metres away. How far have I travelled to reduce the aspect of such majesty? Europe and I can get no higher, although three climbers are trying to. The peak sits impassively: a benign giant reduced to a hummock from this height.

Robert and I set off immediately when the others arrive. Juliet is coaching a tentative Steve to stop; like me he needs something to run into to make it happen. We draw into a small valley formed by Mont Blanc on the right and a rocky outcrop to the left. Robert makes no concessions, immediately skiing through to the other side. My legs have started to shake, a straining leash against the force of gravity. Sweat runs from the edges of my hat to a dripping point under my chin. When I stop again I must put a more relaxing track on, maybe Massive Attack. I wonder what Bepe and Sophia are up to, most definitely at her parents or some distant relative close by. Home tomorrow, this trip has been exhausting. I will read all his books tomorrow night and do his bath, no matter what hassle I get from Sophia. Wonder if she remembered to check my mum and dad were okay to arrive on Thursday at the hotel? I see my knees disappear and it scares me, how deep can I sink?

"…Left Dan." Short, sharp and in panic.

"Keep fucking left Dan." Robert reiterates what I couldn't hear at first. The snow has fallen away steeply behind the outcrop and I am careering towards Robert. He must have stopped at some point because he is going so much slower than I am. I am going to pass him; yes I am going to miss him. I skate on past but I feel my ski clip something and am tossed limply into the air.

I laugh as I fall, thrust into abundant virgin snow. One ski comes off as the other flails overhead. Robert has disappeared from view as I slide head first towards the aching blue of a crevasse he was obviously trying to warn me about. I try to take in the beauty around me as I am flipped up to land in an upright sitting position. I turn my torso to the hill. No sooner had it started it was over. I have fallen and laughed.

I try to push myself up with my hands but sink deeper face first into the snow. I glimpse what it might be like to drown in the stuff. Robert grabs my jacket near the nape of my neck; like a mother cat carries a kitten and pulls me up.

"Shit, you scared me then."

"I was a little scared myself."

"Here, I found this up there for you." He embeds my right ski in the snow, parallel with my other. He bashes packed snow from under my boot.

"You came tanking around that corner towards that crevasse. I thought you had a death wish for a minute. You know it's just a lark don't you? You are such an easy target; you should handle yourself better. You know I don't..." I thought Robert was extending both arms to start to hug me but he just brushes my jacket free from snow instead as the whole group catches up. They direct their anxieties at Robert.

"This is bloody tough Robert; you need to slow down..." Johnny challenges him.

"Will you lead us and stop pissing off and leaving us." The first dissent I have heard from Max.

"If it wasn't for Juliet I would be stuck back at the ridge." Steve reluctantly voices appreciation for her help.

"Can you stop being such a prat and just guide us down. Look at Dan, he's covered in snow," says Juliet.

"I'll try." The shortest sentence he has ever ushered. I am physically weakened but mentally heartened; nature is making him bow down.

CHAPTER 37

Dan 14.40

Rugged rocks sneer down on our presence; funnelling our ski parade into more treacherous terrain. We start to pay it due respect, delicately navigating each turn through treacherous waters. My piratical mates are transformed into a bonded crew, formed around their selfish desire to steer onto the clear sea of ice below us, with the treasure of life intact. Cannon fire for once is directed away from the ship; focus switches to the common enemy of the surrounding burst of extreme nature.

"Together now, but not too close." Robert takes the lead, halting effortlessly after every turn to check the group's safe passage.

"There's a dead body. Watch out Dan." Max exaggerates to alert me to a dead rabbit in our path. Blood spots melt innocently into the snow, leading away from the remaining fur, bone and scarlet innards in the direction of a long-departed predator.

"I wouldn't have imagined foxes at this altitude." Juliet points a finger at the murder suspect.

"Maybe it was Robert having a snack?" Johnny suggests from behind me.

"No, he only eats babies and prostitutes," Juliet offers sarcastic defence.

"Did someone mention food?" Robert shouts up at us all.

"If we have to stop it may as well be now, but five minutes only. It's getting on for three o'clock. We need to get past these crevasses so we can relax. The last train down from Montenvers is about four thirty." Robert offers us a break, although concern permeates, taking the pitch of his voice up a notch.

I realise my shin marrow is pulped. The steeper terrain and deep snow has trashed my technique and my shins misguidedly try to hold me upright in my boots. I clack my right ski off with my pole to seek some pressure relief.

"No, no, no. I told you to keep your skis on Dan. You could be standing on a snow bridge over a hidden crevasse for all we know!" shouts Robert.

"We might have known where to stand if you had bothered to make sure we had a guide," Juliet risks pointing this out again.

"Let it go bitch."

"Guys, just stop for a minute. Look up, look up, it's just magnificent." The mountains silence the squabble with Johnny's assistance.

Each munching chin is pushed upwards and snivelling cold noses point skywards. The muffled sounds of confectionery and bread being pulped bear witness to our slight presence here. Johnny points out the enormous mountainous presence around us. We can ignore it on the move, but stood here all six of us acknowledge its uplifting joy. I watch Juliet taking it in; she is of this earth not rushing through it. She settles eyes on mine and mouths a wow to me, I grin childishly at her silent attention. Johnny sees our connection and I blush.

"Right. Enough is enough. Keep the pace steady through the next bit. Follow me." Max is trying to rally Steve. I feel guilty at inwardly relishing Steve's discomfort, for fear of jinxing my progress. The group dynamic is chastened now; we know it is not just our ability that determines our progress. I pick up speed on our first turn. I jab my poles into the snow to slow down; at first they sink into powder but eventually stick into the underlying ice, snapping my wrists back on contact. I stop but am pulled backwards as I have skied past the poles. I pull my hands free from the straps as I am too far down the slope to pull them out. After three deliberate side steps up the slope I am reunited with my poles. It seems an age since Sophia and I last spoke. As I am about to ski on a hesitant Steve comes inside me so I let him pass; all enjoyment has been sucked from his face, even his brittle veneer of confidence at the top has been shattered now. His legs are forced into an unsustainable snowplough, his whole body leans back from the slope, his hands held close in front as if he is about to box someone. No sympathy arises in me, just guilty triumph over his pricked ego.

"Just let yourself go quickly over the dip here, the hill will slow you down as you come out. It might be a crevasse so just move quickly over it. Come on, it's three o'clock now." Robert is handing out more tactics. Steve rattles through the dip and halts on the opposing slope. Robert reaches his pole down and pulls him up and away to the right.

"Last man over lankster."

I pull my legs parallel, determined to avoid the ignominy of Steve's tattered snowplough style. Fast over the crevasse, fast over the crevasse I goad myself. I picture the deep hole underneath my feet, all ice caves and edges, and shoot over it effortlessly. As I rise up the opposite slope everyone comes into view on my right lined up behind Robert. I smile at them confident of my fluid technique. Having skied so well the weight lifts from my feet and I pop over the ridge they stand on as well.

"Stop Dan," Juliet screams.

"Hey Dan, where are you off to? Max adds with inappropriate calm.

I maintain my parallel ski stance in the deep snow and sail past everyone. There is no control; they are jammed into tramlines again. There is nothing in my technique other than to force an ignominious fall. I drop onto my right side and explode into the snow.

I am falling and laughing: ripped from my skiing heaven to an icy earth. It's a juicy fall one which sloshes my thoughts round like a drunk's glass and bellows pride from my lungs. Suffocating ice particles in my mouth make me gag. I am perversely relieved to surrender to gravity but it makes me want to cry in anxiety over my future. I set a false defiant smile into the gorgeous late afternoon sun. This is for the sake of my ego and assorted friends, but it fools no one, especially me.

Hell I know why I fell; I fell because I am me. I am the common denominator who surrendered to this downfall. My stags may have bullied me into this but it was unwise, I let them come together. I can't even blame the fall on that bastard Robert, he has tried me from the moment I let him set the trip destination and manipulated it right to the point of this off-piste jaunt. The fall started when Sophia's dad bullied me into getting married just because he had booked some country club; how weak am I? Parents like myself sneer at their children saying that pride come before a fall, and so they should. But what would my children think of me in this predicament?

The heart of a crevasse defies all expectation; how can an accumulation of something so white be so vibrantly blue? These blue lines drop away in every direction, encircling my journey. My flight instinct kicks in but I am weak. I cycle my legs casting off huge splashes of snow, but they are irrelevant to my efforts to slow down. Cavernous crevasses and shattered seracs must be sharpening their stalactites to welcome me to their wintry isolation. I belatedly turn my torso uphill and flap my gloves at nothing in particular. My desperate acts slow me down but not enough. I am too close now, I wait the moment of take off, I know it will come. Play it out now, whatever is to be, I am sick of this life of suspended…

No resistance now but some relief. My jacket puffs out as I become airborne.

Flashes of blue and white surround me, but it's only black and blue below me. My poles and skis still attached.

I am going to fly over it. No, it's too far. I've got a family. Just be over now, whatever.

CHAPTER 38

Dan 15.06

My stags wait for the main act to come back on stage.

My body pulses; I am in hot water again. "This Charming Man" is the broken record in my head; its jangly chords open the song with promise but are cut short and re-start. Johnny Marr can't seem to help himself and Morrissey never gets a chance to sing. I shake my head to move the needle on an imaginary record player beyond its scratch. It works but what's that rustling noise? It wasn't there before. When do I have to get out of the bath? It's just a relief to have stopped. I've lost track of time but Chris will be here in a minute. Why can't they stop, what are they all planning for me now downstairs? Robert is such a bastard; someone beyond redemption is planning my stag weekend.

My head is freezing and my right arm numb underneath me. The back of my skull is so cold on the enamel; the heat being poured into my body must exacerbate it. I played with Bepe in the bath the other night, his tongue pushed through his teeth in determination as a pirate failed to fit into a constricted plastic porthole on his boat. He rambles as he descends into his imaginary world. "He's under on top." "It's not clicking Diddy." "He chirps to an imaginary friend." "He into the dump away."

Why are they all pushing me? It's a sport. Juliet turns up as well, why couldn't she leave me until after the wedding? I can hear her voice now; she must be in the bedroom with Chris. I must do some ByeFly before we go out.

That light on my face is fabulous; heat caresses my cheeks, but bitter cold invades my skull. It snaps at my neck. Why am I marrying? Let me go Sophia, quietly Sophia, you deserve better. Shut up Juliet, I am relaxing. Let me be, I still have time before we go.

My back is cold now; the enamel is now carrying a freezing cold charge under my body. It reaches my calves and grips them. I am an intermediate skier now, which is an achievement.

I lift my left hand to grasp the bath side, but I can't find it. The rustle develops into a scratch like sandpaper on sandpaper. Shut up Juliet, go away Max, and piss off Robert. Their voices call to me in the bathroom. Go away it is my time now. You can't come in here. Enough of your bullying. I have my limits you know. I reach higher for the bath rim.

The water must be freezing now. I have been in too long. The cold is coming for me with my stags. I can't reach the bath side, but it must be there. It's enough now, get up Dan, go and face the music outside.

"Are you okay Dan? Answer me. Answer me."

I pull my head onto my chest, stopping the piercing cold from my skull and neck bones. Just get out of the water now. Leaning on my left elbow I release my right arm. Get up and out. I reach my right arm again across my body in search of the bath edge.

"Don't move Dan," Juliet screams from behind me.

"But I have to get out of the bath, it's cold now." I weakly retort.

"Don't move a muscle, we will get help."

There is no bath is there Juliet? I am engulfed in blue crystal walls. It is a crevasse I am in not a bath. I am relieved to be at a stop but cannot contemplate how much danger I am in. How am I getting out of this place?

"Don't move Dan, you are on a ledge. You are fine if you stay still. Be patient and we will get help."

CHAPTER 39

Juliet 15.06.

"WHY DO MEN PUSH TOO FAR?"

Dan's brown woolly hat is abandoned on the scar his body left on the piste. It has lost its purpose; no longer protecting his muddled mind. Semi-erect but lop sided, despite the best efforts of its earpieces. A puff of steam billows out from its residual warmth. If he is alive he needs his hat. What has this fall done to my son?

We have all stopped dead in our tracks but Dan's silently scar the crest in front of us, hiding the truth. There is neither sight nor sound from Dan. We must assume the worst.

"He is such a dick, that lanky twat. Has he learnt nothing from skiing with me?" Robert is unsympathetic of Dan's plight.

"We have learnt that he is as much of a lanky twat on skis as he is on terra firma!" Max joins in and boys chuckle.

"You didn't tell him to stop quick enough though dickhead." Robert surprisingly lashes out at Max, ready to deflect any potential heat.

"I thought he knew because we had." Max doesn't take it on the chin, but knows he might be culpable. They talk without any thought that this could be serious.

"He has probably killed himself down a crevasse or something. Did anyone see that *Touching the Void* film? It was brilliant; the guy falls off a mountain, almost kills his buddy, crawls to safety, only waking up because he was lying in shit." Robert continues.

"He trusted you..." Johnny's speech is tightened by worry. A tear of fear for his friend paints a line down his right cheek. He quivers as shock and cold reach into him.

"Let's help him. He could be seriously hurt!" I pull my right ski out of the deep snow, and set it as far down the slope as I can. The other three boys show fear of guilt and recrimination; they all re-appraise their hand in Dan's fall.

The whole trip feels like it has been seeking out an inconsolable level of embarrassment or tragedy. Push and push till the stag falls, it's been there from minute one.

"If he is, we can just get someone to get him out. I bet anyone one hundred notes he is just lying in a heap over there. Any takers?" A small cloud marches past the sun casting this him into shadow. Not even Max dares tempt fate by taking the bet.

"Haven't you ever read the door at the top? Four times you say you have been here. This is off-piste. No patrols, no rescue service. Who the hell is coming to help except us? Let's just find him."

"Okay. For fuck's sake keep your hair on. Typical woman losing her head while…" He tails off. He has resisted the rescue for fear of what he may find. He is hoping for just another ritual ridicule for Dan.

"I'll go first, let's side step down till we can see something. Keep on different paths so if one of us falls they don't take the other one." Max stands up to Robert's resistance. With his left ski edge at ninety degrees to the slope, he reaches down with his right leg. Once that one is stable he pulls the left parallel and goes on.

"Shall we stay here for now Steve? The others can signal when they find him." At the peak of his fear Johnny can still look out for his fellow man. Steve looks wrecked; trying so hard not to show how out of his depth he is.

I follow Max, making quicker progress to the right on the line of Dan's fall.

More clouds above; I see them skittle over the ground.

I stop below Dan's hat and pick it up with my left hand. I press it to my cheek. It is frozen already but it doesn't convince me his trail is cold.

I want to find him first. I cross a lump in the ground that must have sent him airborne. The sense of risk increases with each step.

What is down this path? Is my friend bloodied and smashed on a rock? Is he intact in a bank of snow? Is he here at all? There aren't many more steps to the crevasse edge. My breath runs shorter. The trail ends with no resolution.

"The bastard is over… shit, how did he get there?" Somehow Robert sees him before I do and laughs through it.

I have to traverse backwards to make Dan come into view. He is in real trouble now. He must have flown from this lip and hit the far wall to fall twenty metres onto a ledge. The orange from his jacket burns into the icy blue around him.

"Dan we're here. Dan you okay?" Nothing. His face points into the wall.

"Are you okay Dan? Answer me. Answer me!" I scream at him.

I feel immense relief as he manoeuvres his left leg to place it alongside his right. His movement is slow indicating either his injuries or a perilous hold on the ledge. I wave reservedly to Steve and Johnny; their figures collapse together as one backlit shadow in celebration.

"Don't move Dan!" At least he is here alive.

"Don't move a muscle, we will get help." He lifts his left arm in acknowledgment as we can only see the top of his head.

I can't see the extent of the ledge he is on. Surely someone with the right equipment can reach him from the far side. I scan for means of a way over. The crevasse narrows in the distance; enough for a jump or a short ladder?

"Hey, lanky you had us worried then!" Robert shouts over. I traverse forwards to get near Max and Robert.

"We can't hear him that far away. Can either of you get a phone signal?" Max ignores the obvious fact that all our phones are redundant at this altitude.

"Has anyone got any food?" Max retrieves a square bar of white Ritter sport chocolate.

"I will throw it over." Robert wraps his index finger around the edge of the bar and tosses it spinning in a perfect arc over to him. It seems destined to hit his feet but the wind takes it higher; it bounces off the ice wall above him and falls below where there is no redemption, as blueness turns black.

Steve and Johnny are unwisely stepping down to join us. "Stamp your bottom edge into the slope for grip," I instruct them as they get within earshot.

"Robert, how long will it take to get down from here?" We need to weigh up our options.

"It could be up to another hour down for a girlie like you." Now we know Dan isn't dead Robert is on the front foot again, challenging so as not to be challenged.

"Can we ski it in poor light?

"Nah, beyond here the middle of the crevasse breaks over steeper terrain. It is all technical turns in short spaces. Once past that it's easy, but you are only at the glacier edge. The train stops at four thirty. After that you would have to walk off the glacier in snow boots into Chamonix on the valley floor below. I don't think we would get much of a night out tonight!" Robert is in denial.

"If we can't reach him what's our best bet?"

"We can't reach him but a rescue team could. We can't risk our lives by staying out here in the open." Another of those moments where they search each other's faces for non-verbal signs of consensus, but it doesn't last for long.

"So what do we do Robert? Did anyone pick up a map of the Vallée?" I ask.

"I got one to take home," Johnny offers me the folded ski map from his pocket. The centre spread shows routes dotted down the Vallée from Italy or France.

"We can't have travelled far. Look there is a hut somewhere over to the left of us, it must be above us I think. Climbers use it as an overnight stay. The Refuge De Requin."

"It's not a very good map but if we go over to the left it seems to be on a rocky outcrop. Let's head for that to get help. If we don't find it we won't be far from the Aiguille in the morning."

"In the morning! We are not going to survive a night out here." Robert laughs but talks softly as he realises Dan will probably have to.

"Come on boys, we have a stag to rescue." I don't wait for opinion, as it is the only course open. I hug Johnny to bolster his faith. He holds me asexually like he is holding a flower.

"We only have thirty to forty minutes of sunlight. You can't read the terrain properly once it's disappeared." Robert says unhelpfully.

"Let's climb back up to where we were guys. I will tell Dan what we are doing."

I plant a pole to mark the spot in view of the path. It skids off the ice at first. I try again and get a hold, the handle judders as I release it. I reach down and push light snow into ice at its base until it stands steady. I reach for my phone to reassure myself that the signal is dead. I hopefully open a map App, but it shows no up-to-date terrain. I drop a pin on the map but am unconvinced that it has been recorded.

"Who are you gonna call?" Robert jeers at me, misunderstanding my motives.

"Ghostbusters?" Max can't resist. Forgive them for they know not what they do.

I take a picture in each direction. The ball of orange to my right floods sunlight onto my stricken friend. How I hope you can feel it Dan. The night will take every glimmer of warmth from your body. Chamonix hides at the bottom of my picture. The relative sedateness of stag japes and foolishness are not visible. Out west lie the more snowy peaks of Italy. I turn ninety degrees to make my final click, feeling my waist pinch and my jacket pull. The top of Mont Blanc is still visible.

"Dan, we are going to get help. I've marked our spot. I know exactly where you are. Not sure how quickly we can get back, but if it's not tonight we need you to hang in there till morning." Nothing.

"Dan do you hear? Maybe the morning." He lifts an arm and rolls his head; his nose is exposed but nothing more.

"Think strong thoughts Dan. Hold on to Bepe. Hold him in your arms tonight. Ethan wants to meet you tomorrow. I will bring him to your wedding next week if you want. Hold on to them Dan," I implore him.

"It will all be over soon. Love you Dan. You hang on in there; keep as warm as you can. Can you hear me Dan?" He lifts his arm gingerly again; his right seems trapped.

Time and light slip away. I turn and start the climb behind the others. No one else has offered him any words; they skulk away.

He had better come out of the hole he has dug. He never gave me any reaction last night. What will Ethan be to him? What have we all done here?

CHAPTER 40

Dan 16.04

Merciless back pain. Oh Mercy Mercy me. That's it, the last one.

I can move now but waves of chill reach my insides. Chill, chill, Big Chill, William Hurt. I am in pain, but the pain will be over soon, over soon, one way or another. Lord have mercy on me. I shiver to generate heat but don't feel it. I slip off a glove and reach inside my jacket pocket. I pull the iPhone right up to my eyes and hit W.

Number 7. "What's Going On" by Marvin Gaye.

Marvin Gaye pleads to mothers around the world to stop the rot. Then he pleads to theirs sons to do likewise as there are too many brothers dying. Is this English brother dying? Marvin's pastor dad, too harshly judging his son's life, shot him in his prime. What's going on now Marvin? I am only glad he didn't live to see the state of things now. Ruining this world. I feel a little flush of warmth at realising I have had my own hand in it. What have we left my sons; my God what have we left you? This feeling is temporarily good as it deflects my mind from the real source of pain. But it is all too late; too late in its thinking. I didn't do enough to stop this.

I try to count the cost of my fall. Maybe I have a busted back, a broken right hip, a broken right arm. I certainly have an overfull bladder. The bladder, the bladder I can't hang on for much longer. Have mercy on pee. I am alive though. I have a chance.

Concentrate now. Thoughts are trains for moving past my pain; get on the train through pain. Anything that I can manage to concentrate on deflects pain or cold. I have one ski on and one ski is gone. The back tip of my left ski supports my foot, pushing it up at forty-five degrees, stretching my hamstring. My bodyweight is on my jammed right arm and immobile hip; I half-face the twenty-foot ice wall that imprisons me. Snow compacts under my left elbow and it drops an inch. Another ineffectual shiver ends in my free right boot. I am stable so don't dare look down behind me; hold onto this security for now. Sun is still up top, but it can't strike me here. My mind races around my body looking to feel warmth. My diaphragm works hard, stoking the heat in my chest. Mercy, leniency; I am not dead from the impact, but can I escape? Am I doomed to let the ice trap soak up my life force? Juliet will sort them out I am sure.

The shivering won't stop now. It starts from my right arm and bum cheek. The cold is unbearable. How many times must I say that before I am rescued; every minute of the night? Maybe it is half four now; a couple of hours till dark. Maybe I can last till then, but overnight? I lift my head and push my jacket hood underneath. My teeth clatter more. I won't look down behind me. This celebration of my new life has been a disaster; merciless. The only relief is being away from the stags. A further shot of pain in my right arm dares me to move it. I get a shot of pins and needles, but its out. It's not broken. However, I am lying flat on my back onto ice. Still I don't look left.

Focus on the mundane, it can be sublime. I remember Bepe as I hugged him on the road last Wednesday. He emanated warm milk and Jammie Dodgers, like the sweetness of fresh bread. He finished them as we left the car, pointing at the red packet as I lifted him out of his seat. "Dodgers," he exclaimed, expecting me to add the rest. Kids haven't suffered the accumulation of life and plaque to pollute their breath. Did I let him down? I can't see Ethan at all, what life has he got? I knew Juliet and I were connected.

"Noooo. Aaaagh." I rail against the pain. I shuffle alternately from left bum cheek to right, holding as much of my body off the ice as possible. I conduct this ice dance with increasing frequency; a few minutes on each side becomes thirty seconds. Each time I feel the tug on my jacket as it rips away from the frozen ice it is attached to.

I stir up increased mental pain to combat the physical. The fear as the snowboarder ran towards me on the railway bridge the other night.

The lash of Robert's tongue serving out more embarrassment. The constant fear of losing my job as Max invents ever more complex deceits to motivate me. I taste the prostitute's make up and the burning of stomach acid and red wine in my throat. Being asked to marry Sophia by my father-in-law; what a jerk I am. I would love all of them again.

My right arm has some feeling again; I strike my knuckles on the wall to re-focus. It's me who has let me down most. For the first time I let all of my back rest on the snow and just soak up the pain.

I almost lost my son a few days ago and now he risks losing me. I gained a new son yesterday and nothing occurred to me to stop today. I hit the ice wall again with my right fist but the glove keeps me from harm. I have to talk to them. I take off my right glove again, putting the open end on my nose and it bellows unexpected warmth onto my nose. My iPhone and headphones were back inside my jacket, with a half-eaten Snickers. I bite the bar three times before any breaks off. I chew it through involuntary chattering. I push an earpiece into each ear scraping the skin. I press the Voice Memo application.

"Bepe, Ethan, my boys… my boys, it's a struggle." I pause after a few words biting my inner lips to damp the shivers.

"You don't know me… but I hope you can hear this." What do you hope for Dan?

"You may hear…" this message at some point in the future when I am long gone or I may grow old with you both having never heard it. I can't bring myself to say anything like that as I am incapacitated anyway.

"I just want you both to know… stuff bout life…about me." I need to tell them something especially as I may have no life left.

I pluck up the courage to tilt my head left. Nothingness roars up at me; black spills from its depths. My heart tumbles into its darkness; I make to cry.

Mercy indeed. I have escaped death when it was a much easier target. The body width of this ice ledge holds me and I am eternally grateful. I have dodged the bullet.

Right now, I must speak up for my boys. I hit record again "Number one. Have a passion… mine was music…"

CHAPTER 41

Juliet 16.04

"HOW DO YOU MOTIVATE A MAN?"

Panting; side step; heavy panting; side step; gravel-voiced panting.

My right thumbnail catches onto the cotton lining of my glove; how did it snap? Maybe when I planted the pole to mark Dan's resting place? It courses annoyance through my body. Fibres lodge defiantly into the nail, wedging further into the jagged gap. I draw my thumb away but it won't release. Despite the gloomy light I can see the depression it causes by dragging the glove skin inward.

We are climbing back up the slope away from the departing sun. Five bodies trudge up towards amber light on higher ground. The nail rips further as I extend my only pole.

Oh Dan, when did you become so inept? Hold on there; hold on to that ledge, I will get Ethan to you. If I have let you down over the last eighteen years at least I can do that.

"Where the fuck are we headed again? You can't use a tourist map to navigate mountains." And have you any alternative Robert?

Everyone stops; lactic acid builds in our muscles. Walking sideways and upwards hyper-extends knees and calves. It is only stopping that brings dull pain.

"We made a plan; we don't have alternatives." Johnny and Steve witness me try to shout him down again.

"Even if this hut thing is up there, it will probably be some empty wooden shack."

"The brochure says it's a hostel type place. It's peak season so they

211

probably have someone still there. Climbers or someone," Johnny counters.

"It cannot be too far. It's the only plan we have. Look, the photo on the map shows a rocky outcrop above us like this one." I am convinced of our broad direction, but Robert raises enough doubt in me to wonder.

"Maybe we can come back for Dan tonight?" Steve suggests naively.

"Of course we can. We should make it into town for his last night out I reckon. Maybe I can get Dan to shaft that prossie after all, instead of throwing up on her," Robert mocks disgustingly.

"Is she any good? That's what I want to know. Despite being surrounded by pussies for the last few days, I quite fancy some myself." Max asks Robert. They roll eyes and laugh to themselves. He presumably has the required amorality to see it through.

"We have to save him." Steve feels the weight of events on his shoulders. His voice squeaks and alerts me to imminent tears, but I can't see behind his sunglasses. He knows he can't lose it in front of his male companions. He is now the weakest link: the zeta male.

"Dan's fine, stop bleating. He has probably nipped down to the bottom of the crevasse for that chocolate I tossed him." Max continues to blank out blame; cancerous behaviour deemed benign.

Johnny fears the loss of his friend too much to engage with anyone.

The fading sunlight works against us. I check my rough bearings on the inadequate map, hopefully for the last time. I visualise the Refuge, maybe an hour's walk away. If we bear up the slope but keep right we should get there with a steep bit at the end.

What is it with these guys? Either dumb struck with fear or arrogantly oblivious to the disasters they have created. A path of humility in-between seems impossible. I don't believe any of them. Their self-belief is either over or under calibrated to hide acts of contrition and delusion. They are all trapped in their own drama. They just cannot let themselves see a bigger one with their friend on the edge of life. But none of it helps anyone; in a time of a crisis they underestimate the threat.

I pull my single pole from the snow; ripping a bigger gap in the jagged nail. Snow falls from each ski as I strike out for Dan and Ethan.

It is turning crustier as it hardens out of the sunlight; sometimes giving and breaking into softer snow underfoot, sometimes holding despite me taking my full body weight on one leg.

We plough on; side step, side step, shuffle, shuffle. Sometimes heaviness in my legs dictates a shuffle forward. I watch my skis, not the scenery. I strike out in hope and sometimes can't bear to lift my head in case that is dashed.

I once watched the sun go down on Uluru in Australia. You realise how inattentive your mind is, unable to comprehend a slow lessening of light. Occasionally you wake up long enough to realise that it has slipped away. The same happens here, so much effort pumped into our legs that you feel robbed when you do look up and see how much mountain there is and how little sun. What will Dan be seeing now, his last sunlight?

"Johnny, have you got plans for Dan's last night of freedom next Friday?" I ask Johnny to focus him.

"Just a quiet one… going to some pubs… in Chester, just me and Dan." He pants between steps but the sentence crumbles, as he no longer feels able to pretend.

"I would love to join you."

"When will you let him be? He is marrying someone else next week." Max badly misinterprets my intent. He strides past me by virtue of his longer legs. Robert gives a forced grin as he stretches to get past. Their cold hearts beat icily.

"Let's wait for Steve." I pause and Johnny does likewise. My eyes readjust to even less light. No crevasses appear to impede our way ahead. Steve seems to see treachery all around. Every step is the click of the trigger against an empty chamber; raising the chance of breaking through to an imagined crevasse below.

"Keep in our tracks Steve and you will be safe."

"Yeah mate. We will get out of this no problem." Johnny encourages his progress but neither of us reaches him. Every step hesitantly picked out by some fractured measure of probability of a fall. He reaches us but looks shot.

"Don't worry about those two jerks. I know exactly the direction to head." I doubt if they have a clue other than up.

"Juliet… Juliet. For fuck's sake Juliet," Robert shouts at us from fifty yards ahead.

"We aren't leaving anyone behind you arse."

"Juliet you…" He is stepping down the hill towards us. The weakness of his legs propels him faster.

I mentally sink at the prospect of more confrontation. This knight has held her sword too long; it clunks to the floor.

He reaches me with fierce humility on his face. "Juliet you were right. We will get there." I fall under his weight. He squeezes me across the shoulders and kisses me aggressively on the lips. I now know he doubted we were ever getting off the mountain.

"Come on children, let's get going." Arms go aloft in celebration. Johnny and Steve step up in unison behind Robert. I follow and see two glorious beaming windows of artificial light from a small hut way above us; giving our eyes the chance to recalibrate the greyness around us.

"We may get to Chamonix for a pint after all." Steve recovers his sense of delusion and has one arm around his boss Max.

"I'm having some chocolate to celebrate," Robert adds. I note that he never volunteered to throw that to Dan. "We will be lucky to get there by six. It's up to an hour away. We can see less and less." Robert estimates.

"Let's be having you!" Robert treats the Refuge De Requin as his discovery.

I breathe new life. Ethan's presence elsewhere boosts me up the hill.

"We will get him out now won't we?" Johnny asks.

"We've got every chance." Our best chance is to rescue him tonight, which is unrealistic.

Why can't we go faster? We eat up space in leg-length chunks. I belatedly take off redundant sunglasses. At first we seem to just be moving around the hut at the same distance but then we get closer. No one considers what we may find there; shelter is our only hope. Proximity is being traded for the light we need. The shape of the hut gets no clearer.

Robert booms out a rousing chorus from an English rugby song. He is devouring the space; his rescue is almost realised. I keep the others in touch with Robert. Ethan must meet his father. The time is right to unite them.

What time is it? I haven't looked because of the hassle of getting out my phone. It's five thirty. I can distinguish outlines well enough. Robert and I start to traverse the slope alone, after instructing the others to wait. The unison of our shuffle leaves us without breath. Neither Robert nor I exchange an expression; we know we have to make this happen.

Where is the hut? Suddenly we cannot see the hut from any angle. Inexplicably we have lost sight of the lighted windows, as we get nearer. I had hoped for a progressive climb to the refuge, but the terrain becomes uncompromisingly steep.

What the hell is in front of us? My brain shifts and I recoil slightly as an ice cliff sheers up at me. Its physicality makes me topple back a step. Desperately my eyes try to pick out its form, but it seems impassable.

"You re-trace our steps and find where that fucking hut has gone. I will walk along here and find a way up." Robert says anxiously.

I work my way back to the others, checking over my shoulder every two steps to see when the hut re-appears.

"Why are you coming back?" Steve is close to breaking point.

"The hut must be on top of a cliffside. As we get closer it disappears," I explain.

"It's on that rock face over to our right."

"Did you factor in a rock climb before bedtime Juliet?" Max chides. He, like Robert, perceives no barrier, they are almost off the hook.

"Let's keep going guys. We've got to stay positive. There may be a path up when we get there," Johnny implores.

"Yes, sure." I don't convince myself. I have been looking down; my heads swims as I search the horizon for shape. I see the small window of light from the hut again, but in the darkness it blinds everything in that direction. Give it up for mercy's sake. We have suffered enough banality and brutality this week. Please let us go, please. Let us rescue all souls from this brutal occasion.

We press on towards Robert and the ice. The steepness of the cliff in front of us can't properly be judged, nor its composition.

"Help me!" shouts Steve, "Help me." The second request fades; the ice in front of us eats it up.

I anxiously rip off my ski gloves to assist him. A deep chunk at the top of my thumbnail comes with it. My whelp starts as an expression of surprise pain. It ends as a cry of exasperation.

Could we be rescued from here? The distance isn't the problem. We are fifty feet under the hut, close enough to hold a conversation with anyone there. But there appears no reason for anyone to do so. We may as well be with Dan in his crevasse.

The men around me howl abrasively, the pack of wolves baying for relief. Steve prays on his knees. Robert throws a ski pole at the wall. It hits the ice cliff abruptly and falls to ground, now we can what is set in front of us. Even the wolves have limits; every thought produces the same stark outcome. However tantalisingly close, we are abandoned. They had no comfort for the prospective newly wed, but have to respect our plight.

It is not the woman who is wailing. I may wish for a hand to pluck me to up to safety on the ledge, but screaming won't make that happen. They moan in despair and guilt. We have found our way here but I need to find a way back to Ethan.

CHAPTER 42

Dan 17.52

Focus on the light to get me back to my boys.

"Number one. Have a passion boys... mine was music. I could play but listened better... Music locates you. Whatever... pick something you can share with others... Maybe I let music exclude me." I pause again for my teeth chatter to die away.

I shift onto my side to give my back the chance to warm.

"Number two. Think. Think brilliantly. Think... Thoughts are things." A fading pink blanket still burns visible on the mountain tops. Sun long gone from view, leaving today's crime scene red-handed. My sunset? I will myself into that light.

"Create your own reality. I spend too much time creating for capitalists..."

Non-stop now, my shuddering body is racked with the jitters. Maybe it will create my warmth and be my salvation? My right ski anchors me in roughly the same spot. No room.

"She's as cold as ice. He's as cold as ice." Both things shriek in my head. Again and again they take my focus. "He's as cold as ice." I'm sure now. Guinness Ice, Bud Ice, this ice, that ice.

I realise I am still recording. "Number three. What was number three? Magnificent Seven I think. No take responsibility boys... I have to face up now... Get married... love you. Face up boys. Take responsibility for your self, your kids... don't blow it. Don't blow it.

I hear the iPhone chirrup. There is no power left, it has been drained away more in the extreme cold. In my jacket pocket, put the phone in my pocket. I struggle but it slips into my jacket just as it has done a hundred times in the past few days.

Wrap up. Zip up. I have had my right hand exposed for too long and my jacket open at the top.

I hear feet I am sure. Pitter-patter. Pitter-patter. Light feet I'm sure.

Sophia, Sophia. I shudder to think when I last thought of her. Marrying her, marrying her. Life with or without me? All I see is her future anger. Anger at the lunacy that got me here. Anger at cancellation. Her day, her dad's doing. Sophia calm down, calm… A wave takes over. My extreme chattering chips an incisor, I ingest ivory.

Those boys, the boys, the men, the stags. Johnny will remember me. Johnny will cherish me. Where are they? The Aiguilles is too far for them to get back to. They have pushed me too far. Where could they go? Will they take care of Juliet? Robert and Max will keep themselves alive.

Where is the edge now? Can't look, must not look.

Feet dance into fresh snow above me and stop. Is someone up there? Not human, no chance. Rabbit, fox or maybe a bear?

Sophia and Bepe will just stay with her parents now. There will be no new house for us, no new nuclear family formed. Not needed, superfluous. I can't shake this wave off. Numb from shoulder blades to calf. Sweet Bepe will be lost in over compensation, he is a brat in the making even now. I am losing him to that already. Ethan is lost to me. Never recover now. What was Juliet thinking? Pushing me, pushing buttons.

"Aaaah!" The sound scampers down the wall and loops back. I am surprised at the noise even though it was mine. My left elbow had fallen away and I panicked. I shuffle right towards the wall. I push my right shoulder up to it. I will be vibrated off the ledge by my chattering. Can't sleep now; have to control it or let myself go. But I am so tired of the shaking, tired and aching.

Walking again, that is no rabbit at the lip. A fox? How hungry? He's thinking of me. My god he wouldn't. A wolf? An easy jump but no way back up, but can he calculate that? The black figure turns and scampers back above my head from view.

Pitch black and sadness fills the gaping hole. Two, three figures are back, weighing up the jump.

"Nooo…aaagh!" I scream at them. Preserve yourself, self-preservation… society.

"Aaaaagh!" Has the desired effect. The horizon is clear but I'm not on it.

Pitch black. A shudder rises. Uncontrollable jerks start at my back and arms and flow to my feet. I somehow relish the sensation of being pounded on the ice; it stimulates warmth.

It's not enough; I've not been good enough. I am the boy who didn't cry wolf. My shudder fades out. I have been my worst enemy, my lousy defence. Best to let it be.

CHAPTER 43

Juliet 17.52.

"WHY IS IT ALWAYS A WOMAN?"

Their noise has gone. No more fighting, enough now. I am fighting for breath but know the next one will come.

There is blood on the snow but I am no killer. It is my blood and I am a saviour. Salvation is close.

Why am I praying? On my knees and shins in the snow as I hold my body together in a ball. I cradle my sore arms, that were almost ripped from my body. My shins are screaming cold. An exploding heart beats in my ears. It's stopped now. Ethan is close. Elbows dig my calves as I huddle all the pieces of my body back together. Breasts snug against thighs. Holding my kneecaps, I rock for warmth, but such pain. Shoulders scream of distress; one pull away from dislocation. God has had a hand in it; but I have had both. I have so much life to save now, so much to rescue from itself.

The window light restores sight. Why am I holding back? Light streams around me, great strands of it. I lift my head to see the source of the blood. My palms are exposed through my gloves. The wounds leak blood consistently. I cleanse them with snow. Blood drips into the substantial kidney-shaped pool in front of me. A pair of palm prints to my right trace the last parts of my crawl. Just stay here a while. Suspend your life for a moment. My body is intact and I have a soul that's clean. I feel such a roar gathering. Take this moment to release.

The wooden door is within easy reach. I push onto all fours and recover myself to stand. Blood being called to my core makes my first steps wobbly. It is my upper body that screams, but I still stumble. No call bell here. Two stone steps later I elect to fall against the wooden door and cause an alerting thump. The bump in the night brings no response. I reach for a rock at the foot of the steps and bring it in one motion to the door, clattering into the metal door catch. I won't fail here. Each effort brings life.

After a neat click overhead, the rock flies from my hand when it doesn't meet the expected door.

"*Merde. Hal, Hal!*" is shouted back into the building.

I rest my eyes. Job done. I grimace to fight back a cry but my eyelids leak.

Within seconds I am pulled from the doorway. Strong arms lock into the back of my knees and behind my back; swept in like the newly wed bride I have never been. Laid on a table now. I hear metal bowls hit the stone floor.

"*Regardez-moi. Vous avez mal quelque part?*" A full-faced beard hides a man of maybe thirty years. He seems so sure of what he is doing I don't want to interrupt him.

"*Je vois que vous vous êtes blessée aux mains, mais vous avez mal ailleurs?*"

"*Elle vient d'où ?*" There are maybe three people who have joined him.

"*Vous êtes toute seule?*" I think he's asking me if I'm alone. I shake my head.

I remember the howling at the foot of the ice cliff. Robert attempted to climb the wall and slid down within a minute. Max and Steve offered desperate and less frequent screams.

It was Johnny who helped me. I started to bend my remaining ski pole in two. He managed to finally snap it.

"Get us all out of here Juliet." He handed me the shortened pole handle and the bottom end with the ski basket, in great faith. And so my climb began, with the stiffer re-freezing ice taking the poles readily.

Although all hope hinged on me I could feel male smirking on my back; that bint will never make it. After five clean holds from the poles the group fell quiet. Hope had sprung to smother fear. The slope was steep but steady. I kicked footholds in the snow and etched others out with the pole. Half way up there was no banter. Grudging support sustained me. Before long I had fallen onto the beaten path to this door. Gravity had sustained me.

"I am with five others. *Oui, cinq hommes.* Under the Refuge. Below here. No, there are four others, only four. One is lost." The whole roomed clatters. Torches, ropes, zips, belays, crampons, helmets.

"Is your guide dead?" someone asks, but I shake my head. These men seize the chance to help without being asked. This manhood bursts out into the night.

I am safely abandoned; exhaustion means I don't protest and go to help. I am sat in a clumsy wooden chair smothered in sleeping bags; my weariness seeps into it. The fire is waning; it expects to be left to fizzle out. The solidity and steadiness of the stone and oak refuge, its shelter and normality, stand up calmly to the fierce nature outside. My core is impenetrable at first but gradually re-admits warmth. Blissful silence again. Every man departed, except those in my heart. Shivering stops me from sleeping.

SUNDAY 19TH APRIL 2009

CHAPTER 44

Juliet 05.45.

"IS THERE HOPE FOR A MAN?"

God sped me through the darkness. I will hold Ethan too tightly tonight; my head pressed onto his chest hearing the booming heartbeat I created. He will flush at his mum's desperation but welcome it easily.

Where is the door, by my side or at the foot of the bed? I have no sense of orientation. No light through yonder window breaks. My blackberry says 05.45 local time and shows 107 emails that I refuse to acknowledge but couldn't anyway. Souped-up work dramas await me tomorrow. Should I suspend Charles for his wandering hands? When can Primark see me on Monday afternoon? Should we bother lowering our day rate just to get on a six-month contract? How can we achieve a step change in margin without changing the headline rate to clients? These questions occupy me but never engage me; my dispassion is lauded as a strength.

Why am I the only one awake? Is Dan awake or unable to sleep with the cold? Is he taking in the morning through hyperventilating lungs, cursing his misfortune? I hope he is occupied thinking about Ethan and his impending marriage.

No noise in the Refuge de Requin. No one stirs, not a begrudging owner nor an expectant climber. I waited up for all the sheep to come in last night. Robert and Max came in together, nonchalantly knocking the standard of accommodation. They fraudulently talked beyond thoughts of the danger they had faced. It was midnight when Johnny was brought in. He had replaced Dan as the misguidedly generous host having given

225

the others priority. Steve was already asleep by then; the first one relayed up the slope because of his distress. He stared at the fire I had enlivened, sat on the stone floor at my feet, hugging my legs. He nervously swept the corners of his mouth on my ski pants, his bristles scraping the nylon.

"Steve. Take care of yourself for now. We will do our best for Dan." Without acknowledgement he rolled onto his right side into the foetal position.

I called Chris at the hotel when everyone except his brother was safe. He said less than Steve.

"You must call the family Chris. I would do but I can't from here. We will rescue him at first light. We have a helicopter coming. Have faith and give it to your mum, and Sophia…" I know it's beyond him. Maybe he will call his mother and let her spread the news that her son is in mortal danger. Let a woman cope with another woman. The collective word for females is that of a "woe man", that never occurred to me before. This would have been a male take on our disposition if it were intended.

"No, no, no," Chris repeated as if he had failed to guide a lamb safely away from a cliff edge.

I elect to be the first noise. Light shifts up the valley. I have saved them; I must save Dan. I pull back the thin curtain material. I knock the room chair over, maybe on purpose. I wash my underarms and between my legs with the postage stamp of soap and scratch them dry with a thin overused towel. Sweat has cooled in my clothes, moulding them for me to put on again.

I clatter down a flight of wooden steps, heels of ski boots clunking, open boot fastenings rattling. Claude the owner topples three plates onto the table: ham, salami, Gruyere.

"*Bon matin*. Thank you and your friends again for your help. Will the helicopter fly okay?"

"There is nothing to stop it." Claude ambles to the unlit window. He must be able to read weather systems in the dark. A small layer of light blue enters from the bottom of the window the longer I stare at it. The sun is rising to our rescue.

"Great news, thanks so much for calling them."

"You will pay for this." In what way Claude?

"Don't you think he will survive?"

"Maybe not. Only with big strength will he survive. In the head, in his mind." Claude has outlined Dan's biggest challenge. "No. You will pay for your lost friend?" I see that he was really asking how we were going to pay for the rescue helicopter.

"All of us will pay." We may pay twice.

"About a thousand Euros, no?" He advises me, clearly not considering the cost of human life.

"We must get to him before the helicopter arrives."

"No, no. You must not make more mistakes. I have arranged Hal and Jacques to get you down the mountain." Two heads appear, leaning back from their bench, nodding their chewing faces to acknowledge me. They had all come down silently before me. Without knowing, I suspect Jacques is the man who opened the door to me last night. I feel uneasy, reminded of my proximity to disaster.

"Hey Jules. That was amazing what you did. Climbing a seventy-degree ice cliff with two broken ski poles, awesome. Are you a climber?" Hal seems to have an easy Californian sensibility; Jacques looks at me with thunder in his eyes. I move to sit opposite them.

"As soon as the sun is up we are out of here. Got a day's climb to fit in as well." Hal insists.

"Where are my friends?" I ask Claude, doubting whether they are.

"*Chambres cinq, neuf, dix, quatorze.*" Was that last one fourteen? I clatter back up the stairs and knock sharply on all the doors. Max opens immediately and comes down with me.

Back at the table Max joins in "We did okay last night. These guys took turns to come down on a rope and abseil us back up. You couldn't see where your feet went. The snow collapsed but we got through it." His adventure is expressed without considering my own more difficult experience.

Carbs and coffee pick me up further. Johnny brings Steve down. We all settle across the bench from Hal and Jacques.

"L'Anglais sont si arrogants." Jacques is pissed off with us. No one looks at anyone else except me.

"Ils n'ont aucun respect pour la montagne. Ces abrutis d'Anglais. On va rater une journée d'escalade à cause d'eux. Sans doute qu'ils n'ont pas d'autre moyen d'aider leur ami. Ils m'écoeurent." He knows we don't understand but I comprehend. He is berating us for risking ourselves on the mountain without a guide.

"Claude says you will guide us back to our friend. We are so grateful."

"Yes, but where is your guide?" Jacques doesn't have my language difficulty. "You come to my mountain. You have no preparation. You have no experience. You risk avalanche. You lose your friend. You don't know where he is. Yes, I love to help you people. If I hadn't come for water I would not hear the door and you would all be little English popsicles. You don't care for life." His delivery is emphatic, but he looks over my shoulder to avoid eye contact. Robert appears at the column at the top of the table, smiling behind our challenger.

"That maybe true, but I know exactly where Dan is. I have a GPS location; I have pictures of the mountains where we left him and I have marked the spot with my other ski pole. We may make mistakes."

"Causing trouble as usual Juliet? Is this garlic-injecting Neanderthal trying to get in your pants or is he just getting on your tits?" Robert arrives refreshed.

I have seen this before. I once insulted a bouncer at the Mud club on Tottenham Court Road, with Dan loyally tugging me away. When Dan hit the pavement and skidded under a parked car, the obvious lesson was that when a man needs to lash out, most luckily he can't hit a woman. There was real shock on Robert's face when he crashed across the cheese and meat table; so rarely are his insults met. One clean punch to the chin from Jacques was unsuspected.

"I rescue you and you give me this. Outside, we go." Jacques stands up and saunters past the stricken Robert.

"Hey guys. Keep him sweet. He has passed up his day's climb for you. Let's get to your friend and hope for the best, hey." Hal smoothes the tension and follows Jacques onto the wooden veranda. White light at the windowsill; azure blue is in the window's centre.

Robert peels Gruyere from his shoulder and places it on his plate. He rearranges the spread and returns to our table a broken man. Facing people down orally is one thing, showing everyone that he doesn't possess the physical prowess to back it up has made us all see through him.

Our group stares intently at the table. We silently give thanks we are alive; starting to realise the enormity of the hole we face if Dan isn't.

"Guys. Dan is with us; he's hanging on waiting for us. You were all hand picked as his best men; so let's all show him he is special to us now. I came here to tell him I had his child when we were living together, my son Ethan. I had to tell him before his wedding so it didn't cause future upset. Look, we have all let him down so far, but not now. The chopper will be up from the valley floor soon; we have to locate him on the ground. Max, Steve, Johnny, let's go outside. Robert, come as soon as you can."

We assemble our abandoned gear on the veranda. The sun makes a burnt halo over the eastern tips of the Alps. We can't look directly towards it.

"As soon as she comes over that ridge properly we will go. It will be hard crust so take it easy. Jacques will lead; I will be the tail. Give Jacques your phone. If anyone can get that GPS location he can." Hal forms a bridge between the group.

"You English fall in line now? *Alons-y!*" shouts Jacques gliding down the trail leading away from Refuge.

CHAPTER 45

Dan 06.58.

Handbills frantically dance across my face, whipped across the night sky by the downdraft of aircraft engines. They make wing-like fluttering sounds as they flock around me. I catch one and hold it up towards the light of the plane ahead of me. VERBOTEN is hand stamped on it across a swastika, as the lights catch the edge of the rough imperfect paper pulp.

I know a plane is nearing as it rips a bigger space in the sky, both with light and noise. It's coming all right, buffeted by the bills I stand in defiance of the truth. Stand up to this one now; something tells me to stay put. The engine echoes against something, a hanger maybe, the engine betrays an older more imperfect age of flight as they rip and roar satisfyingly. Hang on, is it landing or taking off? Another handbill glues to my cheek; three more rip paper cuts into my left hand. This one advertises ByeFly; my inane words scatter across it in the name of the kings of cheap flights.

I have power here. Everyone looking on expects me to run but I know better. For once I am sure. A pink break in the clouds on the horizon leaks from behind the plane. I listen intently for a change in ferocity of sound and light but they seem constant. With my eyes closed I still can't tell. Let it be taking off please, just get out of here will you? Prove my strength right this time. To my right is a wooden gallery, full of trench-coated wearing reporters waiting to judge. I hope their flashes fade with no image worth capturing. It feels like a time when truth will out.

The engines race towards a take-off, yes a take-off. I am to feel the force no more. The sound closes down into a more singular rasp now; a more closed noise intent on delivering flight. Bills are birds now, the whitest doves searching for a way out of the air pocket that pounds us all. I grab a bird one handed, his shifting eyes tell me he is anxious to leave. I turn and throw him away towards the gallery; off balance I fall over. My right shoulder takes the impact as the bird is sucked up into oblivion above me.

I am on the tarmac as the plane leaves sight. I liked its reassuring force, but it dissipates with every second. I was right to stay. The photographers have gone, abandoned hats and cameras strewn on the steps. I can enjoy the air on my skin as it settles again. The intense cold of the tarmac remains; I cannot distinguish between the pains in each of my body parts.

… Dead cold…

…It's morning…

…Sharp breath stabs…

…No animals above…

…Morning…

…Hand on chest…

…Dare not move…

…It's morning…

…Just drop off…

…Just go.

CHAPTER 46

Juliet 07.52.

"CAN A MAN SURVIVE?"

"There's my pole! There it is." I scream, my high pitch revealing my expectation it would be lost.

Jacques' legs take on new purpose; elegant pushes take him on a direct track across the untouched snow. He breaks the crusty top layer creating a virtual railroad track for us all to ski. Clear blue sky, rising sun, but we feel no heat yet. We speed up but still fall well behind. He manoeuvres directly above Dan, throwing himself to the ground on his chest. He is talking to him. My god he is alive. Married in a wheelchair maybe? Will he have a ring finger? But he will be married next week. He has to get married, he has to.

As I arrive Jacques is sitting up talking into a radiophone, presumably guiding in the mountain rescue team. Part of me resists the conclusion of what I might see if I look over. Is he there at all? He's there; except for his flatter right ski Dan hasn't moved. Conserving his energy? Maybe just waking up? Does it take longer in hypothermia? Has he signalled to Jacques? Come on Dan, something. We have to get him out; we have betrayed him here.

"*Non, aucun movement. On voit sa tête et ses mains. On peut l'atteindre avec une échelle. Pas trop d'espoir, mais ces idiots sont assurés.*"

"Hey Frenchie, what's the score? Is my mate alive?" Robert pushes past; our synthetic jackets brush each other with a swish. He unclips his skis and starts to shout into the crevasse. "Dan, you lanky git, are you okay?"

"*Arrête-là!*" Jacques breaks off from the call to shout at Robert.

"What do you mean? I will look out for my friend if I want to."

"No. *Arrête.* Stop there you idiot."

Robert is enraged. "I will do what…" With the phone cradled into his ear by his shoulder he clasps Robert's leg and snaps his right ski back on as if manipulating a puppet.

Taking the phone from his ear, he shouts. "Everyone. Ground unstable. You must keep them skis on. You must stay back now…" Robert dutifully clips the second ski back on having fallen foul of his own safety advice.

"Okay, okay, you will see. Over…" The valley dampens the rumble of the rescue helicopter. Each rotation of the blade brings relief. A potential solution is rising through the valley. Oh please let them do it.

"Dan, Dan, mate," Johnny breathlessly calls out, but his fear takes all meat from his voice; it is the pained cry of a loved one. Still no movement but words are drowned. The red helicopter rises into view. We have all seen the Hollywood scene, but we are living the rescue. I can watch that movie again.

Someone can do the rescue better than me now. Two men rip out of the sliding door, carrying a rolled up metal ladder, heading straight to Jacques. Within seconds of assessment, the ladder is being secured into flat ice well away from the edge; the second rolls it over and follows it. I watch him kneel beside Dan; checking for a pulse on Dan's neck, for the warmth of his breath.

He stands with a distinct thumb up. Johnny and I hug each other in hope, but realise he may have only signalled for the stretcher.

Jacques has made it down the ladder to help. They barely have room to flatten the stretcher, but they lift Dan on all the same. Straps cocoon him. With everyone back up the ladder, the two helicopter men raise Dan from the crevasse and lay him on the ground beside us. He skin is grey blue; a cut has matted black hair on the back right side of his head. Ice has formed on his sideburns and lips.

We all remember Dan again. No longer a desperate suspended memory; now a fragile life before us. Robert collapses to his knees, arms tucked into his thighs. He rocks at Dan's side screaming to him above the noise of the chopper. He grabs Dan's arm and shakes him, pleading for resolution.

"Waiting did you say? Waiting for what Dan?" Dan's lack of response is crucifying him. Robert's behaviour had reached a crescendo, a build up that requires a fall.

"Let him go. Let them take him you idiot." Max shoves Robert roughly away from the stretcher, sending him sprawling. We see two ghosts, one broken by nature, the other by himself. Dan's ghost is picked up and pushed into the chopper.

"You must go now," Jacques shouts into my ear from behind. I pull out the ski pole I left behind. Crystals have formed most of the way up the stem, so it takes some persuasion.

"No, no. On the helicopter, you go with him." Jacques holds out a gloved hand that I take. He kisses me on both cheeks. "You have saved him. You saved all of them." I am knocked back by his simple but apparent conclusion.

"But the others? How will they get down the Vallée?" Jacques points to himself and Hal. He puts one arm around my shoulder, pushes my head down and we run under the rotor blades.

CHAPTER 47

Juliet 09.49

"HOW DOES LIFE GO ON?"

The helicopter door slams with a categorical "whoomph". It cuts me off from the other sources of this wholly male melodrama, all of who stare forlornly at me through the window.

I am alone with a sober Dan for the first time since my revelation. Ignoring the helicopter seats, I kneel alongside his stretcher. More importantly he is alive. How did he survive this ordeal? He is strapped down for the journey, loosely draped in one light blanket. The doctor goes to work; he checks Dan's eyes, his pulse and each part of his body without moving him. The results cause a deep frown. The doctor looks confused when I pick up another blanket and try to put it over him. "Warm slow, very slow," he advises.

"You made it Dan." I talk to a silver-grey frozen face, which matches the lack of response.

"We can get you to Ethan and Bepe now." Keep motivating him.

"We will both be at the wedding next week if you want." His fragility is in stark contrast to the prospect of the tumult of a wedding. But he is alive.

The rotor blades intensify and my stomach is pulled skyward. We bank away from the group below. This is an almighty land, blessed with soaring vistas blighted with constant danger. The rotors bring comfort that I am in a balanced world again and the chopper tumbles down the valley. The terrain directly below Dan's fall looks pristine and progressively steep. However, it is followed by a short spurt of massive crevasses. I wonder if we wouldn't have lost yet more of the group; Steve certainly would have crumbled. Stupid Robert, you are such a stupid man.

I have done a good job, no, a great job. I gave hope where there was none. Within seconds I can draw a longer breath of the thin air; I haven't breathed for a day.

The doctor has stopped attending him. I am transported back to the week-long bout of gastroenteritis that he had, he was laid up so badly that I had to take three days off college myself. He sat propped up by cushions and me, sipping vegetable soup. Spilling it repeatedly left a crusty layer at the top of my all-yellow, daisy-print duvet. I feigned illness for three days for him. We watched the last throes of Brookside. He felt cosseted but I felt compromised. I had planned to leave him the previous week when I found out I was pregnant. This helped me decide to leave as I could see a life of this to come; there would always be something with Dan. I could only dump him when he felt better.

The doctor is leaning in between the two seats at the front talking to the pilot. I fear touching him now. It feels like I might break off a limb. Is he resting or in a coma? I take courage and reach for Dan's left hand; the curve of his stony fingers feels like I am holding stone. His fingers are black; no more copywriting by this hand Dan. I remember a chemical hand warmer I have in my pocket and crack it open for my own benefit.

I try to look anywhere but his face so that I am not constantly looking for unfounded life signs. However, loose bloodied headphones are evident in his stone and orange jacket hood. I unzip his coat slightly and his precious iPhone tumbles out with them attached. I carefully place the dead phone in my zipped pocket to await his recovery. What did he use it for last night? Seeking solace from his carefully chosen friends?

We drop down again and follow the now flat valley floor. On the bottom reaches of the glacier, boulders are frequently peppered onto the ice. It is getting quite warm now; sun magnified by glass onto the humans inside. The glacier thins out even more as we bank left over a forest towards Chamonix. The town is intermittently visible on the valley floor below a cloud layer to my right.

"Dan we are minutes away from Chamonix now, minutes away."

The doctor is back at Dan's side, repeating his checks and suddenly shouts. "*Non, non. Merde. Alons-y. Vite!*" He has tried to find a pulse in a wrist, an armpit, and the neck. He starts resuscitation. The glide of our ride has fooled us all. Frantic chest pumps stop suddenly. The doctor only glances at me; he cannot witness my tearful eyes. We have all lost you. Your precious soul lost on a sea of machismo. You let them kill you Dan, you bloody fool.

I can't cry the wail of a lost love but I release something similar. My love for him tightens my lower lip into a clown-like frown; it quivers as I hold a wall of emotion back that I don't need to. You waited too much for this life Dan. Were you waiting for me? You deserved something better Dan. You deserved better than I could give you.

I will be taking him home in a body bag. I will ring Sophia and tell her. We can arrange for funeral directors to meet the plane at Manchester. She won't get her day of reckoning now. I am sure I see the hotel roof as we follow the train track to the helicopter station. An overgrown X marks the spot as we hover and land. Dan is dead on arrival.

CHAPTER 48

Juliet. 15.40

"How does a boy become a father?"

At departure Gate 40 fate plays a farewell trick on us. Am I the only one who realises Dan's age of departure is written large above the heads of the stewardesses at the gate? Forty years, barely half a life Dan.

What a mournful day; endless form filling to confirm a death. We are boarding as planned except Dan isn't in our luggage. I recall waiting with the marginally disappointed party of hens leaving four days ago. It is better she stayed at home than end up like this. They will never know their luck. Hens wouldn't have let this happen. The party would have wanted their share of embarrassment for the bride to be, but nothing more sinister. Stags evidently don't know when to stop.

"Boarding rows 1 to 30 only please. That's 1 to 30 only." I am the only one of our party to make this cut. A stewardess with scrunched-back blonde hair calmly makes the announcement. Every one of her eyelashes stands artificially to attention around her vital green eyes. They flutter and threaten to crack. I let all the others queue in front of me. The unnecessary "I was here first" jostling accompanies the queue. I wonder again what Dan last used the iPhone for? Johnny has re-charged it so we know that isn't lost.

"Give it to me, Robert. I will try again." I request Dan's boarding card and passport.

Everyone looks spent. They have suffered the dual blow of having to ski the remainder of the Vallée Blanche and then finding that their friend was dead when they got back to the hotel. Having had time to become accustomed to his death I was available to comfort most of them. Robert sought nothing from me and has not spoken since we left the hotel two hours ago. He doesn't start now.

A crumpled looking bearded gentleman sporting a worn-in Macintosh and peaked cap is ahead of me. I wonder where Dan was going to sit? A pleasant cool draught of air is released through the boarding tunnel into the stifling waiting area.

They have the boarding cards now and I see a note scribbled and highlighted on the manifest; must be giving them knowledge of my predicament.

"Mr Greenhenge is…" Words fail her.

"You must understand me. He must come home with us or we have to wait for him." Her green eyes strike at me. "You must see our situation," I say again.

"It's too late madam. We know who you are. You cannot get the body released and we cannot accommodate you on any later flight, even tomorrow." I grip the inside sleeves of my jumper and start again.

"But we can't leave my friend here." She pushes both passports back into my right hand but keeps Dan's boarding pass.

"There have to be special arrangements made. Special arrangements you know." She guides me away from the desk where her colleague is calling the next thirty rows.

"I used to go out with him you know. We have a son together, his name is Ethan but he never met his father." It is evident that he won't now.

"I will stay then and sort this out," I resolve.

"Madam. It's just a body now. His soul has flown to god." I didn't mind her sharing her view on what had happened. The pre-school imagery and assumption of my religious belief didn't affront me. Maybe it's the best way to cope at these times.

"He's getting married next week you know. This was his stag weekend. A celebration of Dan's marriage." I don't correct myself but edit the necessary changes in tense in my head.

"We are women, we can do better than this. We are better than this. You must see that; you must call through to the highest authority."

"Get out of the way lady, we are trying to get home here." A man at the head of the queue behind me speaks up for himself and the thirty rows of people stood behind him who are un-amused. No one has boarded since I arrived at the desk.

"Come on lady, get going." An anonymous traveller throws his voice.

"Back off her. My brother is dead and we are trying to go home with him. They won't let us!" Chris booms at the waiting passengers. Heads look to the floor but their bodies still twitch anxiously. Chris's physicality puts any more protest at bay.

"Get Christian on the phone," Robert appears at my shoulder.

"Christian who sir?"

"Why Christian Denslow of course; your CEO. I used to work for him till two weeks ago. It was a personality thing, he just let me go cause he didn't know how to handle me." Robert's revealing speech has no leverage, these girls do nothing of the sort and he melts away.

"Could you leave him? You are a woman. Could you leave him? Let us go later." I further implore. At that moment I feel the futility of it all and can't continue. I am relieved to have tried so hard and still be going home. I have lost power in my voice having asked for a seventh time: twice on the phone, at the check-in desk, with an air steward, with his supervisor and now most weakly twice at this departure gate. We are going home without the stag.

Each step on the tunnel walkway reverberates with a metallic boing.

"You tried. You stood up for Dan. It's been a pleasure to get to know you a little." Johnny catches up with me to soothe me.

"I will have to come back for him." I realise I have taken responsibility for him when probably Sophia will want to.

We settle to seats spread across the plane. The whine of the engines intensifies as we reach the door. I consider how much more substantial a plane feels, weighed up against a helicopter

"Row 28, window seat on your right, Madam." I leave the boys to seat themselves, they don't deserve my attention. They gave Dan too little. Scott and Ethan are the only men in my life. I place my ski jacket overhead. I am glad to get out of it, smelling so sweetly but distinctly of sweat as it does. I had no option but to wear it. By the time we got back to the hotel it was an hour past checkout. The hotel staff had kindly dumped our belongings into whatever luggage and brown paper bags they could find in each room, so they could prepare for new guests. The pre-booked return journey with the shuttle van was only saved after a ten-minute wait for him to be re-called. My arguments with the French medical team about why he hadn't survived were futile. "Warm and dead," they kept on saying; Daniel warming too quickly had killed him. It has all unravelled now. The push back and departure are suspiciously quick; presenting no further opportunity for English dissent.

There is some serenity in our ascent as we leave so much pain and anxiety on the ground. I look down on the spine of the Alps, cast miles away towards Italy. At this height I can still see mountain ski villages. I ponder my ability to reach them from the surrounding peaks. Maybe we are over the Vallée Blanche again but who can tell. I feel a pinch of pride at just being here but grief soon eats that up again.

I wait for the seatbelt sign to go off, before putting on the headphones that Dan wore at his end. I flick his iPhone to life. What was he doing with it, just playing music or did he leave something. Johnny had shown me its Apps and how to flight disable it. The phone App reveals his last calls which were all to Sophia. He has a note: "Pick up rings" is his token reminder. The photos are a strange set of scenes starting inexplicably with a baggage trolley from the airport. Then scenes from Chamonix: the train station; snowy trees; the hotel and lobby; what looks like his dinner on Friday night (his last supper); one of the river he fell into; at the bottom of the Telepherique; ending in some glorious photos at the top of the Vallee. Remarkable memories in his life, taken with a distinct absence. After the picture taken with Bepe and Sophia at the airport and a random picture of his shoes, there is no evidence of himself or indeed anyone being with him. He is wiped clean from his own story. This intrusion into his life shows how much we can get from the modern day digital trail, but also how little.

Finally, I look in music and there in playlists is "Dan's Magnificent Seven." I vow to listen to that after the boys have heard the selection.

The Clash's "Magnificent Seven" and Stevie Wonder's "Another Star" I recognise".

The plane drops a little and I fumble the phone. Suddenly, Prince hoarsely cries out. I rip the earpieces out and press the screen repeatedly to make it stop.

Maybe this one; there is a "Voice Memos", showing a picture of an old style microphone. I record a stupid "testing testing" message but where does it go? I hit a strange button at the bottom and a series of date-stamped memos flash up. One was recorded at 17.52 on 18/04/2009. That was fourteen minutes fifty-two seconds long, another at 18.33 which was twelve minutes thirty-four seconds long. I hesitate to listen, as he is not yet beyond the grave. What if it was recorded specially for Sophia? But what if he thought I might find it and listen? What if he says something stupid to Sophia about Dan and I being in love? She would never get over her grief. Maybe it's for Ethan?

This was his last ordeal of his shambolic fatal trip? I hit the start button.

"*Number one. Have a passion boys... mine was music. I could play but listened better... Music locates you...*"wind catches the speaker and blurs his speech for a couple of seconds. Silence reigns, I imagine he must be readjusting himself on the ledge. This is a slow death. Minutes of breathing, rustling and wind whistling elapse before Dan says "*Number two.*" On the last voice message he eventually says "*Number 3...*" It is excruciating to hear. He starts as usual with good intentions, to pass something of himself onto his boys just in case. He ends by underlining his inability to heed his own advice. Only those with willpower survive; Dan has killed himself.

I realise now that if I hadn't made my odd journey as a stagette, that Dan would have died without knowing about his first-born son.

My sobs flowed easily without consciousness. I looked up at Johnny and the green-eyed stewardess standing in the aisle. They watch over me but don't intervene. Grief at last, I am relieved to see it come. Near death he saw his failings; he needed to act on them years ago.

CHAPTER 49

Juliet 18.30

"HOW CAN I LOVE MY BOY MORE?"

My luggage spins across the interlocking rubber mats. It jostles for position like its owner at the edge of the conveyor belt. This petty behaviour is man at his worse, no, mankind at their worst. The reclamation of personal space and belongings is the last tired act of our journeys. Everyone dreads the ignominy of lost baggage and the hoop jumping needed to recover anything. Instead they all desperately hope they can sail their trolley past everyone else having reclaimed their full set.

Steve picks up an over-sized light brown leather weekend bag. He looks like he is shouldering blame for the death of his work partner. Johnny's politeness has let his rucksack go around once already. Each person at the belt edge won't relinquish a hard-fought front row position; they lean to one side but don't move their feet. He almost falls onto the conveyor belt in an attempt to grab it without having to disturb anyone. Chris is different. With no deference to this game he parts the crowd easily enough through naked insistence and the size of his frame. Three sets of people either side of him get rearranged at the conveyor belt. He is there to stay, but discomfort of being on home soil without his little brother is taking hold. He unrepentantly takes possession of a 1970's style Head shoulder bag and throws it around his neck. I have lost track of the others but have made everyone promise to walk out to our families together, in case there is any need of support or explanation.

My leg muscles ache rewardingly from skiing. If I close my eyes my body still feels in motion; the muscles seem to anticipate a drop to the left here or a stop there. I need to get to the bathroom to clear airplane germs and debris. I have to admit that all my other muscles are tautened by the unfathomable grief that waits in England. Get me home to my life before I even contemplate Dan's funeral.

Robert and Max are aptly stood directly opposite me, near to the customs exit on the other side of the carousel. They lean pensively together on respective aluminium and Burberry suitcases. The alpha male allies have stopped competing. Maybe they don't want the job now they realise that in a week or two neither of them will have one. They have collected Steve and Johnny. We stare at each other without expected enmity. There is a bond of a shared life and grief. I have seen their hearts but it hasn't been pretty. The arrival of my non-descript blue suitcase suggests I am without taste but it is more that I lack time to get a new one. I am true to type in this respect; I have the heaviest baggage by far. I can now join the others.

"Let's go troops; I have called ahead for a cab on account for me and Steve," says Max. His mention of a business taxi account re-establishes a status he is about to lose.

"Let's wait for Chris at least," I say.

"What did you pack in there, a body?" Even Robert winces at his joke and looks to the ground.

"Funny, I am sure I saw Chris pick up his bag first." And so he had but I had forgotten we had luggage without a passenger. My immediate question would have been to Dan; how much use is a guitar case as a weekend bag? My second question was why Chris chose to carry Dan's case so clumsily under the same shoulder he has his bag on. We all stare at the guitar case: a leather embodiment of our lost friend. I daydream that Dan is tucked under the other arm, his black hair tousled by his mountainous brother. Everyone remembers the ridicule Dan got when this was produced in Chamonix an age ago on Wednesday.

"Dan skied like he was carrying the shopping home. Maybe he learnt carrying that thing." Robert says as Chris approaches, prompting the rarity of a gentle laugh from all of us.

"Is there a guitar in there as well as his dirty undies?" Steve asks Chris.

"No, just clothes and stuff; the fruit loop thought this was cool," Chris retorts.

"Perhaps all his bumbling was an act. It was a sure-fire cover for a Mafia hit man," Robert proposed.

"He was definitely a failed hit man with his music career," Johnny chips in awkwardly. We can all laugh a little without Dan. There hasn't been enough of this generosity of spirit in the past few days.

We realise we have been putting it off. We all know what happened and can make some sense of it. It all seemed pre-destined now. It is momentarily better to live with the protagonists who experienced it rather than the relatives who don't. We exit through nothing to declare, although everyone has, but won't.

A shriek breaks the camaraderie as we turn out into the space in front of the metal barrier. I turn to see the semi-famous face alongside me that caused the reaction. Another twenty-year-old manicured X-factor product that Dan would have detested.

"Juliet, you murderer!" Shock is less shocking when you are already in a state of shock. I am still reverberating from our loss and re-calculating my life because of it. The faint smile from our jousting black humour a minute ago still inhabits my face.

"Luca, I'm here." Excited tones of love to be rekindled cut through the unfounded accusation. Life and death mingle together. I was mistaken, it wasn't the scream of delight for a nobody I heard; it was a scream for the lost life of a somebody. I cannot see Sophia; why is she here? Why put yourself through this non-arrival?

"You promised me he would be safe." The first thing I really notice is her fingers, turned white from her unconscious grasp of the handrail. Bepe peeps his features through two bars. Sophia's father is grasping her shoulders; both in comfort and necessary physical support. Again she squeals as I face her across the barrier; I feel these men behind me.

"Bo Diddy!" Bepe announces happily. "Bo." I see a lifetime of over-protection for you. These people will spoil your perspective; they will expect too much of you. The metal bars already squeeze into signs of an indulged tummy.

Luca has led his lover away; scowling at us for spoiling his moment. No one dares walk around the barrier while Sophia is like this. Families hastily disperse but loiter waiting for a second act.

"I nearly rescued him you know…" my voice crackles and I try to push grimaced tears back into their ducts. Uttering abuse in Italian comes more naturally to Sophia. None of it makes sense to me so it is almost a relief.

"Aaagh, my Daniel. Aaagh, aaagh, aagh." She starts to fall backward into her father's arms; I can't tell if it's fake. She is full-blown hysterical now, like a born again accepting God's way. I can't find sympathy for her while she is in this place. Bepe looks frightened for his mum now. This is excruciating until…

"Shut up.' Chris stands forward with the guitar case pointed at Sophia and gives no leeway to his never to be sister-in-law. He holds on to the case, assuming longevity of familial association.

"Bo Diddy." Bepe seems to recognise the case and starts to lean through the railings.

"It's all of us. These dickheads did for him not her. She saved them all except our Dan." Chris roughly grasps her on the right upper arm and pulls her back onto her two feet.

"It's over woman…" Chris walks away to his family without looking back. I am sure he is relieved that he has a free weekend next week. The two youngest have been climbing onto a currency booth and jump chimp-like onto his shoulders without causing him to change stride. He offers no further comment and marches away. Screams subside to violent sobbing across the barrier. The crowds are dispersing. People have found people and transportation.

Over Sophia's slumped shoulders I see the love of my life. Bodies walk across my view of him. He has the height of his father and his Goth haircut sways above the crowd. He never took on their style or attitude, just the haircut.

"Jesus, who is that?" Robert spots him first causing even Sophia to look around. She chokes on another potential wail.

Ethan walks like a man proud of his body. His dungarees remind him of the two-week trip he had last summer with Scott, who follows him unassumingly. They were following some band called The Grateful Dead across America. It will probably be the last time he wants to travel with either of us on holiday. They will not have washed anything while I have been away, so it's easier to put on a T-shirt and some clean underwear and throw these on top. I am sure they will smell. Ethan is smiling now.

The stags are aghast. They spent so much energy thinking about Dan that they believe they have resurrected his younger ghost. We all have images of Dan looking exactly like this at Ethan's age; except the haircut. An apparition in denim. Johnny and Steve are unwittingly walking towards a young man they have never met. Max is grey with fear. I walk past Sophia who is crying again but this time towards Ethan. Bepe is unleashed; Sophia has obviously been containing him using the barrier. He runs across the terminal looking backwards waiting for the chase.

"Bepe, Bepe…!" I shout.

Ethan can hear my distress so spreads his arms and captures him. He tumbles him upside down in one movement causing Bepe's rigid fringe to flop back and forth, releasing wild giggles with the stranger. I say stranger, but not by nature.

"Hi Mum. Hi everyone. Who is this little one?" Meeting your brother for the first time can seldom have been so uncontrived. He hands him over to Sophia's waiting arms.

"Bet the skiing was top," Ethan states confidently to one and all.

I allow no more questions and silence him with the most embarrassing public mother hug I can manage. I kiss him on the lowered forehead catching strands of jet-black hair in my mouth.

"Well it's good to see you too."

"Obviously this is a good time to ask if I can have some money to go travelling again in the summer." He has no embarrassment either in public or private.

"Thanks Jules, you stag. I have to go. Got to get back to London somehow." Robert knows I have a chauffeur going south but I don't owe him any courtesy.

"Hope things work out again for you." I don't know if I really do.

"Your dad was a lanky... Err a good lad you know." Robert lamely switches tack mid sentence. Such is their physical resemblance, he had started to insult a dead man, not this boy he doesn't know. Ethan is confused and unimpressed; maybe he thinks this man is his dad? Robert skulks off leaving a disaster in his wake.

"You saved us!" Max exclaims.

"Saved them from a wicked hangover by not letting them drink, hey Mum. I knew you would be a nightmare on a stag do. Remind me not to invite you to mine. It's a bloody daft idea." Ethan at least thought he could understand Max's motives.

Scott reaches me and kisses me, causing me to turn too sharply around the barrier and drop the carry handle of my wheeled suitcase. I then softly embrace the broken Sophia. Her resentment is dissipated; she is now happy to hold the woman who last held her man. She briefly crumples into me and I am relieved.

"I am so sorry Sophia. I tried and tried but they just wouldn't stop. He was really happy with what he had achieved but they kept pushing him. He slipped from me in the rescue helicopter." This was almost an accident waiting to happen for her. Although she knew the characters she can't have realistically foreseen the outcome.

I look to her father for help. "Here is his passport and here is the number to call to enquire about his release. They said maybe Tuesday." I really hope it isn't. How shocking it will be to be attending your groom's funeral on the day before your proposed wedding. Perversely, it might be convenient for those travelling so they can still use their hotel bookings.

"I would like to meet Ethan..." says Sophia. Even through her grief she has deduced the purpose of my trip and seen through my lies of four days ago.

"Of course, the boys need to meet of course..." She knows now. Seeing Dan in him has imperceptibly moved life on.

Ethan, Scott and I don't look back. I hold Ethan's hand, squeezing it with the pride of a mother.

"Was it a good trip then?" I can't answer. "So then Mum, which one was my dad?" I know he is curious but it seems no more than that. I hope the loss of Dan a second time will not unduly harm him.

"So, which one was my dad?" he repeats.

"It's a long story darling. You missed him, but I know he missed you. He has given me something for you but I... it's a long story." We walk into the spring evening. The day's temperature has been knocked off balmy by a cool wind. We go over the zebra crossing to the multi-storey car park.

"Your dad gave me this for you. It's virtually new. He said it's got some stuff on it already that he left on for you. Treat it as a very early seventeenth birthday present. You always said you wanted an iPhone." A flush comes over me. Can a man explain a lifetime in a voice recording? Can his son gain anything from a distance?

"Wicked Mum. He sounds like a great guy. Is he Mum?"

Acknowledgements

Lovingly: thanks to my wife Maria for her unflinching support and continued love. Also to my boys Joseph and Luca, for helping their dad grow up.

Fatherly: Dad you demonstrated the right and wrong paths to male responsibility.

Motherly: Mum you had a writer's dream; maybe I delivered it. Thanks YELS.

Brotherly: Mark and Peter for pursuing different paths so I could find a way to mine.

Inspirationally: John Summerfield, you showed belief in me at a time when I had none.

Perceptively: Ailis Murphy for helping me understand my motivation to write this story.

Developmentally: Jackie Tasker for her early analysis of my characters.

Medically: Dr Frank Hargreaves for advice and assistance with medical research.

Linguistically: Mark Sampson for help with the French translation.

Respectfully: to the lives of the Hillsborough '96 and those who've fought in their name.

Transactionally: to my business partner Steve for building our company together so I could pursue this dream.

Finally: Captain Norman Giles for stirring something in me in December 1941 by writing "To my son – a letter for life" (re-printed in *The Times* on December 27th 1985).

Dan's Magnificent Seven
The "Tracks of his Years"

"Another Star" by Stevie Wonder. Tamla/Motown, 1976.

"This Charming Man" by The Smiths. Rough Trade, 1983.

"The Magnificent Seven" by The Clash. CBS 1981.

"Human" by the Human League. A&M/Virgin 1986

"Sign "O" Times" by Prince. Paisley Park, Warner Bros 1987.

"Unfinished Sympathy" by Massive Attack. Virgin, 1991.

"What's Going On" by Marvin Gaye. Tamla, 1971.

An honourable mention goes to "You only Live Twice" by John Barry.